Wandering Magik

Carys Bateman

Acknowledgements

To my first reader, Ian.
Told you it had changed a bit.

To the members of DAC (Disability Arts Cymru)
Writers Group who first heard of
this book a long time ago.

Especially to Alan, Denni, Wendy and Mari.

To Ali and Gill, who read later versions and gave me
the boost to continue when I had almost given up.

To Dafydd who told me about Novel Experientia.

To Novel Experientia and all who sail in her,
especially my editor Andrew, who really got this
story, and Amin who works so hard trying to sell it.

To you folks for buying this
and taking a chance on me.

Thank you!

For

My Nain and Taid for love.

The Boy Wonder for belief

And

My Littlest and Best for love and everything else.

Look what I made!

THE STORY SO FAR

Danielle Wintersborn is running for her life. As a slave belonging to *Lord Willoughby*, she was drugged with Numb, a substance that took away her will and should have killed her many years ago. Through a household accident, she missed out on one of her two daily doses and found her mind beginning to clear. Sent out late in the evening to secure more of the drug, the streetwise *Mr Poole* saved her from attempted rape and wants to help her again but doesn't know how to, as interfering between slave and master would be a death sentence for both her and himself. Although expecting her to have no memories of him, *Mr Poole* still gave her his name and a way to get in touch before watching her disappear down an alleyway back to her owner's home.

Arriving in the house, she is met by *Samuel,* her Keeper. His job is to keep watch on her, to make sure she stays in good health and kill her if need be. She is escorted to her mistress, *Lady Willoughby*, a noblewoman angry at a world she can't influence, taking out her frustration on the slave.

A short time later, *Samuel* sees that the slave is no longer as unaware as she has been, offering to help. Learning the master of the house, *Lord Willoughby,* plans to leave the land of *Bisra* where they reside , Samuel goes in search of *Mr Poole* at the slave's request.

With some finessing *Mr Poole* is able to escort Samuel and the slave across land to the port, where they get a ship to *Mertam*. On their travels, Danielle (now also called Dani) discovers she has the gift of Healing Magik, explaining how she has managed to live so long but also something else to worry about.

Bisra has banished magik, deeming all who are of it or use it as Abominations to be put to death in Punishment Squares which exists in every city, town and village. All who are seen as different or working against the rules of the *Mages* or the priesthood of the

Shining One are sent to the Square for public punishment but not always death. Abominations have no hope of living once the charge is made.

Danielle and her escorts reach port safely and, with some sleight of hand, take ship with *Mr Poole's* brother. On the journey, *Danielle* begins to learn more about her fledgling abilities from *Neera*, an Elemental of Air, as well as from *Zutana*, an Elemental of the Sea. Plans are made to help *Danielle* and *Samuel* escape from the clutches of *Lord Willoughby* and his son, *Markus*. They find new friends and an old enemy, so all does not go as planned.

Danielle escapes on her own, encouraged by the ship's crew, leaving death and heartbreak behind her. As she runs, she meets up with *Pandam*, a gnome sent to help her by *Neera*. With the gnome comes a shadow kat and the three of them escape into the dark and travel to *Pandam's* home.

PROLOGUE

The rain that had been so heavy, turning the day into night, just a short time ago, had lightened to just a shower and the sun finally peeked out from the clouds. Danielle stood behind a wooden screen, drying herself off and putting on fresh clothing. An occasional sob sounded but she bit back her tears. There would be time to grieve later, once she was truly free. Until then, she would hold those she loved and would miss close to her heart for however long she lived.

After sorting through her knapsack of belongings and adding items from Samuel's bag, Dani had a short rest. As she did so, Pandam left to sell off the extras no longer needed. Once he returned, Dani awoke and ate before cleaning up, banking the fire and getting ready to leave.

With a cautious look outside, the gnome and the Healer left the safety of the hut. Pandam spoke a few words under his breath before crumbling some dried herbs in his hand and blowing them at the door of his shack. There was a tumbling of sparkling light which, when it faded, hid the hut from sight. Dani looked at Pandam, her brows raised in question.

'Ismagickeephomesafe,' explained the little man, his words running into each other. Looking carefully around, the two disparate creatures slipped out into the night. A few steps away from the hidden hut, a dark shadow joined them. Dani recognised the huge shadow kat that had pulled at her to get her to move after the fight between the two men at the dock: one trying to save her, one determined to end her.

The shadow kat walked by Dani, its back level to her waist. Its fur was all shades of grey, the colours seeming to ripple, fade and reform along its body as it stepped soundlessly with them. Sometimes moving ahead, sometimes dropping behind, it continued to prowl about them. After Dani had lost sight of it again, she realised that shadow kats could literally disappear and reappear when they wished. Pandam walked quickly but stayed at a careful distance from the kat and Dani noticed that he was very wary and nervous of the animal.

So, these will be my companions for the next stage of my journey, she thought wryly. *A gnome who is a mercenary and who I am already beginning to dislike for he holds so much hatred beneath his skin. And a shadow kat, full of magik and mystery, who joins us for reasons of its own. I hope nothing will harm us. And I hope I will reach journey's end before I die.*

Dani looked up at the moonless sky and gave a quick thought to the other people who had travelled with her previously and who had meant so much to her, especially Sam, Mr Poole and Bili. Sending a silent prayer to the gods of Mr Poole's belief, she wished them all love and luck.

Knowing that she might not reach the end of her journey, wherever that may be, Dani followed the gnome and the kat from shadow to shadow as they moved through the dark.

CHAPTER ONE

Danielle squinted as the rain lashed down, desperately trying to keep the gnome in sight as he slid from doorway to doorway, from shadow to shadow and between the dim light from the oil lamps. Although only mid-afternoon, the rain was coming down heavily again, leaving it looking as dark as night in the town. Apart from the difficulties caused by the weather, the fact that the creature she was following was small and seemed to meld into his surroundings until he was completely invisible just added to her confusion. Only with supreme concentration was she able to see his progress through the narrow streets and twisty alleyways that made up this part of Mertam. The further away from the docks they moved, the more turned about she felt. Then she realised that the huge shadow kat, another of her new companions, was keeping pace with her, which finally released some of the tension from her hunched shoulders.

Dani still felt dazed with all that had happened to her in such a relatively short space of time. Too many thoughts and memories were roiling around in her head as she stumbled along and it was only after she tripped for a third time and found herself clutching onto a wet, furry, back did she realise that the kat was no longer ahead of her but walking by her side, slowing her down so that her pace was no longer outstripping her balance.

'Thank you,' she murmured and grinned as she felt a vibration under her hand. The creature was purring.

More than an hour went by and, to Dani, it was as if she was walking in a nightmare. The rain hindered her sight and confused her, the chill settling deep into her bones while the gnome seemed determined to lose her among the labyrinthine streets. It was only when the kat gave a snarl of warning that Pandam came scurrying back.

'YoumustrunquickerBigyouaretooslowtooslow!' His voice was both hoarse and squeaky, and the way his words ran into the next ensured that she had to listen closely to him to understand what he was saying.

'I am not as quick as you, Pandam, and I don't know where we are or where you are taking us. You have been paid to keep me safe. Rushing ahead so fast that I become too exhausted to follow will only get us both caught. Do you think you will be safe if you are found in my company? Willoughby would have you sent to the Mages to boost his standing in this new land just as easily as he will me. I would die in pain, but it would be so much quicker than your own end, I think.'

Pandam stopped his impatient pacing and thought for a moment. She was right, this Big, damn her eyes. If the humans realised that a magikal being had been living openly among them for years, his punishment would be severe. He thought of the silver-eyed air elemental that had contacted him with this job and knew he would count himself lucky if the Mages got to him first if he caused any pain to this woman. Neera would make him pay in ways that would make the Mages look like petulant children. Gritting his sharp teeth, he gave her a nod of acknowledgement, slowing his pace a little as they moved on.

For another two hours in the rain, they walked, crept, ran and even crawled down alleyways, across roads, behind shops, over walls and through gardens. They stopped every now and then to hide from the Watch, nosy individuals who might sell information for a drink, or just to give Dani time to rest. Eventually they reached a dilapidated building, two storeys high and Pandam pulled her inside quickly, with the kat following.

'Sit here, Big,' said the gnome, speaking with exaggerated slowness, pointing to a small, battered stool. 'We rest now, move in the morning. If we are keeping moving now, the Watch follow, maybe catch. Wait here, food will come soon.' He stalked off, shouting out to whoever was in the next room.

Dani gave a sigh of relief at being out of the cold and wet but moved to seat herself at a chair more her size. Not only was she tired from the journey itself but the need to hide ,and the fear of being captured, was a constant beat in her head. *Mind you*, she thought, *it is something I need to get used to. I have a feeling that my journey is going to take a lot longer than I originally thought and take me further than I ever knew existed. I wonder if I will end up killing the gnome first or if he will kill me*. With that thought she gave a snort of laughter which had the shadow kat looking at her in puzzlement. With no sense of stupidity, Dani explained and the huge animal dropped its lower jaw, giving a rasping chuff which Danielle rightly understood was laughter.

Dani looked around the room they were in. From the outside, the building had seemed dilapidated and ready to fall but she could now see that that was a deliberate illusion. The room was cosy and warm, with a fire blazing in the hearth and furnishings made for all different heights. There was a kettle simmering on an iron hook over the welcoming flames as well as a big cauldron of soup sitting at the edge of the hearth and the scent of burning applewood permeated the rooms. Against one wall was a long table set with bowls and tankards upon them, while across the opposite wall were stacks of small three-legged tables with more stools set under them.

When she had finished looking around her, Danielle allowed herself to study the shadow kat in detail as it sprawled comfortably on a rag rug in front of the fire. She had heard of this type of magikal hunting cat, had even heard a tale about one on the first part of her journey on Bisra, but never expected to ever see one in the flesh. When it walked by her side, it came up to her lower rib cage. It was much bigger than she had expected from the story. Its coat was thick, made up of flickering shades of grey that seemed to change and mutate. The way it walked close by her from the docks, and now laying sprawled by her feet, made her feel safe and protected, despite the danger she was in.

Dani's mind flew back to earlier, and the horror that happened at the docks . Everything seemed to be going so well at first, but then there were the shouts of "traitor!", followed by the man stabbing and stabbing and then the whispered *'run, Dani, run'*…but no, she wouldn't, *couldn't* allow herself to think of that, of her loss and the pain that was trying to take her over again. Holding back a sob, she clenched her fists and breathed deeply until the wave of anguish passed.

She concentrated upon the internal pull she felt, the one she had begun feeling on the ship that had grown stronger as they travelled the ocean. She knew she had to follow this tugging but for what reason, she had no idea. She knew that she was dying; being without the drug, Numb, guaranteed that, but she also knew that she had no choice but to go where this compulsion led her. Giving a gusty sigh, Dani smiled down at the shadow kat who had raised its head with the noise.

'Sorry, kat,' she said, 'I am just trying to work out what happens next.'

The kat stretched and gave a great yawn, showing off massive yellowed fangs, before giving a quiet snuffle before laying its heavy head upon her foot and snoozing again. Its coat had begun to steam gently in the warmth of the room and Dani grinned as she noticed that her own garments had begun to do the same.

'Well, I am so glad you are as worked up about the situation as I am,' Dani smiled at it, before sitting back in the comfortable chair and allowing herself to fall into a light doze.

Dani woke with a start a little later as the inner door opened, and a small woman bustled in. Although of a similar size to Pandam, this woman was of a completely different build. Instead of wiry with a small potbelly, she was plump and rounded. Her skin was smooth, pale cream with pink cheeks rather than leathery green with warts. Her hands had the usual three fingers of a certain type of magiker, as Dani had seen on the others she had met, but these were plump with short nails and many rings decorating the fingers, whereas Pandam's hands were thin and elongated with sharp claws instead of nails. A mass of white hair was pinned up haphazardly upon her head and wobbled about as she moved around briskly.

'Hello, my lovely,' said the small woman. 'My name is Mallie. Pandam has told us all about you. You best come with me into the back room. He shouldn't have left you in here, anyone would think that he wanted to get you caught. He knows we get some of the Watch a'coming in for some tea or some soup and hot cakes through the evening, blast him.' As she chattered on, Mallie flitted from one thing to another; stoking up the fire, moving the kettle so it was sitting further over the flames, putting spoons into bowls, slicing and buttering bread and piling them up on a large plate. Finally she picked up Dani's knapsack and bustled through to another room. Exchanging a baffled look, Dani and the shadow kat followed closely behind her. When Mallie shut the connecting door behind them, Dani felt, rather than heard, a slight whisper and the door gave a tiny "thunk" and she knew it wouldn't open again unless it was by someone who knew the magik needed to make it happen.

Gazing around the room, Dani felt her jaw drop. There was a lot of magik at work here. Firstly, the room was at least twice as wide as the one in the front, if not more so. There was a blazing fire, windows that looked out on a meadow full of sunshine, flowers, butterflies and birds. The wood burning stove was sending out lovely smells from the pans bubbling away on its scarred metal surface. Over in one corner were seven chairs of different heights but all looking soft and comfy. Pandam glared at her from the one he lounged in and deliberately turned his back, while the short man who had been listening to him raised his white bushy eyebrows in surprise.

'Don't you be being rude in *my* house, Pandam the Guide!' Mallie sounded really annoyed. 'You have been paid good gold for looking after this lass, so don't you let your dislike of the Bigs cause her any more trouble or I will be the first one to spread the word that you are no longer trustworthy. Fancy leaving a charge in that room when you know the Watch will be here at any time.' She moved around the kitchen area, removing a plate of hotcakes from the warming oven and placing them on a large tray, along with another loaf of bread, a dish of butter, another of jam and a last containing some sort of syrup. A slight noise came from the outer room. 'That'll be the first of the Watch now. You take this, Brim, my lover, and I will feed our guest.'

Pandam glared as the other man stood quickly, smiled brightly at Dani before he swept a low bow to Mallie, grabbed the laden tray and lifted it easily and left the room, the door making a soft "swoosh" this time. Dani noticed that there were differences between the two men, despite both being gnomes. Brim was perhaps an inch or so shorter than Pandam but much plumper. His skin was ruddier than Pandam's and in all other ways seemed a match for Mallie. His white hair was shorter and puffed out from his head in a mass of curls. He was obviously a lot stronger than he looked, just like Mallie, the tray being so heavily laden that Dani wasn't sure she would have been able to carry it, and certainly not with such ease.

'I ain't staying here to be insulted,' Pandam snarled slowly as he stood and headed for the door set in the rear wall. 'I will be back for her tomorrow, make sure she's ready.'

Before he could step out, Mallie spoke something that Dani didn't catch as it was drowned out by the snarl of the kat.

'Iwon'tbringanytroublehere,' the gnome now sounded almost worried and forgot to slow his speech down, making Dani concentrate with some difficulty. 'IamjustgonnagoandgetsomeinformationabouttheportalandI'llstayt herewithmybrothersuntilitistimetoleavetomorrow.'

'Your word,' Mallie gritted out.

'My word,' Pandam said after a pause, before disappearing out of the door.

Dani raised her eyebrows as the door closed almost with a slam and Mallie scowled at it, angry at the gnome and his attitude.

'Are you sure you want him to guide you, sweetheart?' she asked. Dani looked surprised and then thoughtful.

'I didn't know that I had a choice,' she replied eventually. 'Surely he wouldn't cause me any harm, especially when Neera and I have paid him well in gold and gems?'

'He might,' said Mallie. 'He hates most beings but those he calls "Bigs" are top of the list. I don't know why; he has never said, and I have never asked.'

'Hmm,' Dani pondered for a moment. 'I will see how we get on. If he is still causing trouble once we are out of the city, I will find someone else to help me. Either that or I will find my own way.'

'I have an even better idea,' Mallie said. 'I will pass the news to others that you are travelling with him and ask that any travellers keep an eye out for you both. That way, if there is trouble or you decide to go on without him, there will be other magikers willing to take his place. You don't need to struggle alone, little one, especially as Neera was the one who asked us to help you.'

She was amused at hearing the much shorter Mallie calling her little one, but made sure she didn't show it. Dani was surprised though, as the Air Elemental she knew, although confident, had never made himself seem especially important on the journey over the seas. 'Neera is that important?'

Mallie gaped at the girl then giggled. 'You really don't know, do you? Neera is known by almost every magiker on Yerat. He has been a messenger, a hunter, a bard and much, much more in his long life. He is the best friend one can have but we all know not to cross him.'

'I feel so stupid to have to ask but what is Yerat?

'Why, it is the world we live on, sweetheart. All the islands float on the seas that cover the surface of Yerat.'

'Oh.'

Both women were quiet for some time; Mallie busy making up more hot cake batter and stirring the soup while Dani focused on absorbing the information she had just been given. Brim came back through the door with a tray empty of food but full of dirty crockery, so Dani went to the sink and began to wash them. Her back was to the room, so she didn't see the exchange of approving glances the others exchanged.

The evening passed quickly. Both Mallie and Dani kept busy with cooking and washing pots, while Brim swept in and out of the door every few minutes, swapping dirty dishes for full plates. Eventually, when Dani was about to admit that she had had enough, Brim came in with just a few last cups and told them that he had barred the door. Mallie then dished up the last of the tasty soup as well as a heaping platter of hot cakes and they all ate their fill. Then Mallie waved her hand and a door, previously unnoticed, opened in the far wall.

'There you go, my sweet. You will find a bathing chamber in there as well as a comfortable bed. You get yourself washed and changed and get a good night's sleep. We will see you in the morning.'

By this time, Dani was almost asleep on her feet so the kat stood and allowed her to lean on it, guiding her through to the bedroom where, Dani pulled off her clothing, had a very sketchy wash and slipped her head though the nightdress that Mallie had provided. She couldn't help giving a tired giggle when she saw that it was at least three times too wide yet only just covered her backside.

After a quick prayer to the gods Mr Poole had told her about on the ship, she tumbled onto the wide bed, pulled the blankets up to her chin and knew no more.

<h1 style="text-align:center">CHAPTER TWO</h1>

When Dani got up the next day, she found the shadow kat tucking into a huge meal of chops, bacon and raw eggs. It turned its head and acknowledged her before swiftly going back to the food. Mallie gave her a smile and cracked an egg into a pan and a few minutes later Dani was tucking into her own meal of bacon, eggs, mushrooms and toast with butter. Although she didn't think she would eat all in front of her, she managed to clear her plate. After washing up, Mallie sat her down to explain what would be happening now.

'Right, my lovely,' the motherly gnome said, 'you will be leaving just after the mid-day meal and Pandam will guide you through the gates. Once you are on the move you need to watch him. He won't do you wrong; he is too frightened of Neera for that, but he won't give you all of the help and advice you need either. If he starts becoming a problem, you tell your kat that you want someone else to be your guide and it will find you one. Brim has gone to the ship to let them all know that you are safe for now and you will be moving on soon. I will also make sure that the Air Elemental knows about how Pandam is with you, that will mean that more eyes will be keeping watch. Now, take time to check your knapsack, see your clothes are in good order and move your valuables from where you have them stored now, if Pandam saw where you put them. That way, you are removing temptation from the gnome.'

'I thought about stitching the gems into my coat or my belt,'

'Good idea. Pandam won't come back until just before it is time to leave, so you have time to get that done.'

For the rest of the morning Dani sewed hidden pockets into her coat and slipped the gems and most of her gold inside for safe keeping, leaving just a little for the bribes she might be called to hand out in the near future. She then helped Mallie prepare the mid-day meal as well as making some travel rations for the journey. Just before the meal was ready Pandam and Brim arrived, both wet and hungry. The former was, of course, scowling and seemed to be in a foul temper. Brim went straight to the sink and washed his hands while Pandam had to be prodded to do the same. Then they sat round the table, tucking into pigeon pie, carrots, leeks and potatoes.

After his first edge of hunger disappeared Brim looked at Dani and smiled. 'I have seen the folks on the ship,' he said, licking a drop of gravy off his thumb. 'Neera knows the new arrangements and has sent messages all over. That way, if your kat comes calling you will have a choice over who you have to help you.'

'Wait! What's all this?' shouted Pandam, leaping up from the table and causing crockery to rattle.

'You sit down, now.' Brim spoke quietly but firmly. Dani blinked in surprise. She had been under the impression that Mallie was the driving force of the family but now it seemed that Brim kept his own strengths hidden until needed. Pandam must have seen something in Brim's face because he slowly sat down, grinding his teeth together.

'The reason we have made these further arrangements is simple,' the shorter male gnome continued. 'You hate the Bigs, as you call them, and sooner or later you will be tempted to walk away from our girl. This way, we at least know she will have others to depend on.'

Pandam spluttered but didn't deny the fact that he had already been thinking of disappearing, sooner rather than later. Dani looked at the scowling gnome and gave a short nod, letting him know that she understood him rather too well.

'It also means that the Air Elemental won't come after you now, when you do leave her.' Brim continued saying to Pandam. 'Of course, it looks like the shadow kat has adopted Dani anyway so she would never have been left helpless. This way, it is all sorted, and no loose ends are left.'

The kat raised its sleepy head and yawned at Pandam, deliberately displaying its large, yellowing fangs, which made the old gnome shudder before grabbing up his mug and gulping down some ale.

Twenty minutes later the two travellers and the kat were ready to go. Dani hugged both Mallie and Brim before she slipped out of the door into a dull, grey day. Thankfully, for now, the driving rain had stopped but it was still bitterly cold. The kat followed at her heels, leaving Pandam to shut the door. Then he led the way towards the gates which would allow them to leave the Port of Mertam.

Even as Dani, Pandam and the shadow kat arrived at Mallie's place the previous evening, across the city the Assassin pulled his hood up a little more and leaned nonchalantly against the greasy brick wall of an alleyway, as the rain came down even faster. His dark eyes were fixed on a tall, slightly overweight man, who stood on a platform across the square, telling the large group of people there about his new tax reforms. Mage magik made sure that his voice was heard by everyone in the crowd, and each word made the Assassin more annoyed, even angry, although he couldn't understand why.

Quick as lightning, the Assassin's left hand shot downwards and caught the smaller hand that had tried to pick his pocket. Squeezing hard, he pulled the waif into the dimly lighted alley, and glared down at her.

'Are you mad, girl? Or do you have a death wish?' he growled out. He shook the rain from his eyes and examined his victim. Although only up to his breastbone this was no child. A pale woman stood swaying in front of him, her skin almost translucent and her eyes seemed overly large in her cold, pinched face. The Assassin frowned, realising she was on the verge of collapse.

With a muttered oath he pulled her deeper into the narrow passageway then pulled a slightly stale bread roll out of his cloak pocket.

'Here,' he said roughly. 'Eat this and then we need to talk about your behaviour,'

Taking the roll eagerly, the woman nevertheless raised an eyebrow at his tone of voice before taking a small bite of the bread, chewing thoroughly and swallowing, her eyes shut in pleasure, before taking another small bite. The Assassin watched her, a little surprised at her gentle manners. Once she had finished the bread, she wiped the corners of her mouth with her fingers, looking at the tall man in the eye for the first time. He didn't think she could go any paler, but she did, before staggering slightly. His hand shot out and steadied her as he frowned in confusion at her actions.

'What in the seven hells is wrong with you, girl?'

'You are what is wrong: you are under a *compulsion*. You will find your target and then you will die!'

'Is that a threat, witch?'

'No, no, no, it is no threat. You have been put under a Mage's *compulsion* I tell you. Being forced to kill someone, I think. After he or she is dead, you will also die. I bet you have been getting headaches and now you are standing here but are not sure why. Someone though, someone here is making you angry and that anger builds even as I speak. Am I right?'

The Assassin looked at her thoughtfully, then the orator's voice rose again, and rage swept through him. A small cold hand touched his cheek and he turned back to the small woman, not even realising that he had turned away from her. Shaking his head, he pulled her, firmly but gently, down the passageway and walked swiftly through the streets towards his secret quarters. The woman moved clumsily after him, stumbling and tripping until he gave a growl of frustration and swung her up into his arms. Picking up his speed, he continued moving, eventually walking up a stone stairway and letting himself into a large apartment. Dropping the woman gently onto her feet, he waited until she was steady and then turned and locked the door, slid down the thick wooden plank that fitted into the metal staples fitted firmly into the wall and then handed the large key to the surprised pickpocket.

'Right,' he said. 'You go and get a bath through there, keeping the key on you. I will make something for us to eat and then we will discuss this properly.' With that, he walked into the small kitchen that took up one wall and began assembling vegetables.

Not knowing what else to do, the woman shrugged at his back and looked around her. She was in a large, lopsided room, with a door leading off it to another as well as a heavy, dark curtain pulled partly across a sleeping alcove. The walls were stone and carried very little decoration. The whole place felt empty and unloved, not a home, just somewhere to sleep.

She gave another shrug before trying the shut door. She pushed it open and walked into a luxurious bathing room. Making sure the heavy door was bolted behind her, she turned on hot and cold taps that fed water into a long and deep bath before removing her outer rags, revealing a better set of clothing beneath. She took these off as well followed by a thick sweater, two warm chemises and two pairs of woollen stockings. Walking over to the tub she checked the temperature of the water before turning off the cold tap and letting the hot continue to flow even as she added some herbs from a jar, intended to warm and ease sore muscles. Once the bath was full enough, she slipped into the fragrant water and gave a huge sigh, before she began scrubbing vigorously at the ground-in dirt on her arms.

In the kitchen, the Assassin cut and chopped, putting together a substantial meal for them both. More than once, as he did so, he found himself standing at the locked front door, pulling at the handle and trying to get it open. He shuddered at the thought of someone else in his mind, dictating his actions without his knowledge. He backed carefully away from the door each time, just as if it was a poisonous snake, before going back to preparing the food only to find himself pulling at the handle of the door once more mere moments later. He was thankful that this *compulsion* didn't seem to be able to work with his knowledge or abilities or have any actual knowledge because he never attempted to lift the bar or pick the lock.

Eventually the pickpocket left the bathroom. Her surface rags were gone, and she now wore a plain, long sleeved woollen dress in a rich brown, with a shawl folded around her shoulders for warmth. Her eyes widened and her mouth watered as she saw the display of food covering the table, more than she thought they could eat in a week. Then she leaped forward and touched the Assassin on the arm as he went and struggled with the door again. He turned at her touch, his teeth bared in rage, his eyes unfocused and bloodshot.

'Give me the key, witch.' His voice was a low growl, vibrating with his need to follow the *compulsion*. Taking a deep breath, she touched his temple with two fingers. He calmed immediately, sliding into a trance-like state.

'Calm yourself,' she soothed, as she led him to the curtained alcove. His eyes were completely glazed over, following her like a tame dog. She got him onto the large bed, speaking nonsense in a soothing monotone. Within a moment he lay on his back, arms relaxed by his side, eyes staring up at the ceiling. She climbed up beside him and thought for a moment before she slid over to straddle him. Taking a few deep breaths to calm her own breathing and to pull up the magik she carried within, she then leaned forward and cupped her hands over his cheeks, feeling the slight prickling from his beard stubble.

'You will not harm me,' she crooned. 'I am completely safe with you as you fight this *compulsion*.' She repeated the words three times – a magikal number – then, pressing her palms against his cheeks more firmly, she thrust her mind into his, looking for the threads that bound him to another.

Almost immediately she found a recently buried memory. In it, she looked out of the Assassin's eyes at a tall, emaciated figure, dressed in the purple and black robes, sequinned and embroidered in gold, making the robes unspeakably gaudy. The Mage was chanting words of binding. There was *compulsion* threaded in the binding but also a death curse. If the Assassin had followed the complex spell laid upon him by this Mage, he would not only have killed a member of the town council, but once it was done, he would have begun to bleed from every orifice, causing him to die in screaming agony.

As she probed deeper, her own magik gave her the words needed to neutralise the spell wrought by the thin Mage. As she went even deeper, she found the influence of Black Mýste intertwined as part of the death curse. Releasing the Assassin for a moment, she told him to stay there, went and grabbed a jug of water off the heavily laden table and crammed some sort of meat pie into her mouth as she felt crippling pangs of hunger distracting her. She would have loved to have taken time to fill a plate of food and eat at her leisure but knew she had a long job ahead of her and no time to waste.

Going back to where the Assassin still lay, she saw a man of average looks who could fade into shadow, dark of face, hair and body. Taller than she was by a good amount, he was lean but wiry, his muscles were like steel beneath her body. Settling herself upon him again, she chewed on the pie neatly but rapidly before taking a long swallow of water. Placing the jug on the floor beside her, she wiped her hands clean on a napkin brought from the table before she clasped the man's head again.

'Fight this, fight like you never have before,' she ground out as his memories and the spell dragged her down into his past again.

She saw the Mage in the Assassin's memories and heard his spell coming to an end. As the main part of her mind began reading the woven spell and unravelling it as quickly as she was able, thread by thread, she heard the Mage speak.

'You will kill Borge, then you will hide yourself and die in the shadows. We have no more use for you, and it is time for you to leave our service. You cannot live, remember, you must *die.'*

'Not if I can help it,' she gritted out, continuing to assault the spell.

Minutes passed, time stretching out to become an hour, then two. Finally, after almost three hours of mental battle, she let go of the Assassin's head and slid off him, gasping and panting, trying to draw breath as her body shook and spasmed in pain. He opened his eyes slowly, his head ready to explode in agony but feeling as if he had just recovered from a long illness and seeming to see everything much more clearly than he had for a long time.

They stared at each other for a long moment, while her breathing slowly eased, and then a small smile curved one side of his mouth.

'I am not sure what you have done to me, woman, but you have my gratitude. My mind is clearer now, and I feel more in control of myself although my head hurts like a demon. You, however, look exhausted and starving. So come, let's eat while we talk.'

She gave him a dubious look, shot a glance to the locked and barred door before giving a sigh of resignation and, staggering a little, went slowly to the table.

They both filled their plates with slices of meat pie, potatoes, bread and vegetables. After they had eaten quietly for a few minutes he finished his mouthful and took a sip of the rich, red wine he had poured out into delicate glasses.

'Come then, woman. Tell me your name. I cannot keep calling you "woman".'

'You may call me Wren. And how about you? Do you have a name or are you only known as "Assassin"?'

He frowned a little then, a look of confusion flitting over his features. 'Do you know, I can't remember my name. I have not been anything but "Hey", "You" and "Creature" for so long that my name seems to have disappeared. Didn't you see it while you rummaged away in my brain?'

'I wasn't really looking for that. You not only had a major compulsion and a death spell that held Mýste ready to set upon you, but you seem to have been mind-controlled for a few years, like most of the people belonging to the Mages. Your brain isn't that of a full human so certain things are locked away where even I can't go.'

'I don't understand, what do you mean by my not being "full human"?'

'You have some natural magik in you, my friend, I am not sure what kind although, as you are an Assassin, I assume it is to do with weapons of some sort.'

The Assassin blinked slowly as he absorbed the information that he was one of the "Abominations" that he had been sent out to kill more and more often over the last few years. Taking a deep breath, he ate more of the now tasteless food before speaking again.

'Alright, Wren. What are your plans now?'

'Plans? I have no plans. I tried to pick your pocket because I hadn't eaten in three days. I have broken the *compulsion* on your mind which means the Mage felt the bond snap. They will send hunters or bloodhounds after you. As soon as Verin realises that you have not killed your target he will search you out even harder, to find out what has gone wrong.'

'Verin? How did you know my master's name?'

'I saw it in your mind.'

'And how did you know of the *compulsion*?'

Wren gave a sigh, knowing that she had no choice but to tell him everything. She wondered if she would live after it was over.

'To explain it, I had best tell you my background. I was born and lived in a small village near the sea a few miles up the coast from here. There was my Da, my brothers and me. Da was a fisherman and we children hunted for rabbits and shellfish and anything else we could find to eat. There was a new Server in the village church. He had come to us from Ferna City, a few hundred miles away from here, and he really hated the slower way of life. I have always been able to "know" things, to see when someone is lying and who is trustworthy and who isn't.

'The Server noticed this and decided that if he let the Mages know that there was someone in the village with personal magik, it would help him get away from the place he hated. He sent for a Mage, who came and took me to the Academy here in Mertam. As you know, no-one is given a choice when it comes to Mages and their demands, do as they say or disappear forever. My Da didn't want to let me go but he was told that if I didn't go voluntarily then I would be taken in chains. So, I went. Not that it did the Server much good. His "reward" was to be taken from the village he hated, but then he was sent to an even smaller one in the mountains.' Wren laughed a little, remembering the priest's chagrin as he was told about his "promotion".

The Assassin grinned his amusement at the priest's punishment before nodding at her to continue.

'I was very young when I was taken to the Academy, but I was a tough one. It is a horrible place; we were all encouraged to fight each other, if anyone was badly hurt the attacker was given a mild reprimand for going too far while the victim was ridiculed for being weak.'

'Huh,' said the Assassin. 'That sounds just like the place I was taken to train. My teachers had the same attitude.'

'Well,' continued Wren, 'I grew older and began to realise that I would never fit in with what the Mages wanted.' At the Assassin's puzzled look, she grinned. 'The Mage hierarchy is male only; they look for magik skilled females to breed with. Once the female has lost her fecundity or breeds false, she is then killed off and her body parts, blood and hair is used in spells. I had no thought to becoming a bawd, used by any Mage who fancied me, so I did some thinking, planned and then put it into action once I found out that I was going to be sent to the Breeder's Pen come Winter's End the following year.

'Over a period of perhaps six months I slowly became forgetful and confused before staring into space. My teachers frowned and began muttering to each other. I began getting things wrong, spell components, runes and words getting mixed up and things like that. I also woke up screaming a few times. Eventually, they found me sitting in my own – erm – body waste, covered in blood and drooling. Once the apothecary had looked me over, it was decided that I was no good for breeding or body parts as they didn't know if my madness would pass on to either a child or make a spell react wrongly. I was taken to a small cottage on the Academy grounds, along with a servant to watch over me in case I had a miraculous recovery. I made sure I didn't. After perhaps five more years, the Mages decided that I wasn't going to recover so they threw me out to beg on the streets and took the servant back into the main buildings,' she finished with a grin.

'Weren't you taking a hell of a chance? They might have killed you.'

'Better dead than being used nightly by whoever wanted me, either Mage or sycophant. Besides, I knew it was unlikely they would keep me around, madness isn't something they want to take a chance on getting into the breeding cycle. I knew they wouldn't kill me for spell parts, the madness might cause the spells to backfire.'

'You didn't know that they wouldn't just kill you anyway,' he argued.

'True but anything was better than staying there.'

They sat in silence for a while as the Assassin digested what he had been told and Wren took the chance to finish off her meal.

After tidying away the food and washing the plates and bowls, they moved through and sat on the comfortable chairs with hot drinks in their hands. Wren was beginning to feel drained, not only from the mental battle but also from the unexpected conversation, food and warmth. The Assassin looked at her and smiled to himself.

'Alright,' he said. 'You have no plans and I need to leave Mertam. Does Verin have any way of knowing where I am?' At the shake of her head, he continued. 'I suggest that we leave together then. I can get us both out of the town, and we can escape to the mountains. You can go back to your home and I...' He trailed off as she shook her head.

'I cannot go back to my village. Verin is one of those who taught me at the Academy and that will be the first place he looks. Plus, I know my people are dead. I overheard some of the teachers speaking about how once a child was brought to be tested, their families were rounded up. That's how he put it, "rounded up". When it is decided that the child has enough magik, the family is then disposed of. When I heard this, I began making proper plans to get out.

'Verin will have recognised my magik and how I work from the way his spell has been broken, so will also know that I have fooled them for years. I will come with you gladly and we can see what happens. On the condition that you have a name.'

He laughed and then grinned at her. 'Alright, Wren, you name me.'

After looking at him thoughtfully, she nodded. 'My favourite brother's name was Crow; would that be alright for you?'

'Yes,' he said after a thoughtful moment. 'I like it. Now, as both of us are ready to drop in our tracks, come through to the bedroom and we can both sleep until we are fully rested. Then I will go and fetch supplies and then we can both disappear.'

At her suspicious look, he laughed again. 'I am in no state to want more than sleep, Wren, and I have never forced anyone in my life.'

After another minute's thought, she gave a short nod and they both went and lay on the bed. Wren expected to feel awkward and on edge with sharing a bed with the tall stranger, even fully clothed, but she fell asleep almost as soon as she lay down. Crow lay on his side and watched her thoughtfully for a few moments before he, too, dropped off into a solid sleep.

Lord Jervis Willoughby looked up at the elegant tall building as he stood on the steps of the carriage. At three storeys high, it was at thelimit that Yerat allowed for buildings before it began battering them down. The house had steps leading up to an impressive front door as well as many windows with delicate seeming ironwork protecting the glass. He gave a satisfied nod at what he saw. Just then the front door opened, and the servants marched out. Rubbing his hands together in glee, he saw a butler, a cook, three maidservants as well as a footman and what looked to be three gardeners.

He turned and gave a nod to the man still seated in the carriage, waiting for Willoughby's reaction.

'I thought you said this was adequate, my dear sir. If the inside matches the out, it is much more than merely adequate. I thank you.'

'Don't thank me, Willoughby, you know why we are funding you. Let's go inside and look around there then we can discuss our future plans.'

Willoughby didn't enjoy being reprimanded, even mildly, by someone he saw as beneath himself. With an abrupt nod, he stepped down, waited for the other man to join him before marching up to where the servants waited with blank faces.

Almost two hours later, after walking through every room in the house, both men sat comfortably ensconced in girox leather armchairs, holding apple brandies and discussing their plans.

'What materials will you need for these projectile things you are making?' asked Sevrant Miltop.

'Only a steady supply of Mýste, young Mages to train how to bind the Mýste to the projectile and disposable people to use them on,' said Willoughby, settling back in comfort.

'It won't be difficult to supply all of that. Mýste, as you know, is in plentiful supply and that won't disappear until the Mages stop using blood magik. We have a training academy here so plenty of journeymen Mages are available for you to use. Might help winnow out some of the less able. As for bodies to practise on, we have thousands of peasants that no-one will miss. Where will you make the projectiles? And what do we do if anything happens to you?'

Willoughby didn't answer for a moment, he just stared at the red and gold of the liquid swirling in his glass. Then he looked up with a slight smile just curving the side of his lips. 'You had best hope that nothing happens to me, Miltop. I know plenty of magik, more than enough to cause an Assassin to think twice. If I die, the process dies with me and your hope and that of your backers, of ridding the world of Abominations will also cease to exist.'

'I wasn't thinking of assassination, I would never be so crass. I was worried about accidents. Handling Mýste is a dangerous thing.'

'True, it is dangerous, but no more than surviving the Mage Academy. My apologies if I misconstrued your meaning. Perhaps I will find an apprentice among those you send me.'

'What about your family, your son?'

Willoughby let out a harsh bark of laughter even as he shook his head. 'Oh no, my dear sir. My wife is a termagant, constantly complaining and cold to touch. My daughter is pretty but too soft-hearted and my son, yes, my son.' A heavy silence before Willoughby continued. 'My son is a great disappointment to me. I thought he had great potential, and I was right. Unfortunately, he enjoys the pleasures of the flesh too much to take that small seed of potential and let it grow.'

'Pleasures of the flesh? We can provide him with the most alluring women from our high-class Bawdy Houses…' Miltop's voice trailed away as he saw Willoughby shaking his head.

'No, no, that won't work. My son has found that he needs a variety of different types to keep his member working. It takes all my time to keep him disease free. I want to keep him around though; in case I need a scapegoat.'

'I understand.' And Miltop did understand, and this understanding made his flesh crawl. He had been involved in various plots over the years, getting rid of political rivals, killing, blackmail and thievery, but he had never met anyone quite as cold as this man apart from the Mage, Verin. And that thought reminded him.

'Our Master Mage, Verin, is interested in meeting you. He has heard of you from someone from your Academy days. I think he would be interested in helping where he can.'

'That sounds interesting, yes, let me know when and where and I will make myself available. Now I must send a messenger to tell my wife to pack and find movers to bring my family and their belongings here as soon as possible.

'*And I almost forgot. I need to speak to the best hunter or bloodhound that is available. I have a missing slavey I want found.*'

'*Missing slavey? Won't she be dead or close to it?*'

'*Perhaps.*'

Willoughby didn't elaborate but took a deep draught of his brandy, waiting for Miltop to do what he had demanded. With a face frozen into blankness, Miltop stood and left the room. Willoughby smirked into his glass; he would soon have these idiots jumping to his orders.

He might not have been quite as complacent if he had seen the change to Miltop after he had left the room. Anger coursed through the man and only the fact that his group of plotters needed the arrogant idiot stopped him going back and sliding his favourite garotte around that fat, self-satisfied throat.

Passing on Willoughby's message for his wife, Miltop left the townhouse and stalked off into the night, ready to pass on to the group of rich men in the group of plotters, to speak to the Hunters and Bloodhounds Guild and, finally, to go home and forget about everything until the morning.

CHAPTER THREE

About the same time that Wren and Crow were supplied and heading to the hidden exit that passed by the East Gate with supplies on a small hand cart, Pandam, Dani and the shadow kat were saying their private goodbyes to Mallie and Brim. Hitching on their own packs, they began walking to the East Gate, Brim going with them to see them safely through. The shadow kat faded away from sight so that it seemed that it was just a group of three, with Dani disguised as a young man and the gnomes, Brim and Pandam, as two children.

As they reached the East Gate, Dani found herself looking around for potential danger. Up ahead a big farmer's wagon paused at the huge wooden barricade as the driver exchanged chatter with the guards before they swung the gate open, and it rumbled through . She found her eyes drawn to a tall, dark man who pushed one of the handles on a small trolly while a much smaller woman, dressed in a plain gown, pushed the other. With lowered heads, they walked past the long line and headed towards a tavern a little way down the hill. The Dancing Jester was a typical Gateside tavern, not really the kind of place Dani would have expected the couple to go.

A slight nudge from the invisible kat broke into her revery and she stepped forward. Dani couldn't help being nervous as their own small group reached the guards. Brim moved forward and handed over his own bribe and spoke quietly. The guard he spoke to gave a slight shrug before nodding and soon they were out of the big gate and walking on the busy road.

Brim stayed with them for a half mile before hugging Dani and saying his farewells. Turning and heading down a small trackway, Brim walked towards a farm and his order of milk, eggs and a side of mutton as the others kept walking on the main road.

At the Dancing Jester, Crow left Wren outside to guard the trolly while he went in and spoke to the taverner. A few minutes later the huge man stepped out followed by Crow, carrying a lantern in his meaty fist even though the day was bright enough. With a grunt and a tilt of his head, he led the way to the stables. Once inside he walked to the furthest stall and brushed away a heap of foul-smelling straw, using a mouldering broom set there for the purpose. Wren felt her jaw drop as the straw moved away as a whole piece, revealing a trapdoor underneath.

Crow gestured to Wren who stepped forward and looked down, she saw thick staples set into the wide tunnel mouth. With a slight nudge from Crow, she began down, pulling up her skirts so not to trip. She was glad to be wearing thick soled boots instead of her thin dancing slippers, the latter would have let the chill right through the thin soles and would have easily slipped off the rungs.

Wren expected to head down into darkness and, although she went quite a depth, there were lanterns, lit by magik, set in niches behind the steps. Eventually she reached the floor of beaten earth and looked up just in time to see Crow's boots descending. She skipped out of the way and as he reached the ground he tugged on a rope that hung loosely at the side of the heavy staples. This rope ran to the surface and, as it wasn't fixed to the wall anywhere, ran freely and was used to signal to those above. Both of them stood there, not speaking, looking upwards although Wren had little idea why. She gave a startled gasp as she saw the trolley being lowered smoothly and easily by the man above. Once it touched the ground, Crow undid the complicated knot, tugged on the rope and it disappeared upwards. As it did, the lights above winked out, one by one.

Wren opened her mouth to speak then stopped as Crow laid a gentle finger on her lips and shook his head vehemently. Nodding to show she understood, she took hold of one of the trolley's handles and Crow took the other and they moved down the large, fortified tunnel, lamps glowing before them and winking out once the couple were past.

The day was bright with a cold sun, the temperature low enough for Dani to be grateful for the heavy, warm coat she wore. She wriggled her fingers in the thick woollen mittens that Mallie had handed over and wrapped the matching scarf more snugly around her neck. As she did so, she kept an unobtrusive eye upon Pandam. Both Mallie and Brim had told her to be careful of him as they felt he could not be trusted.

'*He hates the Bigs so much that he would take a chance on betraying his word if he thought he could get away with it.*' Mallie had told her before Pandam's arrival that morning. Brim had nodded his agreement. Even mentioning Neera, the Air Elemental, hadn't stopped the worry.

'*Thing is, girlie,*' Brim had said. '*You and he will be on your own out there. Who can say what dangers might appear? And how will Neera know for certain what has been a natural accident and what has been foul play? Watch yourself, listen to your gut and trust in the kat.*'

Dani had nodded her agreement even though she felt that the two gnomes were being over-protective, before putting the conversation to the back of her mind. She kept watch on him. Although she felt that the gnomes might be wrong, she wasn't stupid. They also hadn't given the shadow kat quite enough credit as it made sure to walk between Dani and the disgruntled gnome at all times.

Moving along the packed dirt road made for a faster pace than Dani had expected. Soon, she knew, they would be heading into a large, wooded area and it was there the pace would slow and they would have to keep a watch out for bandits.

By early evening, Dani was beginning to flag. Apart from a short break to eat the food Mallie had packed, Pandam had kept them moving. Just as they reached the outskirts of the woods they passed the couple whom she had seen at the East Gate. Wearily she wondered how they had managed to get ahead when she couldn't remember seeing them pass. Pandam pushed his way past the two and Dani shrugged her apology before reaching forward and grabbing the short man by the shoulder. Pandam whirled around with a hiss.

'Stop it,' Dani whispered fiercely. 'If you continue with your arrogant attitude, gnome, we will both be caught. Your illusion is that of a child, so act like one, and not like the bigoted scav that you are.'

The gnome ground his teeth before giving a sharp nod. He did a cartwheel and just missed hitting a broken stump before he jumped to his feet and ran back to the couple, who were now looking bemused, and swept a low bow.

'Sorry', he squeaked out, 'I didn't mean to be rude.' Then he gave another bow before skipping back to Dani.

Crow looked after the child and frowned slightly. There had been something wrong with the boy, but he was still tired from having the *compulsion* expunged, getting all they needed to take packed as well as travelling through the tunnel and far enough away from the town outskirts as quickly as possible. Now the tension was easing, his exhaustion was catching up with him and Wren didn't look much fresher. The tunnel had been over a mile long and having to be as silent as possible, ignoring the rats, mice, tranolls and other dwellers in the deep had taken its toll upon both.

Wren had never seen a tranoll and her eyes had widened at the long limbed, hairy scavenger with its big eyes and sharp beak. After one had followed behind them for too long, Crow had taken a pinch of powder from one pouch then more from another. As quickly as both filled his hand he threw them as far behind them as he could. A slight popping sound followed by a bright light sent the scavenger running away down one of the narrow side passages. Luckily the egress was only a short way further and they both stepped out, blinking furiously to clear their eyes from dust and adjust to the brightness of the day. After making sure that the heavy bushes still hid the exit, they had brushed themselves off and headed for the road.

A short way into the woods, where a clearing abutted a small brook of clear water, Crow parked the hand cart and nodded to Wren.

'I know there is at least an hour's more daylight, but I think we should set camp here and get plenty of rest now. As we move through the woods the going will be more difficult. They cover many miles and will take, perhaps, three weeks to get through. Once at the other side there is a range of hills to cross and then we will hit better terrain.'

'Do you know where we are headed?' Wren asked. Not really caring as long as it was away from Verin.

'Yes, at least, I think so.'

'Well, that explains everything,' she snapped. Even as she began unpacking the sleeping bags and the food.

Grinning, Crow began collecting firewood and getting a pot of water to boil and the rest of the evening passed companionably.

Deeper in the woods Pandam and Dani made their own camp much less congenially. The gnome was still angry that she had pulled him up over his actions with the other travellers. Angrier, perhaps, because he knew she had been right to do so. This grated on him and made him regret making any bargain with Neera. Then he grinned viciously; for, unknown to the damned Big and the scary Elemental, he had plans to get himself out of this bargain.

Dani saw his smile and exchanged a look with the shadow kat. Although she *had* been confident that the gnome wouldn't break his word, she wasn't quite so sure now. He was definitely trying to push her beyond her limits. Deciding to keep a more suspicious watch upon him, as well as to demand a few more rest stops, she laid out the food Mallie had provided for their meal while Pandam made a small fire.

There was none of the comradery that Dani had known in her previous journey across Bisra. No excited Bili getting in everyone's way, no Jasper telling tales or exchanging jokes with Smith, Rook or Luke. Mr Poole, Sam, none of the people she had grown to care for. Just this cold-hearted, rude gnome who kept sneaking angry looks in her direction. Before she could fully succumb to melancholy the shadow kat gave a great sneeze and began chasing a bright blue butterfly. Dani burst out laughing seeing the huge magikal creature playing like a tiny kitten. When it came trotting back to her, its bottom jaw dropped in a kat smile, Dani reached down, hugging him tightly.

'Thank you,' she whispered into his ruff. Its steady purring was the only response it gave.

CHAPTER FOUR

The next few days were the same for both parties. Dani had demanded more breaks where she could catch her breath and build her energy as well as eat and drink. Her group was, conversely, able to cover more ground than before. Crow made sure to keep himself and Wren a distance back from them , there was something about the smaller person that set off his mental alarm. Although it would have been easy to overtake them, the former Assassin and the beggar trailed behind in their wake.

As evening approached a few days after both parties had entered the woods, Dani was laughing as the kat batted at a pile of fallen leaves. As the red, yellow, green, brown and orange leaves flew up into the air and a breeze sent them spinning, the kat twisted his flexible body, hitting out every which way at them. Pandam grumbled, annoyed at the camaraderie that had sprung up between the kat and the Big, as he began looking for a place to camp. The woods were a complicated mix of deciduous and evergreens that grew close together, but the whole area was spotted with clearings where the weak sun was able to break through the foliage a little. The biggest problem was not the trees but the many different thorn bushes that seemed determined to snag at clothing, stab at flesh and block the pathways that the Forest Watch should have kept clear.

Dani was still laughing at the cavorting kat when it suddenly gave a yowl of pain and dropped to the floor. She ran over and looked swiftly along its huge body. Its eyes were already clouded over, and she could see that it panted quickly and shallowly, each breath rasping in its lungs. Shudders began rippling the thick fur and it started drooling a thick liquid tainted a sickly yellow. The inspection took a mere second or two and then her attention was drawn to its front right paw. The spasms were speeding up and Dani had a struggle to keep a grip on the heavy leg as it trembled and shook violently in her hands. Lifting the pad of the foot she spied three fine thorns, almost hair thin, sunk deep into the beast's pad. Recognising *Lexith*, a plant that protected its tasty flowers and fruit by covering itself with these hair thin spikes, with some of its thorned roots growing above the ground. Each thorn carried a tip full of venom which, when harvested warily and then distilled and diluted carefully, could help cure childhood pox, heart murmurs and many other illnesses. Unfortunately, this venom was pure and had gone straight into flesh, the kat now dying as its organs began to fail. Usually, *Lexith* was fatal, with no known survivors.

Sitting down as close as she could get, Dani placed the huge paw of the stricken kat in her lap. She scratched carefully at the end of one of the thorns sticking out the leathery pad. As she scratched, she began to hum under her breath and black lightning began to spark from her eyes and rain down her body. As she continued to hum, the energies built more and more strongly, and her hair began to rise, and her eyes became white with power as the black lightning began flashing quickly within them. The long thorns began to slide out of the paw slowly, seeming to go on forever. At last, the three long spikes and another, much smaller piece, seemed to float out of the wounds before being placed carefully next to Dani's knee. Her humming became more insistent and a thick, yellow pus began oozing out of the tiny punctures. Without thinking, she used her warm cloak to wipe the paw clean of the poison, even as she continued to hum. The lightning sparked faster and faster, dancing around the kat's body now, flashing more and more until, suddenly, it cut out. The woman gave a deep sigh and settled down next to the unconscious kat and went immediately to sleep.

Crow and Wren had rushed up to the clearing when they had seen the first flash of the strange dark lightning. Hidden behind a couple of trees they had seen the whole event. Stunned, they exchanged a glance before looking back to see what the nasty little gnome would do.

He was standing there, shocked by what had just occurred then his crafty mind began to work. Not knowing he had an audience he began to mutter as he prepared the camp. Wren waited, watching

Dani, even as Crow listened closely to Pandam and managed to roughly translate what was being said. When he had heard enough, he gave a signal to Wren and they both slipped quietly away.

When they reached their own clearing, the camp was soon struck. Making do with soup and travel bread, they discussed what they had seen .

'I had been told that true Healers no longer existed, that they were all killed when the Plague hit,' Wren spoke quietly, her eyes wide in wonder at what she had witnessed.

'I have seen one other in my travels,' Crow said, keeping his voice low. 'He was an old man who wore his wisdom with pride. I had been sent to kill him.'

Wren looked up quickly, her expression carefully neutral. 'Did you?'

'No.' Crow gave a wry smile. 'No, when I found him, he was already at the end of his life. He knew what I was and yet still asked me to stay so he did not die alone. His whole family had gone before him, so he had no-one.'

'So, you stayed with him.'

'You seem sure of that.' The Assassin smiled in wry amusement.

'If you had killed him or left before he died you would not have the shadows I see in your eyes.'

There was a taut silence before Crow shook his head.

'You see too damned much, beggar maid, I will have to be careful of you. But you're right, I didn't kill him. I sat with him for nine days as he slowly crossed over into the Otherworld. He told me many things about magikers and about different ways that those who worship Kintrelle have changed over the years. It changed me.'

'Changed you how?'

'I began to question what I was being asked to do by the Mages. I thought, hoped, that they hadn't realised but, seeing that I had had a *compulsion* implanted, I am obviously wrong about that.' He shook his head ruefully as he placed his empty bowl on the floor and drank some tea.

'Not necessarily,' Wren surprised him by saying. 'The Mages play politics with each other constantly. If Verin wanted to steal another Assassin from one of his fellow Mages, he would need to get rid of you first. If you died after "going rogue", it would be a perfect way of doing so.'

Crow nodded thoughtfully. Not only did he know of many Assassins that had "gone rogue" over the many years he had worked for the Mages, his own predecessor being one of them, he also knew at least three up and coming rivals with little or no scruples. Verin would much prefer one of those to himself who wasn't always agreeable to his "Master" and was becoming older.

'You were listening hard to the other one with the girl and the kat,' Wren continued after a thoughtful pause.

'Aah yes, the other. We need to follow carefully, Wren. Before we reach the hills and the portal we need to take us elsewhere, the other, a gnome, intends to sell the Healer to a slaver. At first, if I have translated rightly, it meant for both her and the kat to die but now it has seen her power, it intends to profit by it. For some reason, there must be secrecy in case "he", whoever "he" might be, finds out about it.'

'What shall we do?'

'Spoil its plans!' Crow laughed.

Dani woke with a groan, aching in every muscle. She remembered healing the kat and, as usual, doing so had drained her. She knew from experience that it would take a few days for her energy levels to rise, another reason, if he needed any, for Pandam to complain. Shrugging off his likely attitude, she rose slowly. Before she was half upright, the great kat slid under her hand and pushed upwards, allowing her to stand much more smoothly and much more easily than she could have done on her own.

'Thank you, Sir Kat,' she smiled. The shadow kat gave a loud purr and led her slowly over to the fire where a pot of barley porridge bubbled. Scooping out a bowlful and taking some tea, she sat and began eating ravenously.

'You are Healer,' Pandam's squeaky voice spoke more slowly and was almost accusing.

'Yes,' Dani answered calmly.

'You should tell me this. You should, you should.' Pandam seemed to be trying to sound reasonable, but Dani could sense his irritation.

'Why? My magik is nothing to do with you. It is not combat based so it cannot be used to help defend us. If there comes a time when it is needed, I will use it. Other than that, it means nothing.'

The gnome muttered into his tin cup for a few minutes as Dani finished her porridge and rose to get a refill.

'Hurry,wemustgonow.' Pandam began bustling about, rolling up his bedding. He paused when he saw that the Big hadn't moved. 'Come,Isay. Move,move.'

'No.' Dani spoke quietly but there was steel in her voice. 'No more pushing me, no more angry words. I have had enough. When we reach the next safe settlement, you can go. Keep the money, just leave me be,'

Pandam stood up, drawing in a breath to begin yelling when a low growl stopped him in his tracks. The shadow kat now stood protectively in front of Dani, its ruff standing on end and its eyes sparking dangerously. Immediately the gnome held out his hands placatingly.

'No,nogrowl,Inomeanharm.' He slowed his speech again. "We must be quick, keep you safe.'

Dani looked at him appraisingly before going back to her food. She couldn't trust this magiker and the sooner they went their separate ways, the better.

After finishing her meal. She made a batch of flat breads to make sure she didn't get too hungry before the next stop. She had noticed her weight loss from yesterday's exertion and also knew how severely her energy levels would drop unless she ate more regularly than had been the usual up to now. As the breads cooked, she packed up her own bedding and checked the site for anything left behind. Wrapping the warm food in a clean shirt, she set them on her pack, covered the fire and gave a nod of her head to show she was ready. The gnome turned and walked down a narrow trail, leaving Dani and the kat to follow on behind.

Hidden behind the same bushes they had used the evening before, Wren and Crow watched the whole by-play between the others. Once they had moved off down the trail, Wren stood up and looked at Crow in confusion.

'She is not the same as she was yesterday; she looks half starved. And her hair is thicker and longer.'

'It is the Healing gift,' Crow told her. 'As with all magik, there is a price to pay. My Healer friend said that he had to eat and drink three times more than usual when he used his gift, and a lot more sleep. With food and rest, she will be fine in just a few days. He also said that hair and nails tend to have growth spurts, no one knows why.'

'So strange. We are still to follow?'

'Now more than ever.' Crow assured her, picking up his knapsack and heading down the same narrow pathway that Dani had disappeared down a few moments earlier.

The day was wet, with a fine, misty rain that didn't quit. Dani made sure to stop to refuel at regular times, making sure to keep her waterskin full from the trickling burns they went past. Visibility was limited and she was amazed that the gnome was able to move forward so easily, following the almost hidden pathway. The gloom of the day never lifted so when she saw the shadow kat moving in front of her and seemingly to fade away, she first took it to mean that the gloom had masked it from sight. The gnome moved back to her and couldn't hide his grin of satisfaction at seeing her all alone.

'Kat gone?' he queried. 'Is wild, needs freedom. We stop soon.' With that, he turned and moved on, leaving Dani confused. Apart from when he was castigating her, the gnome did his best not to speak to her especially that slowly, so why now? She could feel its thick coat beneath her fingers. The creature felt the need to fool the gnome with its "disappearance" so she would say nothing and stay on her toes.

Further back along the trail Crow frowned in confusion. The pathway to the portal at the base of the hills that surrounded this end of Mertam was in a slightly different direction to the way the Healer and her escort were heading. Now they seemed to be going deeper into the wood, where the trees grew even more closely together, denying even the low winter light entry. Cautiously Crow slowed down, wanting to keep any noise he made to a minimum. Wren followed his lead, staying quiet and only moving when he did.

Thus it was, when the attack came, the Assassin was too far away to be of any help at first. Dani had removed her pack and had taken out some wool and dry kindling from it, hoping to start a small cooking fire. As she bent over, using her flint to light the wool and sticks, a heavy weight slammed into her, sending her sprawling. In doing so, she missed being speared by the arrow that had been sent her way. Rolling to her feet, Dani took in the scene around her. Pandam crouched low over his own knapsack, for a moment Dani assumed that he was going for a weapon to help fight off the swarm of bandits, but a split second was all she needed to realise that he was keeping low, out of the way of any stray arrows.

A sudden roar followed by a scream of pain jerked her head around to see a huge man fall to his knees, the back of his head crushed by the powerful jaws of the shadow kat. Men of all shapes and sizes that had been advancing on the lone woman froze in their tracks.

'Yousignalledithadleft,' The high voice belonged to another gnome, enraged at Pandam. Another roar went up and the gang of cutthroats looked around them in fear, waving various bits of weaponry in front of themselves in a feeble attempt to keep the invisible monster away. Pandam, knowing that his life was now forfeit , tried to save himself.

'Ithadgone,gone!' he shrieked even as another scream echoed out and another fell beneath the lashing claws that cut through flesh like hot knives through butter. Trying to gain forgiveness from the gang, he jumped forward and grabbed hold of the slave-girl even as the kat flashed into visibility and snarled at a group of three standing close to each other in fear. It faded out again and blood sprayed as the men were eviscerated.

'Ihaveher,Healerismine!' Pandam shrieked again. Suddenly there was a cry and another man fell as a swiftly moving shadow sped past him and opened his throat with one cut of a blade. This shadow was not the kat, who was still doing its own lethal dance further away, this shadow was a man who moved with speed and grace as he cut and slashed his way through the men who had thought that this way of life was easy pickings.

There were screams and shouts, mingled with shrieks of pain from the group of bandits; growls, roars and snarls of rage from the kat; then whistles as blades cut through the air as it swung towards an unguarded bit of flesh. Within a very short time the only men standing were the few who had dropped their weapons, the tall stranger in black, Dani and the gnome, who held her tight and had his razor-sharp dagger placed over her kidney.

'Leave,leave,' Pandam shouted, his body shaking with rage. 'Healermine,gonow.'

The unknown man stepped closer, playing a piece of shaped metal over his fingers. 'If you hurt her, you will die.' He spoke calmly, his gaze never moving off the gnome.

'Ha, maybe, Big, maybe. But she will still be dead, ha!' Even speaking slowly, the sound of glee from Pandam was unmistakable. His voice stopped abruptly as Dani placed her hand over the one holding her tightly against her captor. 'What? Stop or I kill.'

'The thing most people forget,' Dani's voice was hoarse, only just above a whisper. Her eyes darkened until there were no whites left, just a blackness darker than the deepest pit. The lighting began to flicker across the gnome, causing him to flinch again and again 'They forget that there is always a balance to be kept. This means that what can Heal…can also kill.'

As she spoke, the gnome froze into place, unable to free himself from her touch. As the others watched he began to cough, his body shaking violently as his eyes bulged out from his head. He coughed more and more, struggling to catch his breath as he collapsed. Blood spurted from his mouth as the coughing became fiercer, his breathing hoarse and ragged, making a whooping sound as he tried to drag life-giving air into his collapsing lungs. With a whole-body shudder and a last almighty choke, blood gushed from his mouth in an arc over his body before trickling to a stop as he finally lay still.

There was a pause as everyone looked at the frail female who, even now, was slowly sinking to her knees and shaking as tears rolled down her face. Her skin almost unnaturally clear and rosy and hair gleaming despite the dreariness of the day.

Crow watched her for a few moments then, after seeing that she wasn't going to collapse, spoke to the few remaining bandits.

'Who told you about this traveller?' he demanded.

They looked at each other and then one spoke up. 'It were the gnome, 'he sends a message from the city to Hacken, our leader, when there is a new pigeon as needs plucking. They has done this racket lots. He sent a sign by a runner saying there was new prey. He never said she were a Healer though, slimy scav.'

'Be grateful,' Crow growled. 'She could have killed the lot of you before the morning. You are all going to find a different job, mates. I come this way regularly and I know many in the forest Watch and the Outriders who would just love to catch road bandits and collect the bounty on your heads. Remember, they don't need the whole body, just enough to prove death, so I really do mean "heads".'

There was a swift exchange of glances, followed by some gulping and a lot of nodding in agreement.

'That's more than fair,' said the spokesman. They started forward as a group, intending to take everything they could from the dead, before all freezing at the ringing of a drawn sword.

'When I said you could go, I meant now. Anyone still here by the time I breathe three times will die.' Before the sentence was fully finished, there was pushing and shoving as each man tried to get away as quickly as possible.

Laughing quietly, Crow turned to speak to the Healer only to shout for Wren as he saw her close her eyes and her body go completely slack.

CHAPTER FIVE

At Crow's shout, Wren came out from where she had been hiding. Rushing over to the unconscious Healer she felt for the pulse point in the neck. Seeing the slave collar in all its ugly splendour, she drew in a breath before pulling the neck scarf up to hide the dainty filigree gold and gems. When she raised her head to call Crow over, she saw the shadow kat watching her, its gaze fixed and unblinking.

'I am not here to cause her harm, kat,' Wren spoke with a calm she didn't feel. 'I want to make sure that she has what she needs.' The kat gave a grunt before settling down to clean itself and to remove the flesh and blood caught on claws and teeth.

By the time that Crow had removed each body to a mile or so away: stripped of clothing, gold, gems and food, and leaving them laid out to feed the forest dwellers, Wren had made a fire and begun cooking. A stew was just beginning to bubble, made from the previous evening's leftovers. She was also frying up the last of the bacon before making some griddle cakes to cook in the tasty fat.

'How many do we expect for dinner,' asked Crow, surprised at the amount of food being prepared.

'Just you, me, a shadow kat and a Healer with a prodigious appetite,' she replied with a grin.

There was a pause before she laughed at his expression. 'Go get us some water.'

'As long as you save me some of those griddle cakes,' he demanded, before picking up the empty bucket and whistling cheerfully as he headed for a nearby brook.

When Dani regained her senses, she found herself tucked up under a warm blanket. A rough lean-to had been made from closely woven branches and very little of the fine rain managed to seep through. A small fire was burning brightly, and the scents of food and tea tickled her nose. She saw a stranger feed a few twigs to the fire then turn his head to give a low laugh to someone further away. Turning her own head her sight was blocked by the huge head of the shadow kat, its bright yellow eyes staring at her intensely. Without thinking she reached out a weary arm and patted its face.

'I'm alright, sweetie,' she said even as she yawned.

'Wonderful,' called a male voice from the fire. 'We have been waiting the food for you.'

Still wary, Dani sat up and saw that, further from the fire, was a small woman, dressed in a bright patchwork of colours. Dani thought she looked a little familiar but couldn't, in her befuddled state, remember where from. As she caught Dani's eye, the woman grinned.

'Take no notice of this greedy man, he is only annoyed because I wouldn't let him eat all the griddle cakes. I was waiting for you to wake up first.'

'Thank you?'

Bewildered, Dani sat up slowly, bracing herself against the shadow kat. One of her hands slipped slightly and she ended up resting her face against its purring sides, breathing in the wild, musky scent of it and felt herself relax fully, for the first time since before leaving the ship.

Crow sat down next to his companion and eyed the cakes greedily. After putting a few on a tin plate with a little berry syrup, Wren passed them to Dani before heaving a great sigh and filling up Crow's plate.

There were a few minutes of quiet as they ate the light, fluffy fare before Crow began to explain his background to Dani and the kat, followed by Wren. After a bit of hesitation, Dani began her own story and her reasons for travelling. She understood that they knew the two most important bits of information about her; that she was a slavey and also a Healer.

'Willoughby?' Wren sat up in amazement. 'Your ex-master is Jervis Willoughby?'

'Yes,' Dani answered, surprised that Wren knew the name.

'Oh gods,' the beggar said, going pale with shock. 'You are lucky to be alive.'

'You know this man, Wren?' Crow asked,

'Yes, he was at the Mage Academy many years before I was. He had a terrible reputation there, which, considering just what atrocities the Academy approves of, should tell you how bad he was. He did a lot of experiments with Mýste and killed many animals and slaves with it. There were also rumours that he had caused the death of more than one apprentice too. A nasty, nasty man, Dani, I am surprised that you survived.'

'I don't think I would have, if I had stayed,' Dani said. 'Apart from the fact that he is planning to do something now that he has arrived in Mertam, his son has become unmanageable.'

'Don't worry,' this time it was Crow who spoke. 'Not only will we help to guide you on your way but, between us, me and the kat will keep you safe.'

As Dani began her thanks her face split in a huge yawn. Within a few short moments Crow had carried her slumbering body back to her sleep space, covered her up and told the kat that they would watch her if it needed to go hunting.

'Hmm, we had better keep all our senses aware,' Crow mused. 'Willoughby being Mage-trained means he is much more dangerous than I might otherwise think. The fact he has used the killing Mýste in spells and experiments as well as caring little for human life also means that we are going against someone who could be the winner in a face-to-face battle.'

'No, he won't be,' Wren spoke calmly and with confidence. 'Now that Dani is learning more about her Healing, as well as having the kat protecting her with its own magik and its claws, we two might not even get a chance to help. Don't underestimate either of those, they could beat our combined abilities without breaking a sweat.

Apart from Willoughby's pleasure in playing with the Black Mýste, we are very closely matched, magikally. If Dani is right, she has a good head start on him and his bloodhounds, so we just need to make sure it stays that way.'

'Sounds like a plan.' Crow looked across the fire at the huddled figure of the sleeping woman. 'Can you remove the collar?'

'No, dammit, I can't. There is only a little magik in its locking mechanism, the rest is tiny wheels, cogs and explosive powders. Not my area of expertise. Could you?'

'No, I have a steady hand and the best coordination of anyone I know. What I don't know is how the blasted things – pun intended – are put together. We will have to leave the sickening thing on.'

'Yes,' agreed Wren. 'She needs to get somewhere safe first, then we will get her free.'

'Sounds like something to be getting on with.' After a short pause Crow continued hopefully. 'Are there any griddle cakes left?'

Dani slept long and deep that night and when she woke up it was to see that everything was packed, ready to move on, and the two companions were chatting and arguing amiably in low tones.

'How far to the portal?' she wondered out loud, once she was up and about. She sat and ate the last of the griddle cakes, as she spoke, much to Crow's dismay.

'At a regular pace, usually half a day. Slowing down for you, I think the whole of today and maybe some of tomorrow. Stop looking so apologetic,' Crow continued, sounding a little irritated. 'That wasn't a complaint about your pace, that was an answer to your question.'

'Right,' Dani heaved out a sigh as she scratched her scalp. A fine length of hair covered her skull now and Crow took a battered hat from his pack and told her to wear it at all times and to tuck the hair up under the brim.

Once the fire was out and Dani's bedding packed away, they pulled on their knapsacks and began a steady walk through the last few miles of the trees. This was so different to what Dani had experienced with the irascible gnome. No muttering or cursing, no lectures on keeping moving, no derogatory mumblings, just stories, laughter and plenty of stops so that by the end of the day, they were less than a mile away from the end of the woods and only another ten from the village and its portal.

Dani was surprised, then, to see her companions stop and Crow began setting a fire.

'We aren't going on?' she asked, surprised.

'No,' Wren answered. 'We will rest here and when we leave in the morning, we will have a better idea on which way we need to go. We'll all be much more refreshed, therefore more able to cope with portal travel. To top it all off, it also means that the first crush for places will be over.'

'Oh yes, that does sound so much better.' With that, Dani settled down to peeling some onions ready for the frying pan.

The evening was just as relaxing as the whole time had been since the fight. Dani didn't realise how much she had needed this act of friendship. She had missed her other friends more than she realised and not being able to grieve for her losses was hurting her, but she knew that there would time for that once she arrived at where she needed to go. The companionship of Crow, Wren and the kat now eased some of the pain she felt.

Since leaving the ship the pulling sensation she experienced had increased, along with the sense of urgency; it didn't hurt her but was insistent. When she explained this, her travelling companions seemed more than happy to travel with her for the time being, which helped her feel so much safer, especially as the shadow kat also seemed content to journey with them for now.

As they sat around the fire under the stars, the shadow kat stood and stretched for a few moments before going up to Dani and snuffling at her hair. It then moved off and soon faded from sight.

'You are a lucky woman,' Crow said quietly.

'I think so too.' smiled Dani. 'But why do you?'

'The kat loves you, which means that you will always be protected. Saving it from infection has given you its loyalty.'

'Why do you always say "it"? I assumed it to be female.'

'Just how much do you know of shadow kats, Dani?

'Nothing much, apart from what I heard in a child's tale, which is that they are magik, but the bard never really said in what way.'

'Oh boy,' grinned the Assassin. 'You have a lot to learn.'

'Hush, Crow, behave,' scolded Wren. 'Right, your first question was why do we say "it" instead of "him" or "her". The simple answer is that the kat isn't either one or the other but both male and female.'

At Dani's look of utter confusion, they both grinned.

'Shadow kats don't seem to choose a gender for long, their sexual organs are whatever they want them to be. Kats, when female, have also been known to become pregnant without a male's participation. Sometimes their disappearing ability doesn't just mean from sight but that their whole body goes elsewhere. That's why we think they can go anywhere they want in seconds and why they can take people through the portals easily. If you knew the place you needed to be, it could probably take you there immediately, without needing a portal at all.'

'I wish I did know where I needed to be,' Dani said in frustration, 'The best I can do is point in the general direction and say "that way for now". I hope that eventually I will be more specific.'

'Don't worry,' Crow said lazily as he stretched out upon his blankets. 'We will get there eventually. Now, we are safe as this area is close to the Watch patrollers, so I suggest we all get some sleep before the morning,'

Taking his advice, Dani and Wren found their own blankets and snuggled down. Sometime after she had fallen asleep, Dani half woke to feel the kat lying down next to her. Burying her hand in its fur and sighing at the warmth, she soon dropped back into a deep slumber and heard no more until morning.

Willoughby sat looking out at the miserable weather, feeling a huge sense of satisfaction. The house was much more comfortable with the added furnishings he had insisted on. Constance, his wife, didn't seem interested so perhaps it was time to remind her that she was his property. A grin flickered across his features as his perverted imagination came up with various painful – for her - scenarios to fit his desires.

When a knock sounded at the study door, Willoughby grin became broader. The snooty butler, Heds, had tried to insist that quality servants did not knock before entering. He had soon changed his mind when Willoughby told him to lower his standards or leave. The butler had looked like he had swallowed a live mouse but inclined his head and had made sure that every servant now knocked on both the study door and the door to the workshop and waited to be invited in. The fact the old hypocrite hadn't packed and left only confirmed that he was a spy for Miltop.

'Come!' Willoughby shouted, making sure to be smirking as Heds opened the door to usher a tall, handsome man in army uniform into the room.

'Mr Blood, sir,' the butler intoned, careful not to look at the man sitting in the chair.

'Come in, man, sit yourself down,' Willoughby spoke eagerly, not bothering to tease or even acknowledge Heds any more as the butler gave a short nod and left, closing the door quietly behind him.

Whether accidentally or deliberately done, the door didn't quite catch, unnoticed by Lord Willoughby, so eager was he to move on with his plans.

'You need someone finding?' The much younger man asked as he took the chair indicated, already taking a dislike to this puffed up, self-important idiot.

'Yes. First though, just how good are you?'

Asking such a question was an insult to any true Bloodhound. The
lands of non-magik studiously ignored the obvious magikal
abilities of both Bloodhounds and Trackers. Of the hunters, only
those with very little skill missed their mark. Used by law
enforcement but employed by the army, Bloodhounds could track
all humans, magikers and animals for safe collection. Trackers had
the same ability but didn't worry so much about the survival of the
prey and, consequently, were much cheaper to hire. Willoughby
was determined to get the slavey back unharmed, though. Not only
was she his property but the fact that she had survived for so long
after the Numb should have killed her meant that she had magik
which also belonged to Willoughby and could be exploited.

After leaving a long enough pause to let the older man know that
he had made a grave error in attitude, the Bloodhound responded
with as few words as possible.

'The best.'

Willoughby sat back, satisfied. He was a good judge of character
and had been rude intentionally. Seeing how the man opposite had
responded, with controlled irritation, told Willoughby that there
would be no aggressive posturing from this man, which usually led
to lethal fights, a constant issue for the younger Bloodhounds.
Satisfied, he told a fiction about needing to find a servant, leaving
out the fact she was a runaway slave, instead implying that she had
left to meet up with her lover, not knowing that her lover had
returned to Mertam.

After he had finished speaking he waited for the soldier's response.
And waited. After a few more minutes he was beyond irritated.
Before his temper snapped the soldier nodded his head slightly.

*'My time in the army is finished,' Charlie said flatly, knowing that
the man, Willoughby, had lied already. 'I have come here as a
favour to my ex-commanding officer. I will need the typical
finder's fee paid to the Guild and the contracts signed before I
begin. As long as you stay true, I will find the girl. Break your
word and I keep the fee, but my job ends.'*

Willoughby gave a growl of anger before he began blustering. As he tried to wriggle out of paying before getting any results and also having to sign a contract, the soldier stood up, ready to leave.

'What? Where are you going?' Willoughby roared, his face bright red with surprise and irritation.

'I assumed that you were told that the payment and contract were non-negotiable. I will leave you to find someone to do the job who isn't connected to the Guild.'

'Alright, alright,' Willoughby conceded the point, having known about the conditions beforehand. With obvious ill will he signed the detailed contract before promising to send the outrageous sum to the Guild the following day.

'You will have until the end of the selling day,' the soldier said. 'Any later and the contract is void, in which case you will be expected to pay a fine of seventy-five percent.'

'That is outrageous!' Willoughby spluttered.

'That is how it works.' With a short nod, the younger man turned and left the study, not caring that he was leaving an extremely angry man behind him.

As Charlie Blood moved down the long corridor, he saw the butler give a half smile as he stepped backwards through an open doorway. Another door opened further down the passageway and a slender woman, her head turned away from Charlie as she spoke over her shoulder, shut the door and moved off. For some unknown reason the sight of the small straight back, the honey-coloured hair piled up to show a slender neck and shoulders and the smooth stride stayed with Charlie as he collected his hat and coat and walked out into the cold, blustery weather.

Not happy about taking the contract, Charlie knew he had very little choice. His ex-C.O was a mean bastard and had said that unless Charlie did the job, he wouldn't be given his last month's pay and his savings would disappear, never to be found again. He needed the money to begin his life as a civilian, he had no choice but to do this job . The only thing that had been in Charlie's favour had been the fact that, as his tenure in the army had finished ten days ago, he could demand that the contract was done through the Guild, giving Charlie a much bigger percentage.

Whistling through his teeth, his hands curled and thrust deep into his coat's pockets, Charlie strode towards the Guild house where he had rooms. Even as he whistled and watched other people, his mind's eye kept seeing that small, slender figure moving ahead of him, always out of reach.

CHAPTER SIX

Dani watched Crow sorting through the packs as he got himself ready for the next part of their journey. Seeing Wren sitting and staring into the flames of the cooking fire, she was struck at just how well the two worked together, yet they had known each other for only a short time. Pondering over their connection, Dani thought of another question she needed to ask.

'Why are there magikal portals in the lands of the Shining One? I thought He hated magik?'

It was Wren who answered. 'In fact, Kintrelle, the Shining One, never did say anything against magik. That is down to the Preceptors, Mages and local councils. As always, when Man gets religion, he takes over and tries to force it into a specific shape, even if that means going against the teachings of the Holy Ones they follow. Crazy, isn't it?'

'Completely. I know Mertam is very much the same as Bisra in the fact that magik is banned. Bisra would not accept an Abomination like a portal, at least I don't think so, so how does Mertam accept one?'

'Money.' Crow said bitterly. 'It all comes down to that, girl. The reason the portal is so far from the city is simple; those who use it can pretend never to recognise another waiting there, even if they are family. Don't worry, they pay a high premium for the use of the portal and only have a limited time during the day to use it. Mainly though, goods are transported from one place to another, ensuring no losses, unlike sea travel where ships, men and expensive trade goods can disappear into a serpent's belly or be lost in a storm. As long as only gnomes are on show when humans are present, blind eyes are turned towards anyone, or anything, who uses them. All you will need to do is point in the direction we need to be going and Niralz will make sure we get there safely.

Having a shadow kat with us will guarantee that no-one tries to cause us any problems. Now, are you ready to move out?'

'Almost.' Dani scrambled to her feet and washed her bowl and spoon before shouldering her own knapsack and followed behind Wren with the kat at her side.

'Actually, Bisra does have a portal, but they keep it well hidden from the common man.' Crow mentioned before walking on.

This part of the journey was much shorter than the other, which Dani was grateful for. The weather had turned freezing cold, with a bitter wind that sliced through all her clothing. Even wrapped in her heavy coat, thick socks, mittens and a scarf wrapped around her head and mouth didn't stop her teeth from chattering. The light was dim even at midday and there seemed to be a strange colour to the sky.

Just as they saw tiny spots of light in the far distance, Dani gave a shout of alarm.

Crow whirled around, his hand on his sword hilt, ready to protect the women. He turned his head rapidly from side to side, trying to see what had caused Dani's fear.

'What's wrong, woman?' he snapped out.

'The clouds are falling.'

Turning around, Crow opened his mouth to make a sarcastic comment but shut it quickly when he saw the real fear on Dani's face.

'I don't und – oh, no sweetheart,' as he began to recognise the origin of her fear. 'That is no cloud explosion or unnatural magik. It is snow, my sweet, just snow. Haven't you ever seen it before?'

'Snow?' The Healer's eyes grew round with wonder, and she turned her face up to the flakes that were falling a little faster now, dancing and blowing in the strong wind. 'The only snow I have seen is grey and dirty. I have never even seen it fall from the sky before.'

'Try this,' Wren grinned before sticking out her tongue and tipping her face upwards. Dani laughed before she followed suit, giggling at the cold kiss of the flakes and the shock of cold touching the heat of her tongue. Who knows how long they would have stayed there if the kat hadn't let out a growl. Crow saw just how thick the flakes were becoming as well as how quickly the temperature was dropping. The wind had picked up, swirling the snow around in a dizzying, disorientating dance.

'Enough, ladies. Time to move.' His tone was brusque as he adjusted his pack, grabbed Wren's hand and, after telling her to hold on to Dani, he began a quick march towards the small town ahead, where tiny spots of light flickered. The snow came down quickly, covering the ground with a carpet of white. The howling wind and the spinning flakes were confusing and frightening to Dani, who was grateful for the kat, who came back to push her onwards every so often, and the grip of Wren's hand on hers, leading her towards safety.

By the time the town came into view properly, both women were struggling to carry on as the snow was falling so thick and fast that it was a true blizzard. If it hadn't been for the strength of the shadow kat that Crow now held fast to, and his own stubbornness, all three would have fallen face down in the snow to be found in summer thaw. The kat gave a sudden loud yowl, causing local dogs to begin barking.

Doors opened and shouts of surprise and alarm let the travellers know they had been seen. People swarmed towards them and each of them was swung up into strong arms and rushed indoors. This included Crow which Dani promised herself to laugh about later.They were hustled into a large house, baths were filled, and they were encouraged to drink hot, honeyed milk, with added spices. They struggled, needing help to remove their wet garments, after which they all slid into the steaming water, Wren's sigh of contentment was echoed from her side where Dani lay in her own tub and from behind the screen where Crow wallowed in his own. To begin with, the water felt too hot, almost burning, but as the minutes passed, their bodies became comfortable with the heat.

The added herbs helped their tight muscles to relax and breath to come more easily.

Although they would have gladly stayed in the baths for longer, drowsy in the warm and fragrant water, eventually tasty cooking smells seeped into the bathing room, and they all reluctantly left the tubs and dressed in loose, warm, robes trimmed with coney fur.

Following the sound of voices, they went into a large room, set with chairs and tables for dining. It reminded Dani a little of the gnomes' home back in the city but much larger. Her eyes widened as she saw the many different species of people sitting around and chatting. People who seemed to be made of wood, or water, some looking like Neera from the ship, others looking like nothing human at all. Short, tall, fat, thin, all shapes, sizes and assorted number of limbs. Her gasp of delight when she saw a child running to his mother, trailing huge wings covered in fine down stopped all conversation. Dani blushed in embarrassment.

'I'm sorry, I don't mean to be rude. You are all so breath-taking and beautiful.'

There was a slight relaxing of tension which tightened again when a short, round man went to stand before her.

'And me?' he rasped out. 'Do I count as breath-taking and beautiful?'

Dani looked at him, his body covered in fine brown fur, his thin hair pulled tightly back into a wispy bun on the top of his head, emphasising his rat-like features covered in warts and wiry hair. Then she smiled.

'Of course,' she said, matter-of-factly. 'Your eyes glow with the secrets of the sea. I saw eyes like that before, on a magiker called Zutana. But I have to say that all the magikers I have ever seen seem to have gorgeous eyes.'

'You know Zutana? He is a strong merman. And that means you know the Air Elemental, Merra.'

Dani looked completely confused as she answered him. 'No, no, my Zutana is a Water Elemental, mated to Captain Poole, not one of the Mer Folk. As for the Air Elemental, he is called Neera. Why do you…? Oh, it was a test.'

'Yes, it was,' said a voice from the back. 'These idiots didn't believe that you were here to escape the humans, as the message said, they thought you might be a spy, despite your looks.'

'Hmm. And now?' Dani crossed her arms and tapped her foot in irritation at the man in front of her.

There was a burst of laughter from the challenger, and he took her hand in his paw-like grip.

'You win!' he said, still laughing. 'I should have realised there was more to you than I first thought, just by your eyes.'

'What about my eyes? They are just grey.'

The curanja, a rat-like changeling of the sea, shook his head in surprise. 'My eyes are black and show dark rainbows and secrets. Yours may be "just grey" but they glow with their own treasure, my dear. Not all magikers have eyes like these, but no pure human has them either.' With a short bow, he moved back into the crowd. The rest of them acknowledged Dani in their own ways: a nod, a wave, a wiggle of ears, before dispersing and going back to their own business.

Dani was quiet as her small group were seated, and various people came and sat to chat with them for a few minutes before moving away for someone else. The toddler she had seen running earlier came up to stare at her out of deep purple eyes the colour of pansies, before climbing up onto her lap, wrapping a wing over her shoulder and calmly falling asleep. Dani snuggled him closer, listening to the conversation his parents were having with Crow. After a few minutes she felt eyes staring and she looked up from her examination of the feather-like hair growing on the youngster's head. His mother was staring at Dani in wonder, causing the Healer to feel uncomfortable.

'I'm sorry, do you want him back?'

'No, if you are alright with him sleeping on you,' the woman said in a light, fluttering voice. 'I am just surprised at how quickly he settled with you, as he doesn't usually like strangers. He has not yet gained the ability to hide his wings, so we have taught him to be wary.'

'His wings are beautiful,' Dani answered. 'I feel myself to be his own age, or even younger as there is so much I don't know. I have had a very enclosed life. Do you know, until today I hadn't known that snow falls from the sky, is white and is very, very cold!'

The woman laughed. 'My name is Flavia; my mate is Humbert, and our son is Humlia. And we are all still learning, every day, so don't feel as if you are the only one.'

Dani introduced herself and they chatted for a while until food was delivered and Flavia carefully removed her sleeping son so that they could all eat.

Dani smiled in pleasure at what sat before her. Slices of roasted girox, lean and dark. Fresh green beans, potatoes mashed with butter and garlic, two batter puddings, all covered in a rich gravy. Without a word, she set to and cleared her plate of everything. She was even happier when a pie bursting with cherries and decorated with almonds was brought to the table, along with some thick cream to scoop on the top of it.

She looked up to see a few awe-struck faces at the amount of food she had managed to get through; as much as many a grown man. Although she flushed slightly, she refused to feel embarrassed. After all, apart from her Healing "gift" burning through energy, it also took a toll on her physically. Every time she gained enough flesh and energy to look as normal as she should, something happened which meant she had to begin all over again. At the moment, she still looked over thin from the rushing about with Pandam and the shadow kat's Healing. Pandam's death bothered her only because that hadn't drained her at all. In fact, she thought that if she had been in a better place, killing the gnome might have done her a lot more good than otherwise. Remembering the shadow kat, she looked around for it but there was no sign.

Once they had finished eating, Dani and Crow were called into a small office. Inside was a tiny being, no more than two or three feet in height, busily moving a complicated set of discs around on a board. When he spoke, his voice was disconcertingly deeper than his size indicated.

'So, where do you wish to go and when?'

Crow looked at Dani who closed her eyes and allowed her inner "pull" to direct her. Raising her hand, she pointed to the east.

'There,' she said, confidently.

'To Predima?'

'I don't know, is that in that direction?'

The small fey creature glared at her, assuming she was acting up, and opened his mouth to growl something but at that moment the shadow kat became visible and rubbed its huge head against Dani's arm. He watched in fascination as Dani raised her hand automatically to rub the purring beast's head.

'Is that beast yours?' he said.

'Of course not,' snorted Dani, inelegantly. 'Who could own a shadow kat? It has, however, chosen to be a travelling companion with us for the time being.'

There was a silence then Niralz bowed his head slightly in apology.

'Alright then, you and all your companions are booked for the morning for the East Portal. Everyone else will be travelling through the South Portal, which is situated elsewhere. There is no charge.'

'No charge?' Crow sounded suspicious of the favour. 'Why no charge and why the morning?'

'You have a shadow kat, sir. Its energy will transport you; the portal is just a convenient place to travel from. As for the morning, Predima isn't safe, especially as it gets dark. You will have a two-day journey to get to another outgoing portal so go early and you can cover at least half. I will give you directions tomorrow.'

Crow thanked him, took Dani's arm and led her out to a quiet corner where Wren sat waiting. The kat was already lying sprawled on the floor.

'Alright, Miss Question Mark, I can see you have questions so ask what you will, quietly. And what did I say wrong?' Crow said the latter as he saw Dani's face drop before she forced a smile.

'Sorry, that just reminded me of something we called a young friend of mine. Bili was either eating or asking questions. I miss him.' Giving herself a shake, she continued. 'Questions, yes. Why do we need a second portal? Don't they bring people in as well as let them leave from just one?'

'No, if they did both journeys from the same place, there would be too much congestion as well as too many faces recognised. There might actually end up being a collision, meaning that those going through the portal explode and mingle their bodies into those coming back. The outgoing portals are always at least twenty miles from the incoming ones.'

'Oh, I didn't realise. And having a shadow kat with us means we don't pay?'

'As to that, it doesn't always follow. Sometimes we might be charged a little, we may even get a portal keeper try and charge us extra. Believe me, I would have soon stopped that from happening.'

'So, what do we do now? We need somewhere to stay. Should I offer some of the gold or gems I carry?'

'No, wait until I can see what you have on you first. That way, you won't overpay and perhaps whet the appetite of any unscrupulous bandit who would follow to rob us.'

As Crow finished speaking a harassed looking boy pushed his way through the small crowd and beckoned them towards him. They all got up and followed him through a large wooden door, down a corridor and into a private chamber.

'Here you go, my lovelies,' drawled the youngster. 'This is all yourn 'til mornin'. The master says you can 'ave supper in 'ere

later, save any worriting you might be 'avin' over strangers bein'
about. Ooohh, thankee kindly.' The latter was said to Wren who
had given a tiny piece of metal with a chip taken from it. Although
of little worth, obviously it meant much to this boy. With a huge
grin, he backed out of the door with an amazed look at the kat
before disappearing down the hallway.

'This is a surprise,' Wren commented. 'Should we be
"worriting"?'

'No,' Crow grinned at her. 'This has a lock on the main door and
on the bedrooms. Anyone that can get through three locked doors
deserves all he can get. Unless he is a bloody Mage, that is. I
reckon we have been given this because of the kat and because
they can't work out what our Dani is.'

'In that case, I am going to take a nap then I might feel less muzzy
headed.' With that, Wren walked into one of the sleeping chambers
and shut the door.

'Are you sleepy?' Crow asked Dani. 'No? Good. Let me see what
goods you have to trade. We will be able to exchange some of
what you have for the coins of commerce, used in some of the
FreeLands and even some of the Coalition lands.'

From then until supper arrived, and Wren woke up, the two
conspirators went through all of Dani's goods with Crow giving
her information on what she had and its overall worth. The small
group then discussed things and all agreed that not allowing
anyone else to join them would prevent future betrayal. Knowing
that they needed to practise great caution as they worked their way
to the outgoing portal would take all their focus without also
having to keep an eye out for traitors.

After they had all eaten, Dani went off to sleep in a comfortable
bed while Crow filled Wren in on Dani's goods. Once he had
shared the information, he took a few of the smallest gems and left
the suite of rooms to go and speak to Niralz about swapping them
for travelling currency. When he came back, holding a heavy
pouch of coins worth various amounts, he made sure to lock the

main door and added a little booby trap for anyone who tried to break in. Then the two separated at the bedroom doors.

The shadow kat walked around the rooms in its invisible form, gliding through the wooden doors with ease. Where it walked, protective magik flowed until, satisfied, it went and lay down on the couch. Heaving a huge sigh, it settled its head onto its paws and slid into a light doze until morning.

CHAPTER SEVEN

The following day saw the three dressed warmly,with full packs, walking through a wooden passageway that, though cold, saved them all from the worst weather outside. The short gnome who led them proceeded into a series of caverns. Crow was grateful for the guide as, even with his superior sense of direction, they would soon have been lost without him.

Their breath billowed out in clouds against the grey stone walls. In places Crow had to duck his head as the roof lowered. Through one tunnel and then another, forking to the left, then the right, they walked for almost seven miles until the gnome pointed silently into a side corridor and led them through the entrance to the East Portal chamber.

Wren and Dani gasped at what they saw. The whole room was lit by energy pouring from the furthest corner. It flowed down in rainbow-coloured waves, looking like a waterfall as it spilled from a gap in the ceiling, in a broad sweep to the ground to disappear through another opening in the floor of the cave.

For the first time the gnome spoke, his voice lower in register and much slower than Pandam's screech had been.

'One of you needs to touch the kat, then the others form in a line. Do *not* let go, or you will be lost in the *never*. This will take you to Predima, although you is fools for going there. Here be a map, the boss told me to give you this and to wish you safe travels.'

'Why is everyone so afraid of Predima?' Crow asked, suspiciously.

'We know there are some Necrotics there, sir. The rumour is, some of the Mages drop prisoners off there, to be eaten. So, you be careful, people disappear from Predima.'

Looking at each other and recognising the need to still travel to this accursed place, Dani caught hold of some of the shadow kat's ruff in her fingers. Wren held Dani's hand and held out her other to Crow, who caught it and laced his warm fingers with hers. Then, with a deep breath, Dani followed the magikal feline through the energy curtain. Just before her sight and sound cut out, she heard the gnome yell out.

'Name the kat! I forgot; the boss says na…' The rest of his words were drowned out. A noise like a whirlwind blowing through a forest assaulted their ears even as bright lights flashed and streaked before their eyes, making their lids squeeze shut in self-defence. Swirling and tumbling, losing all sense of direction, Dani felt a scream building up within. Just as she thought she would lose her senses to panic and fear, she tumbled out onto the hard packed floor of a forest clearing.

A group of gnomes pulled the companions away from the energy field as soon as they landed, clearing the way for any other travellers. All the gnomes held weapons and there were a few who kept watch on the surrounding area. Dani felt sick and sat still, holding her pounding head as did Wren. Only Crow and the kat were unaffected and the small men looked at the kat in awe.

'Where are you heading, folks?' One of the gnomes stepped forward and offered them a drink from his waterskin, while another poured out more into a bowl for the kat.

'Over there,' Dani pointed, weakly. The group looked at her, puzzled but then shrugged and drew lots as to who would guide these idiots to the outgoing portal that lay to the east of the island. There was a huge argument when Crow told them that no-one else would be helping defend them on the journey.

'Are you insane, man?' the spokesman yelled. 'There are Necrotics out there, they have learned to hunt in packs, and they will pick you off, one by one. You will pray for death.'

'That's as maybe,' responded Crow, calmly. 'However, I am a trained Assassin, we have a shadow kat with us, this lady has Mage training and the next one is very good with her knife. We have no intention of letting any of you risk your lives for us. Accept it and stop arguing.'

The spokesman was stumped for words and shook his head in resignation. 'Alright, alright. I think you are all crazy but if that is the way you want it.' With that, he handed over a skin of fine mead to add to their water ration, gave them a roughly drawn map and waved them through the tall wooden barricade with the warning that the accuracy of the map couldn't be guaranteed.

Walking two by two, with Crow and the kat in the lead, they began following the rough map through the trees and out into the open. Even after leaving the trees, it wasn't easy going in the wild country with brambles, ferns and bracken completely overgrowing pathways. As they broke through bushes and undergrowth, they kept pausing, listening for anything that might point to danger, but nothing stirred except the usual birds and beasts.

After the bone chill of the outlands of Mertam, the mild weather here was a pleasant surprise, causing them to strip off heavy coats, thick mittens and hats when they first stopped for food. As they ate, Crow compared the two maps and saw only minor discrepancies. Once they were ready to move on, repacking everything took only a few minutes. As they climbed to the top of a steep hill, Dani gaped in shock. Even the others were a little surprised as they looked down on a huge, broken glass and steel structure, almost smothered in foliage.

Much of the glass had disappeared from the frames but enough was still there for them to recognise what it used to look like. Vines grew up the outside and wove through empty spaces. No more than two storeys high, it sprawled for over a mile and was surrounded by broken concrete covered in weeds and burnt or broken-down hulks of metal machines. Even from the distance they stood at, they could see the faint hovering of Black Mýste around the metal. Crow looked at the map and then squinted at the structure ahead.

'We have a bit of a problem here, folks,' he said. 'If we follow this map, which they have admitted might not be completely accurate, we have to go around that. That will add a good few miles onto our journey and means that we may not get to the further portal today, and even tomorrow might be a stretch. If, however, we go through that, it shortens our journey a lot but adds to the chance we will come up against the Necrotics.'

Everyone pondered this, there was merit and dangers with either choice. Even bypassing the structure didn't guarantee completely avoiding the Necrotics but it was a slightly safer option. On the other hand, that might be exactly what the Necrotics planned for. The disease changed the person into something craving human flesh, a craving few resisted except through death. It did not, however, make the person stupid.

In the end it was the shadow kat that made the decision. Giving a snort of disgust at their procrastinating, it stepped forward and began working its way down the hill, heading for the broken concrete area with the metal boxes. This was a lot further away than it had seemed, and they all got very sweaty and hot as they stumbled and slid down the slope, following the huge animal.

Once they reached the outskirts of the broken building, Dani lifted the heavy head of the kat and looked deeply into its eyes.

'I name you Whisper, the silent pathfinder and I am depending upon you to find us safe passage. Can you do that?'

Whisper gave Dani's hand a gentle butt with its head before turning and walking over the broken ground. The others followed slowly, watching carefully where they placed their feet. Crow was beginning to re-think the decision the kat had made. The ground was littered with broken glass, rusted bits of metal and other detritus. Usually, all of this would have been taken by scavengers and piled up for re-using in the building of new homes, shops or to mend what was already built. That this was all still here was unsettling, as was the fact that there were no homes or dwellings. Along with having to avoid the Mýste, it was an uncomfortable journey, with everyone listening for any sound that might indicate unwanted company.

After a tense half an hour they reached what seemed to be a huge doorway. Now empty of glass, the metal frames were warped and covered in scratches and patches of old and colourless paint. The kat stepped through first and they all noticed that its ruff was raised as it moved cautiously into a huge open area. The rest of them followed silently, watching all around them as they stealthily moved through the cavernous ruins.

Every hundred steps or so there was another doorway, leading into another open space. Some of these were just huge, with very little left inside to hint what they had been used for. An occasional rusted pole or a handful of screws along with rubble and other detritus. There was also no sign of anything using the place, which surprised them all. Considering how big the sections were, many families could have settled here. Tinkers should be using it for a resting place on their travels, but there was no indication of their runes: markings that left messages for those who knew the hidden language. Crow grew more and more uneasy, not helped by the kat who hadn't let its ruff lay flat yet and whose heavy head swung from side to side, tilted as it listened to unknown sounds.

Crow reckoned that they were about halfway through the sprawling structure when there was a clatter coming from behind them in the direction of the opening. They all froze, waiting for they knew not what, but the silence stretched out heavily. Eventually the kat moved forward, belly lowered in its stalking pose, checking behind it even as it made sure that the rest of them were keeping up. Crow realised it was too late to back out now. The only way was forward.

'Be vigilant,' he hissed, his eyes moving from side to side and upwards.

Suddenly the kat whirled around and leaped past them, claws extended, and shredded a Necrotic that had been creeping up behind. Crow swung out with his sword to slice through the neck, completely removing the head. Dani stepped close and looked down at the separated body.

'I wonder if I could heal them?' she whispered. The kat made a negative growl and herded them to start moving again. Now though, they knew that they were being stalked by the living corpses as noises began sounding around them. Slight scuffling, tapping, something being dropped: all this pointed towards them having Necrotics behind them. Then there was a tapping from

ahead.
Wren froze in her tracks.

'They are all around us,' she said, keeping her voice as low as Dani's had been a few minutes before. 'Should we run?'

The kat shook its great head and gave a low grunt as it continued at its slow pace. Up ahead was what looked as if it had been a staircase, the struts bare metal rods and rusted through. The kat led them up the struts carefully to a walkway large enough for them to move abreast of each other. More of the caverns were on this level. By Wren's reckoning, they had passed maybe twenty-five of these things. Suddenly she realised what it must be.

'It's a marketplace!' Still speaking quietly, she rushed on. 'These empty caverns must have been shops that sold necessaries, although who would need so many shops selling the same things. Whoever dreamed it up must have been crazy. No wonder it all failed.'

'It failed because of the Break-up of the world, not because of bad commerce. According to what Lord Willoughby used to say, people crowded the earth, leaving very little green places for health and food growth. All food was grown in – erm – manufactories, I think he called them. Almost everywhere was covered in concrete and so people bought "stuff" to fill in the emptiness of their lives. Then the world rebelled, cracking open the earth, levelling some mountains and causing others to appear and reshaping the whole planet. Huge waves of water – saamies? Sumanies? What were they called? No matter, these huge waves drowned towns and villages by the seashore and some places sank beneath the waves but then others rose up from deep beneath the water. More than half of everyone from all over the world died immediately, then more did in the next few years.'

'How do you know all this?' Crow wasn't as quiet as the two women had been, but his senses were alert.

'I told you, Willoughby was told all of this "his story", he called it, at the Mage Academy, then he told his son while I was there. They used to talk a-after servicing me and I retained much of the information even though I didn't think about it until much later.'

Wren and Crow exchanged a quick glance at her slight stutter but didn't comment. The kat looked at her, rubbed against her hip and then led them into a large, cavernous room. Unlike many of the others, this had more metal than they had seen anywhere else in this strange building. There was also shelving and a few stairs leading to a narrow corridor into a tiny room with a metal sink and broken ceramic pieces on the floor. After looking around them, they went back into the main room and the kat stretched up against a door they hadn't noticed set into the back wall. Its front paws rested at the top of the door and pushed hard. A creaking, tearing sound and then the door fell outwards, falling down an exterior staircase with a loud clatter. They followed the feline through and out onto a small platform and then down the rusted metal.

Many treads were missing from the structure and part of the stairs pulled away from the wall, where the huge bolts holding it had sheared through, so they all moved carefully but as quickly as they were able. Just as they reached the ground, there was a howling from a distance that slowly became clearer as whoever – or whatever - made it came closer. The kat, still in the lead, now picked up its speed and they moved through broken concrete, narrowly avoiding Mýste, creepers and thorns, at a much better pace. Just before they managed to reach the further roadway, a small group of Necrotics jumped out from behind a concrete building set to one side and blocked them, holding spears and grunting low in their throats.

Crow opened his eyes wide at the group in front of them. There was something wrong with this group. More wrong than just being Necrotics. They just didn't look or sound quite right and then it hit him that these *weren't* Necrotics, but humans dressed in ripped and torn clothing, bodies covered in some kind of greyish paint and faeces rubbed in their hair. The noises they were making were just a poor imitation of how a Necrotic sounded and were really a call for reinforcements. All of this ran through his mind in a flash as he moved forward, his sword ready for use. The kat crouched, ready to pounce and Wren followed their lead, murmuring an incantation under her breath as she moved her hands in an intricate manner.

Dani looked surprised but caught on swiftly, pulling both her wrist knives from their sheaths. Instinct had her looking behind her, just in time to duck a heavy cudgel aimed for her head. Dropping low, she thrust up with her knives, one was pushed to one side, but the other sank into the breast of the woman standing behind her. As the false Necrotic screamed, Dani saw filed teeth and spikes through her tongue.

'Eaters!' she yelled, even as the sound of combat came from behind her. The little she knew about the Eaters was enough to have her determined to kill them all or die trying. The Eaters preferred human flesh above anything else and they liked it not only raw but still moving and screaming. Unlike the Necrotics who had no choice as the disease ate into their brains, changing them completely, Eaters *chose* to kidnap individuals and eat them, thinking that any ability or strength of the victim would pass into the consumer. Dressing as Necrotics meant that not only were the diseased blamed for the deaths but, once it became too dangerous, the Eaters would kill the group they had infiltrated, clean themselves up, slip away and start somewhere new.

Even as the word left Dani's mouth there was a roar and more of them burst from around the corner of the building. Grimly, she held her knives ready, knowing they might not survive this. At a rough estimate there must have been at least thirty of the Eaters and only four of them. The thought shot through her mind that at least she had tried to go where her compulsion pulled her. Then there was a huge roar of sound, tremendous heat before a powerful force knocked her flat and she knew no more.

Charlie went around to the docks early in the morning. When the Guild Master had sent word that the full search and rescue amount had been paid less than an hour before the cut-off point, Charlie had scowled deeply. He had double-checked that he could still walk away if the contract was broken, causing the messenger to raise his eyebrows in query.

'I don't trust this Willoughby,' Charlie said darkly. 'It feels as if he lies and cheats the way the rest of us breathe. Pass the word about him, I think that he is plotting something. Miltop spoke to my ex-commander to push me into this, and we all know how much those two can be trusted.'

After being assured that the message would go out to all the Bloodhounds and the rest of the Guild, Charlie made his pack ready, had a filling meal, bathed and slept heavily until first light.

And now he was here, wandering around the docks, listening to conversations and dropping the occasional comment to encourage words to flow.

The fight a short time earlier was still the main topic of conversation. The man yelling "Traitor" as he flew down the gangplank, followed by the frantic stabbing was told by so many people in so many ways, getting bigger with each telling so that Charlie was amazed there was any dock left. He also found out that the ship that the antagonists had descended from had pulled out from the dock and anchored a way off in the distance.

Surprisingly, from nowhere did Charlie hear of a servant girl leaving the ship, in fact, the only females spoken about were the wife, the daughter and a slavey. Charlie turned his nose up at hearing that Willoughby had a slavey. Although slaves were common in Mertam and many other places, he had been brought up to abhor the subjugation of another. Shaking his head to remove his sense of distaste, he carried on walking and listening.

Eventually, he heard of a woman seen running away from the carnage. No-one had a real description of her, and most didn't blame her for running, although there were a few sneers from female workers who thought she might have been going to look for trade. The most information came from a drunkard who also spoke about a gnome and a shadow kat, so Charlie accepted that that story was at least exaggerated if not a downright lie.

Knowing where they would be headed if there had been a gnome, Charlie shouldered his pack more firmly and then headed for the

East Gate, his busy senses picking up words, smells and sights that would lead him on to the next place he needed to go.

CHAPTER EIGHT

When Dani eventually woke up, she thought her sight had been affected by whatever had knocked her unconscious.She blinked rapidly before realising that night had fallen while she had been senseless.

Turning her aching head, she saw Wren stirring something that smelled tasty in a pot over a low fire, while Crow used a whetstone to remove a nick from his sword. At her movement, they both looked round.

'Aah, the lazy one deigns to wake up.' Crow laughed while Wren hushed him before bustling over to help Dani sit up.

'What happened? And why am I the only one unconscious?'

Wren looked sheepish and, ignoring Crow's chuckle, went on to explain.

'One of the things that I forgot about shadow kats is that they can amplify magik used near them if they choose. I heard you shout and sent some of my own spell your way but the kat decided to help me out. It added its own power to mine and, instead of a few flames to singe our enemies, we got an inferno that just missed taking you too.'

'What? How did it miss?'

Crow raised his hand. 'My fault,' he said with no apology in his voice. 'I knocked you to the ground. The flames singed my hair a bit but you're alright apart from a knock on the head.'

'In that case, I will forgive you the headache. How many died?'

'All of them.'

'What?' she croaked out. 'There were so many.'

'I told you,' Wren said. 'It was the kat.'

While Dani tried to understand how magik could be amplified so much that it killed so many, the kat itself came wandering back into the camp. Seeing Dani was finally awake, it came up to her and chirruped a demand for some petting. Dani did so and its purring echoed out into the night.

Wren dished out the food and they spent a quiet evening chatting before setting the watch. Dani went first, then Wren before Crow took the last shift. Although they had wanted to reach the other portal by the following day, Dani being unconscious for so long put paid to that idea. Sitting on the fallen tree trunk that Wren had used earlier, Dani faced outwards and focused her senses on the night sounds, ignoring the crackling of the fire, the soft sounds of clothes against blankets and the grumbling snores from the kat.

Turning her head slightly towards the latter, Dani grinned.

'Well, with the noise you are making, kat, Whisper was surely the wrong choice of name.'

The kat opened one eye, gave a grunt and then rolled itself into a tight coil, a paw over its nose. With a heavy sigh it began snoring again. With a quiet chuckle Dani resumed her watch.

An hour into her patrol, Dani found herself scratching incessantly at her arm. Pulling up her sleeve she was taken aback to see a long, almost healed, scar running down her forearm. One end though was black and swollen into a hard, black lump. Carefully she probed the lump and felt something move inside her flesh. As it did so, her stomach roiled. Taking out one of her knives, she cut a large X over the lump carefully. To her surprise and horror, scarcely had the point of the blade pierced her skin then a broken piece of a human fingernail burst out from the hard ball of flesh, along with some festering pus.

Making gagging sounds of disgust, she poured water over her arm to wash away the poison, wiping it clean and squeezing at the cut again and again. Eventually after many minutes, the cut stopped oozing pus, just a little bright red blood escaped so Dani burnt the cloths full of pus on the fire but, after hunting in the dark and finding it, she saved the nail in a piece of clean fabric. The smell from the burning cloths was horrendous, so much so that, even in their sleep, lips were curled in disgust.

When Wren woke for her turn at watch, Dani showed her the nail and explained what she had found.

'Good gods, that looks and smells awful.' Wren turned her nose up at the stench wafting up from the cloth. 'It doesn't smell like an Eater's nail, more like a Necrotic.'

'A Necrotic? Why would a Necrotic nail be doing among a group of Eaters?' Dani frowned in complete puzzlement.

'Eaters sometimes hide among them but could also be an Eater who was just on the turn and losing the nail speeded it up.'

'That makes sense, I suppose, but having the nail in me and not being affected by it is amazing.'

'How do you know that you aren't affected?' Wren asked in astonishment.

'If I were like most people, having that,' Dani pointed to the broken nail. 'That stuck inside me would have made me sick immediately before making me more and more ill. Yet, after I got rid of the fragment and pushed the poison out, my blood ran bright red. No darkening of colour and no disgusting smell. Isn't it wonderful?'

'I suppose so,' said Wren, doubtfully. 'I am not sure why you are so thrilled about it though,'

'Don't you understand, Wren? This means that I can heal the plague! I can cure the cursed and make them whole again.'

'Yes, you can but will they thank you for it?'

'I-I don't understand.' Dani shook her head in confusion.

'Alright, let's say I had the plague, I was a full Necrotic and had eaten of human flesh. Do you think that I would want to heal and remember those whom I had killed? And eaten? You must remember, most Necrotics start by eating their nearest and dearest. You told us a while ago about your good friend, Mr Poole and how his wife, Lottie, got the plague.* She sent their child away because she had been tempted to bite her. How would she feel, if she had succumbed to that and then you cured her? While ill, she would not have cared who she hurt but later, once she had recovered, she would have hated herself.

'Just because you can, honey, does not mean you should. Now, you look tired and still have a little self-healing to do. Go lie down and we will wake you at first light.'

Dani went and lay down in her blanket, thinking hard. Ever since first finding out that she *could* heal, she had never thought about whether she *should*. As she remembered Bili and his habit of getting into dangerous scrapes, she understood that his injuries, though grave, were not ones she had any moral issues with. Healing Necrotics, after Wren's comment, was something else. She was still thinking about it when she fell back into a deep sleep, her magikal energies focusing on not just her arm but other, unknown, internal injuries.

When she woke up, it was to see Crow sitting by the fire and beginning to cook breakfast. All she could see of Wren was the top of her curly hair. Getting up and stretching, Dani went over to get some of the tea that was steeping in the embers around the side of the fire. Crow nodded and silently handed her a few of the tiny hot cakes he adored.

After a few minutes of eating and sipping the hot brew, Crow tipped his head towards Dani's injured arm.

'How is it?' he asked, *sotto voce* so as not to disturb Wren.

Rolling up her sleeve, they both examined her now unmarked arm and then she walked to her blanket and picked up the cloth bundle. When she opened it up near Crow, they both reared back in disgust at the stench.

'Kintrelle's balls, what the hell is that stench?' he gagged.

'It is the nail fragment from my arm,' Dani coughed and choked on the noxious fumes. She lifted her arm back to throw it in the bushes when Crow stopped her.

'Wait, if a small fragment can affect you and cause that much of a smell, throwing it away might cause a major problem and perhaps call more here. Go and make a small fire, downwind, and then burn it. We don't want to spread the plague.'

'But that's what I don't understand,' Dani said with frustration. 'I thought that the group who attacked us were just Eaters, not Necrotics?'

'Seems to me that there must have been both among them. Your bad luck to get clawed by one turning. If we hadn't killed them, there would have eventually been a full band of Necrotics wandering this land.'

'At least we can tell the gnomes who the gang really were.'

'True. Now I really like you, Dani, honestly I do, but take that shit and burn it!'

With a laugh, Dani did as she was bid. Building a small fire down behind a slope, she opened the cloth and blinked in surprise. Not only had the nail fragment rotted to nothing but a black ooze, the cloth itself was burned through in places as if splashed by acid. With a shudder, she threw the torn and stained cloth onto the flames and jumped back as they flared up high, sending gouts of foul-smelling smoke into the air. Turning away once she made sure that there was no chance of the fire spreading, she went to a small stream and washed her hands in the icy water. Even so, she thought she could smell the noxious scent for hours afterwards.

Walking back to camp, she found that Wren was now awake, and all their gear was packed, and they were just waiting for her. About to ask what the rush was, she caught the smell on the wayward breeze, coming from the dying fire she had just left. With a grim nod of understanding, she shouldered her pack and began to follow the others.

Although they kept their eyes open and wary, the kat still made them jump when it appeared perhaps an hour later. After moving into its accustomed position at Dani's side, it gave a small sniff, wrinkled its muzzle in disgust and shot her a fulminating look. With that, it stepped up to the front and walked beside Crow.

Every few steps it would turn and give Dani a snarl, just to remind her of its disgust. By the midday break, the two women were breathless from laughing at its antics as well as the puzzled looks from Crow, who hadn't noticed much of the byplay.

The amusement didn't stop them all from freezing in a combat stance as they heard a loud crashing through the brush. As the sound got closer they heard a high voice singing as well as the happy yipping of some beast. Then the singing changed to a voice calling out to them.

'Hey, hey, strangers in a strange land! I am here and I am Nobby, come to guide you to the portal, shout out, shout out and say you hear me!'

Before Crow could stop them, both the kat and Dani gave answering calls. The hidden voice gave a whoop of delight and then moved towards them. Within a few short minutes a strange looking shape came out of the bushes by the side of the track just a little way ahead. With him strode a fox, almost twice the size than any seen before and with a glorious deep orange coat with a dark brown cross of fur growing across its shoulders and down its spine. Both beings were of similar height and Dani couldn't help grinning at the two in delight.

'Hello, hello, I am Nobby!' the first creature said again, sweeping off a shapeless hat and bowing low. He had a nut-brown face with a wide lipless grin and a nose like a potato. He was as broad as he was tall, dressed in homespun trews and a long waistcoat made from sacking that still had "flour" printed down one side. Twinkling black eyes laughed back at Dani, seeming to enjoy her amusement at the sight of him. 'I received a message by carrier pigeon that you are needing a portal, but you have taken so long to arrive I thought I would come and see what delayed you.'

'Aren't you worried about the Necrotics gangs wandering about here?' Crow was a little suspicious of this stranger just appearing, seemingly out of nowhere.

'Afraid? Me? The great warrior, Nobby? Afraid?' There was a long pause and Crow was on the verge of apologising, even though he wasn't sure why. Then Nobby burst out in delighted giggles, nodding his head frantically.

'Yes, yes, of course I is afraid! That's why I has magiks and the great fox, Fox! He keeps me safe, and I keeps me hid.' Crow couldn't stop his own grin at the antics of Nobby, as he danced around in circles. The fox came up and sniffed hello to Whisper and the kat replied in kind.

'Does your fox have a name?' Wren asked, smiling.

'Why yes, yes he do.'

There were a few minutes of silence and then Dani, with a chuckle, asked what the name was.

'Well now, missy, there's some thingys to be sayin'. He b'ain't being mine as much as I is being his, see? And so he named hisself cuz he has this right. And because I don't know how to speak Fox, his name is Fox! Took me ages to work that one out!' With a laugh, the wood gnome led the way down a hidden pathway, and they followed after him, still chuckling at his antics.

As they walked, Dani realised how far their guard had lowered since the attack by the Eaters. Hearing Nobby's nonsense talk and watching the fox dancing and playing in the bushes and out, she felt as if a heavy weight was lifted from her shoulders. Looking at the slight turn up of his lips on Crow's face and the wide grin on Wren's, the others seemed to feel the same way as she did. Not only the humans felt better she noted when she saw Whisper playing tag with the fox, appearing and disappearing at will.

Within an hour they came towards a complex and confusing building. Starting at the ground with a small hut built connected to a huge gilly tree. Looking up the broad trunk into the flat branches and intertwined foliage, there seemed to be hints of platforms in various places and, here and there, a roof or two peeping through the close-grown leaves.

'Come, come,' Nobby gestured eagerly, and they all followed him inside the hut's front door, only to walk to the back of the empty building to a small door built into the tree's trunk. Dani had never seen a gilly tree before so seeing the door gave her a surprise. The others knew that gilly trees usually grew around a hollow core, and just expected to be very cramped and crowded in the hut, but with inner stairs to climb up.

Once through the door in the trunk, which faded away behind them, Dani stopped in amazement. Instead of a small, circular room with steps spiralling upwards, she saw a wide-open space with a tall box set in the centre. This room seemed to be much bigger than the space allowed and, looking at the others, she saw her own surprise reflected on their faces.

'Come, come,' the wood gnome hustled them towards the central box, unlatching and swinging open the whole of the front like a door. Stepping inside, it was a little tight for all of them, so Whisper vanished, allowing them a bit more room. Nobby went over to a lever and pushed it down. As it went lower, another lever appeared through an opening in the floor of the box and Crow recognised it as a pulley system. With a jerk, the floor they stood on began to rise, making them stagger a little.

Nobby chatted happily as he tugged on each lever, never sounding out of breath or looking sweaty with exertion. Shaking his head in wonder at the strength shown in this small bundle of a gnome, Crow knew that he himself would never have managed the feat so easily.

After a few moments the platform came to an abrupt halt and Nobby latched the lever system closed before scurrying to open the door. Then, sweeping an exaggerated bow, he welcomed them into his home.

The wide flat branches forked off in different directions, each with a thick rope for balance. Some of them meandered into the distance, while others led to open archways into separate chambers. The visitors realised that the whole tree was Nobby's home, each chamber having a specific purpose. Following Nobby up and around the trunk on one of these "pathways", they entered a wide sitting room filled with comfortable chairs with fat cushions. Sitting with a smug look on his face was the shadow kat. Fox went over and renewed his acquaintance.

Urging the others to sit, Nobby went through an archway, passing by another fox. This one was a shade bigger than Fox and her coat was much redder, without the cross of darker brown, making the white tip of her brush seem to glow. She went over and joined her mate, where he lavished her with attention and then made introductions to the kat. There was a lot of sniffing then a gentle push from the kat had the fox couple swarming it and they began rolling and chasing each other.

The others were laughing at the animals when Nobby came back, pushing a trolley. Following him was a slender, pale woman of unearthly beauty carrying a tray. Putting it down on a small table, she gave a shy smile and gestured to the food while Nobby spoke.

'Here's food, you eat and then sleeps. Take portal tomorrow? Yes?'

Wren looked at Dani for guidance and was pleased when she saw the Healer smile and nod.

'That would be wonderful,' Dani said. 'We can provide some food and…' Her voice trailed off at the emphatic denials from Nobby and the lady.

'Nope, nope, we has lots. Nice for company here. We sits now, drinks. Eats and chats. This is my lady, Gilly Flower, the heart of the tree and my love. She does not speak as we do so will seem quiet. I will speak what she says. And what she says is eats food, drinks drink and then after you must tell us story.'

Gilly Flower smiled at them as she began pouring a clear golden liquid into delicate glass goblets. Wren couldn't help thinking that she looked very much like her namesake. The flowers of the gilly tree were delicate, with star shaped petals surrounding a deep green centre. Gilly Flower herself had a very faint spring green flush to her hair, which fell past her hips and had gilly tree leaves woven in it, as well as her skin. Her eyes were of a darker green and seemed a little too big for her face, while her lips were of the same deep green as her eyes.

There followed an evening full of laughter, a few shivers as Nobby told some spooky stories and a complete break from worry.

Although Dani could still feel the pulling need to leave and continue her journey, though it was a much gentler tugging for now, so she was able rest fully and gather her energy. It surprised her how worn out she felt, and she was beginning to think that she was now entering her dying phase. This worried her as she felt she had quite a way to travel yet but she couldn't control when she would die, only that it was inevitable, and it might not be long enough to get where her soul wanted to be. A gentle hand touched her arm and she looked into a pair of deep green eyes. The lady Gilly Flower then sat by her, and Dani felt her worries begin to fade slightly. No words were spoken but she felt lighter somehow, still tired but less bone weary, she smiled and held the cool hand as Crow told Nobby about the group of killers and the rotting nail.

Eventually the night drew in. Gilly Flower lit some fey lanterns that burnt with a flickering green light and led the group along another broad branch to a set of three adjoining rooms. Dani couldn't shake the feeling that these rooms had not existed the day before, but she felt no hint of ill intent from the magik that had made them.

Each room was neat and comfortable. A bed, made up with fresh scented linen, a table holding a ewer full of water and a wide washing bowl and a bench to lay down a pack. There was a window opening in each room, covered by drooping vines that gave privacy but let in light. Delighted with the lovely room, Dani told the kat that it would have to sleep on the floor due to the narrowness of the bed, to which it gave a huff, picked up her hand in soft jaws and led her through the first two rooms and into the third. There, instead of the narrow bed that the other rooms held, was a bed more than twice the size. Bemused, Dani shook her head in wry amusement before washing, pulling on a sleep shirt that lay at the end of the bed and then lying down on the comfortable mattress. With a huge, gaping yawn, followed by a grunt of effort, Whisper jumped up next to her, stretched out and closed its eyes.

She could hear Crow and Wren chatting to each other as she began drifting off, a hint of flirtation in their conversation. Smiling, Dani hoped that, at last, they were beginning to recognise the mutual attraction they held and would, she thought, begin moving forward

with the intention of getting closer. Her thoughts growing
confused, Dani slipped into a dream where Bili flew on a gryphon,
while she watched him, sitting on a shadow kat, and Mr Poole,
Neera and Sam swam in the deep ocean with merpeople.

The next day dawned warmer with a strong breeze blowing. After
they had all eaten, Nobby asked if they wouldn't mind going with
him to hunt for the rest of the Eaters. After checking with Dani to
see if she was up to it, Crow agreed that they would all go along
and so got ready for a prolonged hike. Gilly Flower made up food
parcels and filled their water skins and waved them off.

'Doesn't your lady hunt?' Crow asked.

'She not leave her tree long, it brings hurts to her so she stays,
protects there with her magiks and I goes and gets meat or hunts
Eaters and dead ones. We do what suits best.'

Crow nodded at this common-sense attitude and followed the
stubby little man further into the undergrowth.

They walked silently for about an hour, Crow's respect for the
wood gnome growing with every step. Not only was Nobby as
quiet as Whisper when he walked through the undergrowth, but he
seemed to be able to communicate with all living beings around
him. They went in a circuitous route, seeming to move in a tighter
and tighter circle, following signs that no-one else, except perhaps
the shadow kat, could see.

A slow signal from the gnome had them all crouching a little more
and, making sure to move incrementally, they were able to creep
up on the encampment of unknowing cannibals. As they all
watched the small group, who sat around on trees chopped down
for seating, a high scream echoed through the air. Crow saw his
friends all freeze for a few seconds then, with the shadow kat
disappearing, they quietly followed Nobby towards another, larger
clearing, moving carefully from one hiding place to another.

When they got there, Dani felt her jaw drop. Tied to a stake in the middle of the clearing was a woman, wearing very little in the way of torn and tattered clothing and covered in bruises, cuts and grazes. Around her danced and whooped fifteen or more men and women, wild eyed and laughing at her terror. Nobby glared out from where he stood, his face set in a grim expression, completely unlike his usually happy air, before he lifted a hollow tube to his lips and blew hard. The man closest to the tied woman, making shallow cuts on the top of her arms and across her chest, threw up his hands and released his dagger before he dropped to the ground.

His knife had flown from his hand and skewered a thin woman who was covered in paint and excrement, her hair matted with more filth and tied up in dozens of different coloured strips of material, who had been standing behind the captive, sawing off her hair. She screamed in pain before falling to the ground and clutching at her thigh where the blood spurted out in time with her heartbeat. The rest of the group whirled around and headed for the place where Nobby and his friends stood. The wood gnome had already filled and blown his pipe twice more, hitting his targets fatally every time before the Eaters had covered half the ground between them.

Crow leapt out, his sword slashing in one hand and, now wearing a spiked gauntlet upon the other, punched out in the opposing direction. Whisper joined in the fray, appearing and disappearing at will, taking down opponents on each appearance. Wren raised her hands and spoke words of command, lifting two of the nearest enemies and slamming them hard against some trees. Both screamed in agony as bones broke, the sound stopping abruptly as Nobby sent a dart into one throat and Dani threw her knife into the other.

More of the Eaters flooded into the clearing, some from where they had lounged about on the cut down trees, others from the surrounding woods. Sword and claws stabbed and slashed, spinning blue lights lifted bodies and slammed them to the ground, crushing bone, small poisonous darts hit throats, eyes or elsewhere.

While this was going on, Dani ran forward, avoiding as much of the fighting as she could. Using her dagger, she sawed through the ropes holding the prisoner. Once free, the woman moved as quickly as she could, hobbling towards the still hidden Nobby. Crow and Whisper stopped fighting then, a sword at the chest of the last one still breathing. Breast heaving, he tried to speak so Crow dropped the sword tip a little. With a strangled shout, the former prisoner ran at him, stabbing the Eater through the throat with a rusty knife she had scooped up on the way.

'Dammit.' Crow shouted. 'We wanted to ask them questions, to find out if there were more people to find.'

Her hand covering her mouth, the woman dropped to her knees and cried. 'I am sorry, so sorry but I c-couldn't…' her voice faded into loud sobbing wails and Wren glared at the Assassin as she found a cloak to cover the former prisoner's near nakedness.

Leaving her in the hands of the women, Crow and the wood gnome went and checked out the bodies. They found a lot of evidence of man-eating. Human bones were used as personal adornments, as weapons and were even used in shoring up tent walls and in other equipment. There were items obviously scavenged off travellers as well as from the huge, empty structure they had travelled through the day before. Nobby thought that this crowd of savages had been around for years, attacking travellers, those who guarded the portals and even each other. Gathering up any evidence regarding the identity of the victims, Nobby finished by setting the brush around the stake alight and then he and Crow began heaving the dead Eaters into the flames. Both men noticed that on more than one body there were signs of the Necrotic Plague beginning to take a hold.

When the men eventually walked back over to where the women sat, they found that the stranger was now dressed in appropriate clothing rather than rags, scavenged from the piles hidden in a tent. She had washed her face and body, removing much of the dirt and any evidence of her tears.

'What happened, why were they going to burn you?' Dani was asking as the men strode up.

'I don't know, I don't know,' the woman mumbled, hiding her face in her hands. Crow looked at Wren, raising his eyebrow in query but Wren just shrugged her shoulders and helped to carry some more clothing, all piled together in a large blanket.

'I will come back,' Nobby said. 'I will collect all things for use and give them to new settlers. More people will come soon, if all the Eaters have gone. We might be able to get proper trails from place to place sorted.' With a satisfied nod and a last look around, he began leading the way back to the gilly tree. Crow and Dani exchanged a look, having noticed Nobby's more precise speech, rather than the simple way he had spoken up to that point.

Wren stepped forward to help the woman who still hadn't given them her name, but she was shrugged off abruptly and the woman moved up to Crow to walk by his side. He looked at her in surprise but said nothing although he sent a quick glance to Wren.

As they walked back down the trail, Crow tried getting more information from the woman who skilfully avoided giving any specific answers. Nonetheless, Crow seemed to be enjoying her company and there was quiet laughter from them both, floating back to Dani and Wren. The Healer looked at Wren's set face and decided to keep quiet for now but was sure that there would come a time when she would be giving Crow a hard kick in his common sense.

Once they were back at the huge tree, Nobby went through some of the gear they had collected before giving the travellers certain pieces to replace their own property. Crow admitted to himself that he couldn't always see any difference between what they had and what Nobby gave but he accepted everything given, with good grace.

'Are you staying today and leaving tomorrow?' the wood gnome asked.

Dani spoke up. 'I would love to stay an extra night, but the feeling is growing even stronger. I must go as soon as possible.'

'And when she leaves, we leave too,' said Crow, forestalling any comments Dani might say about them staying.

The stranger spoke then. 'My name is Varla,' she said. 'What direction are you travelling?'

'We are heading in that direction,' Dani pointed to the east. 'I am not sure where we will end up though.'

'I will come with you, if you will allow it,' Varla said. 'I come from over that way so I will travel with those who make me feel safe. I will be too afraid to go on alone, after what almost happened.'

Busy smiling broadly at Crow who gave a slight nod in embarrassed acknowledgement, she missed the sour look traded between Dani and Wren. As they went to double check their packs and the extra rations that Gilly Flower had prepared, Dani called sharply back at Varla, who seemed more than content to just sit with the men and flirt.

'Come along, Varla. We need to sort your food, clothing and other necessaries out and we need to be leaving in the next hour.'

'Of course, of course,' Varla sounded so reasonable that Dani felt that she, herself, sounded harsh. Following the Healer out of the room, Varla flashed a smile and rolled her eyes in amusement, as if wanting Crow to join in with her silent laughter at Dani's nagging.

'Be careful, Crow,' Nobby spoke more quietly than usual, still using the precise diction. 'Methinks this woman will stir up trouble between you all, if you don't watch out.'

'I think you worry too much, Nobby,' said Crow, dismissing his worries politely. 'Varla won't be with us for long. There is a limit to what problems she can cause. Besides, she is still in shock from nearly being burnt, she will soon settle down.' With that, he and the kat went off to check his own gear. As he went through the archway, the kat looked back and nodded at Nobby in acknowledgement of the warning.

'*You don't like this Varla, do you, Nobby?*' Gilly Flower asked, suddenly appearing at Nobby's side, her face troubled.

'*Her smells like lies, my lover,*' Nobby replied, silently using the mind-to-mind speech he always used with the woman he loved. '*If*

I was they, I would not be believing any words from her gob, I would be checking once, then twice, then thrice. Her has poison in her blood and her wants Crow. Not because her loves or even just wants, only because her wants to cause hurting for Wren and, maybe, Dani. Her has magik, uses spells and herbs, methinks. She smells wrong, love, just wrong. She hides hersen and I can't see the true her. Bad magik, bad woman.' Nobby frowned, knowing that his Gilly Flower saw much but said little unless it was important.

'I think they need no further warning, they have worked most of it out for themselves.Crow needed the warning, but he heeded you not.' With that, Gilly Flower went off to take care of her own business, leaving Nobby with Fox and Vixen.

'There's going to be trouble there, my lovelies, I betcha.' Having said his piece to the foxes sat patiently by his side, Nobby gave a sharp nod before going to get the last of the potatoes from his vegetable patch.

Dani was becoming more and more irritated with her companions. As she sorted through the pile of clothing and blankets they had scavenged from the Eaters camp, she tried getting Varla involved with choosing and packing her gear, but the woman just waved a hand languidly and yawned her disinterest. Wren seemed to have sunk into herself, hurt being masked by an expressionless face and she, too, seemed little interested in helping to kit out the stranger or search through her own clothing. Eventually, after another blank look from one and a languid wave from the other, Dani exploded into wrath.

'That is enough!' she shouted, slamming down the pack she was holding. 'You,' pointing at Varla. 'Unless you want to wear the same things day in and day out for however long we travel together, you had best set your mind to this job and choose what you need, or you will *not* be coming with us. We need no slackers when we move together. And you!' turning swiftly and waving her finger under Wren's nose, Dani continued. 'You need to buck up your ideas, don't you dare give up without a fight. Look to yourself, see what you want and damn well go for it instead of sitting in the corner and whimpering like a baby. Now, get on with it, both of you.'

With that, she stormed out of the chamber leaving the other two women staring after her in complete shock. After a few minutes of stunned silence, Varla picked up the knapsack from where it had landed, before removing everything and checking all that had been packed. Some of the items had been put in because of Dani's temper and were certainly not appropriate for travel.

Wren gave herself a shake before she, too, began sorting through the piles of clothing. The atmosphere was no more companionable than it had been but at least the work was getting done.

After leaving the storeroom, Dani worked her way down the gilly tree's huge trunk and out of the hut into the clearing. There she began to work off her annoyance by going through some fighting forms that Samuel had taught her many moons ago. Each movement brought the memories of him closer, and her temper soon dissipated as she remembered him and all the others, leaving her feeling a bittersweet mix of joy and sorrow.

Crow, having heard her shouting, waited for a short time. Then he, too, went down the tree with her to practise his own forms. They worked in complete silence apart from the occasional grunt of exertion, for over an hour. Watching her carefully, Crow decided that Dani was now over her snit.

'So,' he murmured. 'What was that all about?'

'You.' Was the uncompromising answer.

'What? Me? I haven't done anything.' Crow was stunned at this seemingly, unprovoked attack.

'That Varla, I don't trust her,' Dani spoke quietly but firmly. 'She is already driving a delicate wedge between you and Wren, and I feel it will only get worse.'

'Really? Are you sure? Wait, of course you are sure, or you wouldn't have said anything. I think you are overreacting though, Dani. The woman is just flirting, perhaps because of the shock of her close call although, I must admit, she makes me uncomfortable with the way she seems to cut you out.'

'Idiot man,' Dani said, beginning to feel exasperated all over again. 'It isn't so much what she is doing to you but the effect it is having upon Wren: think about it.' With that, Dani stalked off, the kat following on behind.

Shaking his head in bemusement, Crow finished off his forms, annoyed to find that his mind was going over the conversations that had happened between himself, Wren, Dani and Varla since the latter's inclusion. Slowly he began to realise that the woman had been more manipulative than he had noticed. Picking up a cloth to dry his sweating face, he resolved to keep his eye out for any more games she might try to play in the future. He had no idea what he could say to Wren to put things back to the way they were though. Heaving a sigh, he walked back to the tree to get ready for departure.

CHAPTER NINE

After eating a huge meal, and picking up extra packages of food to tie onto their packs, the group started out to the portal. After being reassured that it was just a short walk away and that there were plenty of places to stay on the further side, they all went to say goodbye to Gilly Flower. Crow went first and gave her a warrior's clasp, hand to forearm. He gave her a kiss on the cheek followed by a look of astonishment before grinning broadly and catching her up in a hug.

'I promise,' he said, seemingly for no reason.

Wren gave him a puzzled glance as he set Gilly Flower on to her feet and moved out of the way for the young mage. Going straight in for a hug goodbye, Wren, too, gave a start of surprise before she gave a blinding smile to the beautiful dryad.

'I will try,' was her slightly confusing comment before she stepped to the platform that stood ready to be lowered. Dani went next, wrapping her arms around Gilly Flower.

'*You are more than halfway through your journey*,' Gilly Flower spoke directly into Dani's mind, and she suddenly understood the shock shown by the other two. She grinned at Gilly Flower and nodded her thanks, but the tree spirit hadn't finished.

'*The stranger will cause trouble in any way she can. She seems determined to cause friction between all of you. Watch her, yourself and the others and keep your Healing magiks hidden if you possibly can. Usually, I can see into the surface mind without any problem but hers is deliberately clouded. She either has a natural shield or she has magik training. Whichever it is, beware.*'

Thinking straight back at the tree spirit, Dani acknowledged the words of caution. She thought, '*I agree with you completely. I just hope the others will be as wary.*'

'I have spoken to them so they should be on their guard. Now you go with my love and the blessing of my tree, which is no small thing. Once you find your true place, tell a tree and the message will find itself back to us. Be safe, my friend.'

'I will, Gilly Flower, and many blessings to you.' Without conscious thought, Dani sent a tendril of Healing out into the tree spirit, kissed her cheek then stepped away to the platform.

Varla stepped forward for her own farewell, but Gilly Flower didn't seem to notice her as the dryad turned to give Whisper a fuss. The trio on the platform all saw the brief flicker of rage flow over Varla's face before she quickly hid it, gave a brief nod, and joined the others to go down the tree.

Once they were on the forest floor, Nobby set a quick enough pace to ensure no spurious chat and they made good time going through the gradually thinning trees towards an outcropping of rocks.

The closer they got; the more Dani became uncomfortable. A faint humming, only just audible, seemed to be coming from in front of them. With a glance around she saw that the others also seemed uncomfortable except for Nobby, Whisper and Fox.

'Nobby,' she called out. 'What is happening?'

The wood gnome turned his head, his usually cheerful features set with a blank expression. 'Hmm? Oh, dear me, dear me, I forgot!' A quiet mumble followed and the increasing pressure that Dani had been feeling suddenly eased, much to her relief. Crow and Wren echoed her thanks and, after a slight hesitation, Varla added her own comments.

The outcropping they were heading for stood directly in front of where they needed to go. Climbing over the first fall of rocks that reached taller than Wren sat upon Crow's shoulders and moving past more debris from a landslide, they came to a most amazing sight. Dani had expected the next portal to be very similar to the first she had seen but, instead of a waterfall of light deep inside a cave, here was what looked like a giant soap bubble caught on the branches of a deformed ash tree. The branches grew in such a way they formed a huge oval with the part nearer the ground being slightly broader and flatter. The colours weren't as vivid or as flashing either, here there was more of an opaque look with the occasional shimmer across the surface of the "bubble". The humming that had caused them to feel uncomfortable came from the opening, even Nobby's magik now unable to completely dull the sensation. The group came to a staggered halt and stared at the magnificent sight in awe.

'Here is the portal,' Nobby said quietly and unnecessarily, enunciating every word carefully. 'It will take you to another land called Hackta. Tell the gnomes at the portal that we have cleared away the Eaters, or most of them anyway, so they can begin to let groups of pilgrims through. No singles though, not until we are sure that it is all cleared completely.' Once Crow had given a short nod of understanding, Nobby continued. 'The capital is Drintoth, go there and tell the council that there is room for the open-minded. Although many follow the faith of the Shining One, there are very few of the fanatical there. None of the more rigid followers would want to come to a wilderness where it takes hard work and brute force to carve out a place. Once people are established properly, there will be such a mix of faiths we should be able to prevent any of that Shining One madness ever happening here, if the gods are willing. Now, time for you to be going, remember what my Gilly Flower told you.'

Ignoring Varla's curiosity at his last comment, he began to chant, his voice rising and lowering into a hum, slowly weaving a melody around the energy of the magik from the portal. The opaque surface began to clear and vague shapes blurred into being. When Nobby waved his hand and nodded a goodbye, still humming, the shadow kat caught hold of Dani's hand gently with its mouth and Wren grabbed on to the other. Crow and Varla joined the chain, and they stepped on through the wide opening.

Once through the other side they found themselves in an open field, two gnomes waiting to greet them. After passing on Nobby's message and getting a pleased response, the small group went through a gate in the hedge at the end of the field and went towards a large Portal Inn, to rent some horses.

An hour later, after freshening up and grabbing a quick meal at the Inn, the group rode towards the capital city of Drintoth. Crow was in front, followed by Wren and Varla riding side by side in a heavy silence and Dani travelled behind with the shadow kat. The road was wide but busy, so it was easier moving this way than altogether in a bunch. The kat kept, as was usual now, invisible to any strangers.

Dani found everything fascinating, her head in constant motion as they went past scores of fields where crops were being reaped. Men used huge scythes to cut down the long, red stalks and women and children gathered everything up into piles. Very few of the workers stopped what they were doing to watch those passing by, but Dani admitted to herself that, as it was so busy, very little work would have been done if they had. It was a bright, sunny day but the wind blew chilly, so she was glad of her cloak. She found the changes in weather and the growing cycle confusing to her mind as she moved from place to place, season to season and time zone to time zone. Crow's convoluted attempt at an explanation had just made it more entangled.

The tug of energy that was her guide, that which had come to life as the drug effect had faded, was guiding the Healer towards the direction of Drintoth now, so she was quite happy to follow along the roadway.

Wren fumed in silence. Once Crow had relegated Varla to a place behind him, after she had ridden by his side for a few hundred yards, chattering like a magpie, Wren had tried to start a conversation but had been studiously ignored by the other woman. After being snubbed three times, Wren stopped trying and concentrated on staying in the saddle. Unlike the others, she had never ridden very often so was still a novice on a horse, something that Varla took great delight in pointing out.

Dani's stomach rumbled, and the sun had begun its slow descent when the huge gates to Drintoth finally hove into view. Dani remembered that back on Bisra, there had been wooden gates around the city of Harmony that were just a handspan taller than the average man, whereas here were metal gates three times that height. As she sat, her mouth agape in astonishment, she noticed a giant of a man, more than twice Crow's height, finish speaking to the guard and walk inside, just clearing the top of the framework. That is when she saw the rest of the crowd. All were moving steadily to the gates, wanting to get inside before evening curfew. At Crow's impatient gesture, Dani caught up with them and they waited in line as it moved slowly forward.

'Stop gawking,' grinned Wren. 'Anyone would think you had never seen a city before.'

'I haven't,' responded Dani. 'At least, not like this.'

The noise was earth-shattering and there were colours bleeding into one another as all types of people moved around her. Big, little, short, tall, fat and thin as well as every shade of the rainbow for skin and hair as well as clothing made her head spin. Getting through the gates was simple enough but the riot of noise and colour followed them inside.

Crow leaned over his horse to speak to a passer-by who pointed as he answered. Thanking him and tossing a coin in gratitude, Crow moved his horse's head and walked it slowly in the direction pointed to, the others following closely behind him. From her position at the back, Dani saw Wren give a hand signal to a young ruffian that was headed towards them. Whatever it meant had him nodding before turning away. She spied Varla giving a slightly different sign to someone else but couldn't see who it was in the crowd. Frowning, she filed it away at the back of her mind to ask about later.

Half an hour of steady walking had the small band pulling up outside an inn called The Purple Orchid. The proprietor bustled out to speak to them while the ostler took the reins of the four horses and led them away once the knapsacks were removed from the saddles.

The small man had a wide grin and welcomed them inside where he led them to two rooms with a bathing chamber between. Crow had a quiet word and was led down a short corridor to another room, where he stowed his things. After a quick discussion, they all decided to freshen themselves up then meet downstairs for food in an hour or so and there they could plan the next phase of their journey.

Later, as they sat around eating a roasted fowl, potatoes and leeks in a creamy sauce, Crow announced that he would go to the city hall, where the council leader resided during work hours.

'I will go along on the morrow and pass on Nobby's message, then…'

'Do you think that is wise?' interrupted Varla with a sniff. 'How do we know that the land the wood gnome lives in is as free as he says? What if there are hidden pockets of more murderers he has not yet found? We will be advising people to go and be slaughtered. I cannot agree to this.'

Before either Wren or Crow could say anything, annoyance rolling through them at Varla's attitude, Dani spoke, her tone quiet and gentle but it shut Varla up immediately.

'You seem to think that you have a say among us, Varla. You forget, you have been allowed to come with us only to save you travelling on your own after your "ordeal". You said you lived in this direction, so tell us where and we will find you an escort for the rest of the way. As for Nobby's knowledge; as a wood gnome he can literally hear messages on the wind that blows through the trees. The animals bring him all he needs to know from the whole land surface. If he says that there is safety there and pilgrims should be given permission to go, then that is exactly what we shall tell those in charge here. Now, allow us to make *our* plans while you decide on your own.'

Varla glared at her before snapping her mouth shut. Lowering her eyes, she hid the rage dancing in them and breathed slowly and evenly to calm her temper.

'We will go to the market in the town square,' Wren spoke easily, trying to suppress her pleasure at Varla's set down. 'One of the serving maids says that you can buy and sell anything there and there is a trading house for gems and metals in one of the houses on the north side of the square. I thought we could have a good look around, find out where the portals are placed and see which one Dani needs for the next part of our journey. If you are happy with that, Dani?'

Dani gave a nod, swallowing a mouthful of her mulled cider, enjoying the mix of subtle flavours.

'I have been here before,' Crow said. 'The trading house has very experienced brokers and tries to give fair prices for goods, unlike some other places I know of. I don't need to warn you about pickpockets or thieves, I assume?' The latter was said as he aimed a broad grin at Wren, who burst out laughing. Before she could say anything, Varla again interrupted.

'My apologies, my friends,' she spoke in a subdued tone. 'I misspoke a few moments ago but all I can say in my defence is that I worry about your safety, particularly about Dani and Wren. They seem to have very little understanding of the wider world. Perhaps it is because you saved my life. I do sense stories and secrets that you don't trust me enough to share yet, so now that I have eaten my fill, I will go to my room as I am tired and that will give you a chance to speak openly with each other without having to be careful of what you say.' With that, she sent them all a sad smile before heading for the stairs.

'Do we believe her, folks?' Crow asked, his voice low as he watched her ascend the wooden stairs.

'No!' said both women and Whisper gave his own yowl which sent a wave of silence over the large room as the other customers were made rudely aware of the kat's existence. At this the three of them began to laugh which lowered their personal tension again.

Later, as the food scraps had been cleared away and Dani sipped some more of her warm drink, she remembered the signalling Wren had done earlier so asked about it.

'That was just to let the Thieves Guild know that we are not here to cause problems but that we aren't easy prey either.'

'Does this mean the same then?' Dani managed a close approximation of what she had seen Varla do.

'No, it doesn't,' Crow answered, after a short silence, his teeth gritted in temper. 'That is a high sign to anyone watching from the Assassin's Guild. That Guild works exclusively for the Mage Academy. So, our little "victim" has hidden some very important information from us. I think I need to have words with her.'

'Don't say anything to her yet,' Wren advised. 'We need to know who has hired her through the Guild and which of us she is after. It could be any of us. Let's stick to what we have planned: to find a direction that Dani needs then get any items from the market we still want. Hopefully we will find a way to shake Varla off and move on without her. If we don't manage that, we will make other plans. Now, it is time to get some sleep, I think.'

Drinking up, they moved to go up the broad wooden stairs to the sleep chambers and then separated at the top. Crow went down the corridor to his chamber while Wren and Dani separated at their own doors. Dani had a large bed that Whisper had already made itself comfortable on, which made her laugh as she undressed before pushing the big kat to one side and climbing in. Wren went into the room she was sharing with Varla and saw a muffled-up shape on the sleeping cot in one corner. After undressing and murmuring a quiet good night, Wren climbed onto her own cot and settled to sleep.

It was only as she was about to fall asleep it hit her that she hadn't seen any movement from the opposite corner, despite the sound of heavy breathing and occasional snores. Without changing her position, she sent out a small *searching* spell over. When her spell showed just a bundled-up set of Varla's clothing within its own spell, she gave a grim nod of satisfaction. Something else to share about this sly woman tomorrow.

CHAPTER TEN

Dani struggled to get up the next morning, her limbs felt heavy, tired and achy. Wren, recognising the signs, brought her some eggs, bacon, mushrooms with extra toast to her room and stayed while the Healer ate a good breakfast and drank two mugs of tea before giving a sigh of contentment and falling immediately back to sleep. While Wren saw to her, Crow dressed and went out to speak to the Council Leader, so she was unable to tell either of her travelling companions of Varla's behaviour the night before.

Varla had snuck back into the room via the window in the early hours of the morning. Wren had set herself to wake at the slightest sound or change in atmosphere but had not needed to do so as she had still been awake, puzzling over the enigma of Varla and being honest with herself as to why she didn't like the woman. It wasn't just because the hanger on flirted madly with Crow, although that was annoying, it was more that she constantly tried to undermine the connection between Wren, Crow and Dani. Now knowing that she had hidden links to the Assassin's Guild only increased Wren's mistrust and dislike.

After leaving Dani fast asleep after her breakfast, Wren went and spoke to the Inn's proprietor about not disturbing her until Wren, herself, returned. Reluctantly, she handed over a coin, exchanged by Nobby from some of Dani's gems. He had been more than generous, but the capital city was eating away at their monetary funds. Pulling a warm cloak around herself; for although the sun shone brightly, the wind was sharp, she accepted the basket offered and wandered out to the market square where stalls full of produce, of fancies, of pastries and much more were laid out for her pleasure. Humming with delight, she began her shopping.

Crow wound his way through crowded streets, full of those going to sell, those off to get early bargains, those who worked indoors so were able to make a later start than those who had already been in the fields two hours or more. Everywhere shone with prosperity. He saw very few beggars in comparison to other places he had travelled.

His eyes widened when he saw two members of the priesthood of Kintrelle step aside for a tall, winged mother trying to corral three youngsters who were all determined to run or fly in opposite directions. The older man, a Server by his robes, gave a bellow of laughter as he caught one youngling by the ankle just as the female grabbed hold of another's shoulder and a huge, burly ogre caught up the last attempting escapee. There was much laughing and hilarity as the children were returned and placed in a connected harness. Despite being scolded roundly by the harassed parent, none of the three looked noticeably downcast and the gathered crowd began to move again. Crow did notice that although the elder of the two priests had joined in the fun wholeheartedly, the younger one had smiled only with his lips sneering when he thought no-one was watching.

'So, all is not in harmony,' Crow murmured to himself before deliberately catching up with the two men.

'Excuse me, good sirs,' he said to them. 'I am looking for the Council chambers or the Guild Hall or wherever the City Council meets, could you direct me, please?'

It was the older man who responded. 'Why, certainly, young one. We are walking most of the way there ourselves, feel free to walk with us.'

Again, Crow noticed a flicker of distaste from the younger priest but decided against commenting. Instead, he gave a smile and said how surprised he had been to see their robes in a city full of magik.

'Well, you see,' again the older man spoke. 'We belong to the Holy Church of Our Blesséd Kintrelle. He, our God, told us to be tolerant of all, *including* the magikers. It was only those who misuse magik we are supposed to condemn. Unfortunately, as with almost anything man gets involved with, His teachings have become corrupted over time. I know that in other lands the magik users are known as Abominations, but I am thankful that we here are more tolerant and liberally minded.'

His companion gave a snort of disgust and strode ahead. The priest shook his head and looked at Crow.

'I am Fidell,' he said. 'Methinks that young hothead, Arto, will not stay with us for much longer. We have tried but the bigotry seems to have sunk deep into his bones. Ah well.' With that, Fidell pointed to a large building just ahead. 'The place you need to go is the third green door from the gateway. The Leader is a good man and will listen with an open mind to all you have to say.'

'Thank you,' Crow said, handing over a contribution for the Church, before striding off in the direction indicated.

Wren filled her basket with herbs for her spells, plus some for a tea that might help Dani when she was so tired, as she wandered around the market stalls. She also got some long-lasting travel bread, some pastries as well as a few pieces of fruit to keep in Dani's room until she had gained enough strength to move about again. Heading back to the Inn, concerned at how expensive everything was, Wren saw the back of Varla's head as she moved quickly a short way in front. Before Wren could see properly or follow, Varla seemed to disappear. With a shrug, Wren headed back to the Inn.

Dani had woken up earlier and eaten a little. Now she was trying to get the energy to move as she was not only starving but needed to relieve herself. As she wondered if she could manage, Wren came in and handed her a meat pie, still warm from the oven.

'Eat this,' the mage demanded. 'And listen to what I have to tell you about Varla.'

'Wait just one moment,' Dani begged before hobbling her way over to the water closet and breathing a sigh of relief. Once she had washed her hands and face and felt a little more refreshed, she got back into bed and reached for the succulent pie.

As she ate, she frowned as she heard Wren's tale. Her frown deepened when she was told about Varla doing a magikal sending to pretend she was asleep in her bed, to sneak back into the room a short time before dawn. Dani had been wary of Varla before but now it seemed that the woman had a bigger hidden agenda than the Healer had thought.

'Have you told Crow?'

'Not yet,' replied Wren. 'He was off early to deliver his message to the city council, so I haven't seen him to speak to today. What *is* going on with that woman?'

'No idea. You need to make sure Crow knows everything though. I still feel as if she wants to drive a wedge between us all but you and Crow specifically. I just wish I knew why.'

'We'll find out. And if we keep nothing from each other, she won't succeed in her plans, if that is what she intends.'

After a few more minutes chatting, Dani felt her eyes beginning to close again. Wren left her to go into her own room to get on with some mending. Before starting, she sent out a little spark of magik to investigate Varla's travel bag. A sudden glow lit up the room, showing a ward in place over the woman's bag.

'Hmm,' Wren mused. 'Now why would you feel the need to bespell your stuff? And why hide your spell-making ability? Well, I have nothing to hide from anyone, but I do like my privacy so I can't blame you for not wanting snoopers to go through your things. I am, however, as sneaky as you but a better spellcaster than you are.' With that, Wren set a hidden spell to let her know each time Varla tried looking at anything that didn't belong to her. Even as Wren set the spell, it gave a slight flicker of light, letting her know Varla had already been through her luggage today.
'Alright. Now if you were the innocent you are trying to portray, why would you feel the need to go through my luggage? You, Varla, are no innocent lost in the wilderness.'

Collecting what she needed, Wren went back into Dani's room and sat in the big, padded rocking chair close by the window and relaxed while she mended shirts and breeches. The shadow kat arrived back from its own concerns a short time after and Wren found herself explaining the issues regarding Varla to it. It gave Wren an assessing glance before nodding its powerful head. Soon after, Crow arrived back, and Wren found herself explaining everything yet again.

'It is obvious that there is much more than meets the eye to our first meeting with the woman,' Crow said. 'If, as seems likely, she is an Assassin or a spell maker, she was tied to the stake through choice. I wonder which one of us she is after?'

'It could be any of us,' Dani spoke up drowsily from her pillows, making Wren jump a little. 'She could have been hired by Willoughby, my ex-master. Or perhaps because they felt the stirring of magik, the mages back in Mertam set her on either one of you. You say that the mages would kill one or the both of you, so the choice is wide open.'

'So,' Crow pondered. 'Do we kill here now or wait to try and find more information?'

'Wait,' Dani said firmly. 'We can get rid of her, or just disappear, at any time. We all have skills she doesn't know about. By waiting we may get valuable information that helps us further down the line.'

'Alright,' Crow said. 'Makes sense. Now, do you want to know what happened to me today?'

Immediately both the women's full attention was upon him. Grinning, he told them about meeting Fidell and the large house that stood as the council building.

'It truly is huge,' he enthused. 'Very elegant too. I went in and asked to see the Leader. I got passed down from person to person for what seemed an age before I finally ended up in a smallish room, very elegant though. It had murals painted upon the ceiling, well-crafted furniture and everywhere smelt of polish. There was also a bloody snot of a secretary who tried to bar me from meeting the big man He was pushing to know what I wanted and what I was going to say, I was pushing back and saying that the message was for the Leader's ears only when the big man himself opened a door to find out why his secretary hadn't answered his buzzer. On seeing me, the man gave a start then invited me into his chambers. I didn't smirk at the secretary too much!

'I passed on Nobby's information, then I asked if he knew Varla. He kept staring at me all the time until, in the end, I became uncomfortable and asked him directly what he was doing. He apologised profusely and explained that I looked very much like his brother; so much so, it had shaken him up. He asked if I knew my parents or my background as a child and when he heard that I had no clear memories of things before the Assassin's Guild, he wondered if I would speak to one of the Bloodlings, who would be able to give me answers regarding my family. I have told him I will think about it but, at this moment, I don't think I will bother. Do I really want to find a family that I don't remember at my age? Anyway, he seemed to understand that I wasn't really interested and changed the subject. I mentioned that we have someone with us who needs complete rest, and he has offered us a house to live in, rather than paying for rooms here. I have come to collect you and we can all move in now. He has sent food to fill the cupboards there as well as paying our bill here, he says that Nobby's information has been well worth the money. I have agreed to stay there only as long as Dani needs to as he would like to talk with me more as well as meet you two. I haven't mentioned your mage abilities, Wren, and I haven't given away any of our Dani's secrets either.'

'And did he?' asked Wren.

'Did he what?'

'Did he know Varla?' Wren asked impatiently.

'Oh, no he didn't but he will be asking his contacts about her. Come on sleepy head, we have a carriage for you. Can you get the bags, Wren?'

Just as Wren was about to ask if Varla was included, the woman herself knocked on the door and let herself in.

'I have heard that we have a house given by the Leader,' she exclaimed.

'Well, I have,' said Crow, bluntly.

'Oh, I thought you said that we could stay together,' her voice faded a little as she turned away.

'It's alright,' Dani yawned. 'Go get your stuff and bring along Wren's too.' Varla ran off almost as if she were afraid that Dani would change her mind.

Wren and Crow turned identically incredulous expressions toward Dani, making her giggle.

'I haven't gone mad,' she assured them. 'I just think I would rather have the poisonous spider where I can see her than wondering what she is doing when she is out of my sight. If we make sure to share her machinations, she cannot play us one off against the other the same way she could if we kept quiet. Besides, having her with us will make it much easier to find answers to why she wants to stick around.'

With that, Dani struggled up out of the bed. With Wren's help, she got dressed as Crow left the room to pack his bags. Shortly afterwards, they were all seated in a covered carriage, pulled by two matching bay horses. When the innkeeper saw whose coach it was, he refunded most of what he had been paid, so that the group left with a much heavier purse than expected, much to their relief.

Charlie left Mertam without fanfare, sure now of the direction he needed to go. His employer, Willoughby, had given him quite a heavy purse for a travelling allowance and was annoyed it would not be coming out of Charlie's eventual fee. The blasted scav had tried to argue about it but Charlie ignored him. Having the gift of finding people was rare and Charlie was the best and expected to be paid his worth, especially as he knew that all of this would have been explained to the foreign lord before his name and abilities were ever mentioned.

The biggest problem – apart from his new employer – was that Charlie had his doubts about the story regarding this escaped servant. Being a Tracker and a Bloodhound meant that the tiniest scent, the oddest word, even the denials given to direct questions guided Charlie to the prey. Something did not ring true with this Willoughby man though. There had been lies of omission in their conversations, if nothing worse. While searching for this woman, Charlie would think seriously about whether he should hand her over at the end.

The eatery that many of the Watch went to for food was run by Mallie and her husband, Brim. Charlie's innate abilities let him see the two gnomes without their human glamour as well as helping him sense what type of magik they used. With just a few words he could have had their place closed and both sent to the Punishment Square as Abominations. It wasn't that long ago when he would have done exactly that, but things had changed so much in such a short time that Charlie had, instead, given Mallie a veiled warning to be careful before he left her establishment. When he had stepped past the following day, the place was closed and shuttered.

Stepping through the East Gate, Charlie felt a slight shiver, but it wasn't the cold that caused it. Although rain had come down very heavily during the night, it was the scent of prey that made him shudder. Long years of practice had helped the young soldier take control of his abilities as well as to keep them hidden from others. It was now easy not to sniff at the air like a dog or whine when catching the odour of the prey he was after, but he couldn't stop the excitement rippling through him.

He spoke to the gate guard then walked out onto the road that led to the portal. The guard had remembered the girl with a youngster, a boy, but they had seemed angry with each other, which is why they had stuck in his memory. Charlie didn't care what had caused the memory to stay, just that it did.

Following the pathway into the trees, he heard a couple of woodcutters chatting about a fight in the woods, where a group of bandits had been beaten by a small group they had hunted.

'Aye, some deaths that day. Mind you, I did hear that one was an Abomination. And that there was magik being used!'

'Oh aye? And did little winged fairies come down and bop them on the head too? Garn with ya, there ain't no 'bominations round here, especially so close to the city. The Council wouldn't allow it.'

'I agree with you, you dolt, I am just passing on what I heard.'

Both men clammed up as Charlie stepped up to them. After some reluctance – and a nice bribe – they told him about the fight and where it had taken place. One of them even described some of the bandits involved and where they could be found. Charlie gave a nod in appreciation and marched on.

Using his hound ability, Charlie followed a faint mixture of scents he had recognised on the journey so far. He had first smelt it at the docks, again at Mallie's and now here on the roadway. From the direction it came from, it seems as if whoever it belonged to had veered off the pathway. The main scent was a gentle citrusy smell that had a not unpleasant astringency to it. There was also a heavy, animal musk scent, full of magik and fierceness. Then there was the last scent, oily and slimy, magik overlaid with trickery and the sourness of hate.

Bloodhounds and Trackers have internal magik that had never been outlawed by Kintrelle's followers. Charlie thought that there many reasons for this, the main one being that they were useful to the rich and the powerful. Someone with Hound magik had a sense of smell that could follow trails even through wet weather, if whatever had passed wasn't too long ago. A Tracker followed their instincts and almost invisible clues: a shared glance, a blush, refusal to speak or lies told were all sifted so quickly and then a feeling was accepted and a direction chosen. As Charlie was one of the extremely rare few that had both abilities it meant that he was successful in over ninety-five percent of his hunts, whereas the average for other Hunters or Hounds was below sixty percent for recovery.

The last few years in the army of the Shining One had become a time of stress, bullying and oppression. Charlie had become more and more isolated and unhappy with the way things were going. Then they changed some of the commanders, including his own, which was when Charlie had had enough and handed in his papers. Doing this last job would, he hoped, guarantee that he saw his money again but also made sure that no-one came after him. Using what was owed would enable him to disappear.

As the thoughts rushed and flowed in his mind at frenetic speed, Charlie continued to follow the scent trail. Moving off the pathway completely didn't come as too much of a shock as he had been expecting some kind of betrayal of the woman. Finding where it had happened did give him pause though.

He stopped and closed his eyes, inhaling deeply. After a few seconds his eyes snapped open, and they held an unearthly shimmer. He could smell magik belonging to the woman, but it held a deeper, unknown flavour that made the hairs on the back of his neck rise at the untold strength of it. The wild magik seemed to appear and then disappear and, finally, there were two other players now in the game.

Turning one way and then the other, Charlie found a story beginning to become clear in his mind. Following the scent of decomposition, he then turned up the bodies of the killed bandits.

Taking his time, Charlie moved around, step by small step as he pieced together the whole story. Raising his head, the glimmer in his eyes now much more pronounced, he began heading to the Portal at a gentle pace.

CHAPTER ELEVEN

The journey to the house took the small group of travellers less than half an hour, some of that time had been taken up with waiting for carts to move out of the way so as to allow them passage. Dani, between yawns, looked out of the window of the luxurious carriage at the bustling crowds who walked, flew, rode and ran. There were beings of every race, colour and shape. Young, old and ageless all vied for her attention as her eyes moved speedily from one group to another. When she saw the robes of the Shining One, she instinctively shrank back into her seat, adjusting her neckerchief to ensure that it covered her slave choker. Seeing that Crow gave a nod to the elder man in his white robe, more delicately decorated than his companion's overblown gaudiness, Dani realised who it was from Crow's description earlier. This must be the priest, Fidell. Taking up her courage after a few minutes, she peeped out at the masses once again, seeing the back of the priest's robes disappearing into the crowd..

Eventually, the carriage pulled up in front of a building of whitewashed stone. There were windows deeply recessed into the thick walls beside the heavy wooden doors. Taking a key from his pocket, Crow let them inside, and he went to help the driver bring in the luggage, which seemed to consist of much more than the single knapsacks they had been carrying on their journey so far.

As they walked into the house, they all blinked at the change in light from the brilliant sunshine outdoors. They stepped into a huge room, with soft seating, a dining table and heavy chairs for six as well as a kitchen area. Through an archway, stairs led up to the next storey. There were also three doors leading off from the big room. On the opposite wall of the front door, was another door of the stable type. Opening it up took them out into a courtyard. A flat terrace had a table and seating for outside dining, a vegetable garden as well as a small orchard. Deeper within the garden was what looked to be a stable block while much further away were big wooden gates that opened up to the outside thoroughfare. A huge wall enclosed the garden and outbuildings.

Stepping back inside, Crow opened one of the inner doors to see a pantry full of different foodstuffs, dried herbs and spices. Wren beat him to another door which, when she saw it, had her gasping with delight. A bathroom, with a bath that was plumbed in. Around a corner within the room were the conveniences as well as a marble sink with sweet smelling soaps and unguents. Dani opened the last door and gave a cry of pleasure. This was a room made for both sleeping and living. A big bed, covered in blue velvet with curtains of the same fabric and colour tied back at the windows. A couch with an overstuffed armchair was set by the unlit fire and shelves full of pretty objects as well as a few books and parchments covered the walls. With a sigh of delight, Dani walked in and dreamily removed her boots, picked out a book from the shelf closest to her and climbed up onto the bed, where she piled a few pillows behind her for comfort before opening the embossed leather covers of the heavy tome. Crow stuck his head round the door and laughed.

'So, this is yours, hmm?' Still grinning, he brought in her knapsack along with a platter of bread, butter, fruits and little pies. 'Settle yourself here, sweetness, Wren and I will check out upstairs.'

All he got was a distracted nod from Dani as she began to read the first page of the book and bit distractedly into one of the little meat pies. Leaving her in peace to enjoy herself, Crow stepped out with a grin which soon dropped from his face when he heard Varla speaking in an oh-so-reasonable voice to Wren.

'I am not trying to be difficult,' she was saying. 'I just don't think it is sensible for Dani to be sleeping down here when I will be doing all the housekeeping. Being down here would be much more convenient for me...' She broke off abruptly when she realised that Crow stood there listening, a cynical twist to his lips.

'Dani chose it first, she gets the room. Secondly, who says you will be doing all the housework? You seem to be forgetting that you are with us because we allow it, rather than being an integral part of our company. Once you tell us which way you are going, you might find that we end up travelling in different directions. Now, enough of this, let's go on up.'

Ignoring Varla's oily obsequious acceptance of his words, the same words that she had ignored completely when Wren had said them, he went up the wide, low steps that turned a corner halfway up. There was a corridor separating two doors, with windows at either end, allowing in some of the bright sunlight. Opening the first door showed a room like the one Dani had chosen downstairs. Books adorned shelves along with precious glass, shells and crystals. Wren exclaimed with pleasure when she saw that, behind a curtain, was a place to wash up.

With a grin at her delight, Crow took his own bags to the bedroom opposite, nodding in satisfaction at the breeze blowing gently through the open window, bringing with it the sounds and scents of the streets below. Frowning, he realised that, unless Wren allowed Varla to share her room, there was nowhere for the hanger-on to sleep. Wondering if this would settle the issue of Varla for once and for all, his thoughts were interrupted by a shout coming from the corridor,

Stepping out of his room he saw Wren looking at the farther end, so he followed her glance. There, almost hidden, was a narrow door which Varla had found and opened. It led to a narrow wooden staircase that went up into a wide-open space that covered the whole house. The ceiling was almost flat, with beams set at a very slight angle; there were two beds, cupboards to hold belongings as well as a wash station and tiny convenience. Although bigger with floor space, it was much barer in furnishings and decorations even though a comfortable chair sat near the unlit fire.

'Well now,' Varla exclaimed. 'This is even more perfect than the room downstairs. *I* will take this one.'

Crow saw Wren open her mouth to say something sharp and gave an infinitesimal shake of his head, remembering just in time that Dani wanted Varla to stay close. They were both so irritated with Varla's attitude of entitlement, neither one of them noticed Varla's eyes taking in the movement of Crow's head or the flash of satisfaction that flickered quickly and then disappeared over the woman's face.

After an awkward moment or two, Crow led Wren back down the stairs to unpack and check in on Dani. They found her asleep on the bed, the food tray placed carefully on the floor. After removing her shoes and covering her with a blanket, they left her door open. Wren went through to begin to prepare supper, only to find Varla had already begun the preparations. Wren helped to peel and chop in silence as Crow went to check on the kitchen garden. After collecting some of the ripe thistle-berries, he deliberately waited out of sight, grinding his teeth in annoyance as he heard Varla sniping at Wren, who sensibly refused to answer. He stepped into the room, cutting off Varla's latest remark, and handed the fruit to Wren with a wry smile.

When the roasted fowl, vegetables and potatoes were ready to eat, Dani wandered through, rubbing her eyes and exclaiming at how hungry she was. There was very little conversation as the meal was devoured, although they all exclaimed over the berry pies that Crow had made. He raised a cynical eyebrow at Varla's over-enthusiastic remarks, just giving a slight smile in acknowledgement. After they had all eaten enough, Wren, Dani and Crow cleaned the room as Varla went upstairs to her attic room. Once she was out of sight the shadow kat appeared and was given a helping of the meat and some of the small, fruit pies.

'I understand your reasoning regarding having Varla around,' Wren groused once they had all reconvened in Dani's room and shut the door firmly. 'I even agree with you. Just don't expect me to like her.'

'Don't worry, Wren,' grinned Crow. 'Neither of us expect miracles. She does hold her secrets well though. I will have to devise a way to get her to open up and tell us what we need to know. The longer I am in her company, the less I trust her.'

The women murmured their agreement before Wren asked about Whisper. Dani grinned and looked down at the sleeping kat.

'I have no idea what it is up to, so your guess is as good as mine. I think it is searching out information of its own. It will let us know when it is ready.'

'And how is the tugging motion? Are we heading in the right direction?'

'We seem to be although it isn't as insistent as it has been up to now. That usually means that I need more rest and must stay in one place for a short time. *Again.* Dammit, it is so frustrating, when this exhaustion hits, I am useless for anything. It isn't always when I have done any Healing, either. I wish I could either heal myself or be done with it all.'

'Stop being stupid,' Crow snapped, surprising the two women with the force of his irritation. 'Think about it, Dani. From, what, the age of twelve or thirteen, you were given Numb. Not only did the drug control you and force you to do your master's will, but it also ate away at your brain. You survived over *four* times longer than any other person, who all died from brain bleeds or other issues caused by the damn poison. We don't know what is going on inside you. My guess is you had a lot of damage within – your brain, maybe your blood or other organs or all of them combined – and your Healing Gift spent the twenty years hiding while just managing to keep you alive. Now your Gift is freed up to do so much more than just keep you breathing. And don't forget, you are still learning what your abilities are as you seem to be able to do more than Heal, but even just Healing takes a lot more energy than people realise. And the other stuff you can do, the sensing of people and if they can be trusted, the glimpses of the future and so much more that we haven't seen yet.

'Don't you get it, woman? You are a walking miracle that should be dead, not wandering over Yerat, trying to find your mysterious home. Everywhere you go you are leaving a mark, a good mark, so stop complaining when sometimes you are hit with exhaustion or hunger or whatever.'

He stopped his rant abruptly as he saw three sets of eyes, wide open and staring at him in wonder. Feeling suddenly embarrassed about his unusual outburst, he left Dani's room, grabbed a drink and went up to his own quarters and closed his door firmly.

'Well,' said Wren, still surprised at Crow's outburst.

'Well indeed,' replied Dani, sounding a little dazed.

The kat gave a loud snuffle, as if echoing the women's surprise, which made the women grin at each other and shake off their shock at Crow's words.

With just a few more words exchanged, the women separated and Dani, after having an apple with a little cheese, snuggled down to sleep, mulling over what Crow had said.

When Dani finally awoke the next day it was to find that Crow had left to go and speak to the Leader here in Drintoth, Wren was out doing the day's marketing and Varla was nowhere to be found. This didn't bother the Healer as she took a long, soothing bath and reclothed herself in fresh garments before washing those she had been wearing. Going to hang them out on the line, she saw a young boy, perhaps twelve or thirteen years in age, leading a group of four horses to the stable along with a sturdy mule. Strolling along next to him was Whisper. Dani frowned slightly, puzzled as to who this was and why the horses were here.

'Hello,' she called out and the youngster turned around, a huge grin on his face.

'Hi, lady,' he chirped, his voice cracking in the middle of the second word. 'The Leader has sent these along for you people, so you don't feel stuck here in the city. My name's Blue and I'm here to take care of them.'

Dani gave the boy a smile, which he returned, flashing a dimple in his right cheek. Studying him, Dani saw a short, slim youngster with a look of determination in his blue eyes. His curly, sun-bleached hair could do with a trim and, although his clothing was patched and worn, he was clean and looked ready to work hard.

Dani introduced herself then went to the horses. The first was tall and muscular, a stallion with a black coat that was splattered with dots of white, a front right sock and a white blaze on his forehead. He tossed his head before bending his elegant neck to nuzzle at Dani's cheek, much to her delight. Standing patiently by his side was a gorgeous red mare with black mane and tail as well as fat, black spots on her rump. She wasn't as arrogant as the stallion but happily accepted a petting as her due. Two more mares followed behind. These were of matching colours: a heavy cream body with a much lighter mane and tail. They also stood a little smaller than the other horses.

'Nightsky, Ladybird, Dazzle and Dream,' Blue gave Dani the horses names. 'And the mule is Brick, for brick wall, 'cuz he is dead stubborn.' The boy grinned in delight, smacking the grey, long eared animal on its flank.

Dani grinned in return before stepping back to allow him to lead the animals into the stables and she went back to the line where she pegged up her few bits of clothing. After that she went along the vegetable patch, pulling up weeds as Whisper basked in the sunshine. Eventually she felt weariness catching up with her again, so she said goodbye to Blue, who was grooming the already shining coat of Ladybird. Whisper lumbered to its feet and followed her into the house.

Standing just inside the kitchen door to allow her eyes to adjust, Dani saw Wren unpacking a basket of foodstuffs.

'Hi honey,' she said brightly, only to drop the smile when Wren sent her a black look in return. 'What the…what's wrong?'

'Nothing. I'm sorry, Dani, I am just really fed up. Varla is the housemaid? Yeah, right. She left first thing and I haven't seen her since. I went to the market once I had cleared away the breakfast things. While searching for the ingredients for our evening meal, I asked about her there, but no-one had seen her. What exactly is she staying with us for? Oh, I forgot, she is "helping".' Wren paused and huffed out a frustrated breath. 'Oh, don't listen to me, Dani, I am just sick of her and her attitude towards you and I, even as she fawns over Crow.'

Dani gave her a hug then gave a helping hand to empty the basket. Putting the fresh loaf of bread into the cold room, the two women then began to prepare the evening meal. A piece of pork for roasting, a cabbage, some carrots and potatoes from the garden and stuffing made with yesterday's bread. Going outside for the herbs needed for the meal, Dani took Wren over to the stables to introduce her to Blue and was delighted with the way the two of them seemed to connect immediately. She left Blue introducing Wren to the horses and one stubborn mule and went back to finish preparing the meal.

Exhaustion hit her as she put the meat in to cook so she grabbed some bread, a pear and a nectarine as well as a piece of cheese before heading back to her room. As she climbed into the wide bed, the shadow kat jumped up to join her. Dani hugged the big neck, breathing in the wild, musky scent and felt herself relax, the tension leaving her shoulders and the headache that had been brewing for the last hour eased off. Taking a bite from the pear, she caught the juice on her fingers and sucked them clean. Keeping her ears open for anyone coming into the house, she spoke quietly to Whisper.

'I do understand why Wren is fed-up, but she seems worse today, not just irritated but hurt. I wonder why things have changed from last night. Varla must have said something, I think. But then, Wren isn't stupid, she knows how the scav will try and manipulate us all, so why is she letting the woman get to her?' Dani gave a huge yawn. 'Oh well, nothing I can do now. Whisper, could you stay invisible and find out what's going on?'

Instead of fading from sight, the kat licked up the side of Dani's face, making her splutter, before wriggling and twisting its body. The Healer gaped at the huge kat as it messed her covers as it rolled onto its back, waving the enormous paws in the air.

Dani gaped then rubbed her eyes and stared in wonder. The kat was huge, with a soft grey coat covered in stripes and mottled patches in a deeper grey but as she watched, Dani saw that the kat was becoming smaller and its patterned coat became one solid colour. As it continued to roll and gave out the occasional hiss,

Dani tried to get it to stop, not liking the sounds it made as it seemed to be in pain. Then, eventually, rolling onto four unsteady legs, the now tiny black kitten gave a sneeze which knocked it off its feet.

'Oh, my goodness,' she exclaimed. 'I know that a kat is magikal, but I never expected this.'

With another sneeze, the kitten made its stumbling way to the edge of the bed before tumbling off the side. Dani moved swiftly, hanging her head over the edge of the mattress to see the kitten making for the main room wobbling slightly. Grinning, she got up to follow it, all feelings of tiredness temporarily forgotten.

CHAPTER TWELVE

As Dani followed the small "kitten" into the next room, the garden door opened and Crow walked in, looking despondent and weary. Seeing Dani, he pasted a smile onto his lips, but his eyes stayed drawn. Dani went and hugged him, feeling a slight bolt of her Healing slide into him without conscious thought. Reaching around him, she put the heavy kettle on to boil.

'What is it about this place?' Dani said in exasperation. 'One day and two of you are already miserable. Did you see the horses?'

'For my part, I am tired and irritated, not miserable.' Crow responded. 'I went to the Leader's office first thing, like I was asked to do, and his secretary once again plied me with questions before he ignored me. It was only when a captain of the guard walked by after a few hours and saw me sitting there that I found out the Leader wasn't even in his office today. So, I wasted time that I could have spent here, plotting the next step on our journey or helping in some other way. The only bright side was that the captain reminded that scav of a secretary to hand over a bunch of currency that the Leader had put on one side for us. I hadn't eaten and wasn't even offered any water so Pelagro, the captain, took me to a local eatery for a drink and a snack. He says that if we need anything, send word to him. He also says that Blue knows where he will be. Have you met Blue?'

He listened to Dani enthusing about the horses as he absent-mindedly fussed at the small kitten. Wren stepped silently into the room to see the Assassin lifting the tiny creature up to his cheek and rubbing against its face. Despite her feelings of hurt, she felt her heart turn over.

'We have a new companion?' Wren spoke as she stepped forward, focusing on the kitten and refusing to look at Crow. Dani saw his confusion at the slight, quickly masked behind a blank expression, and mentally rolled her eyes. This seemed as if it could be Varla's meddling but unless Wren spoke up about what was bothering her, the situation would have to continue a little longer. The idiots might even learn something about keeping secrets, or rather, *not* keeping secrets.

Wren gave the kitten a light rub on its head before she checked on the meat and got the rest of the meal cooking. Crow handed the kitten over to Dani before slipping upstairs to get washed up.

Varla came in just as he disappeared and stopped when she saw the kitten, now chasing a piece of string Dani wriggled in front of it.

'A kitten? I hope I am not expected to take care of it?' Before Wren could explode in anger at the comment, Dani answered calmly and coolly.

'Firstly, whatever this animal needs, I will provide. Secondly, as you don't seem to be able to do the job you insisted on staying with us for, I wouldn't expect you to do anything for me or mine. Thirdly, be very careful just how demanding you become, you walk on thin ice as it is.' With that, Dani walked to her room and shut the door.

'Oh, perhaps the ice is thicker than she thinks, what say you, Wren?'

'I say nothing to you, Varla, except call us when the food is ready.' With that, Wren walked past the smirking Varla and headed for her room, her bland expression hiding her turmoil.

After Varla heard the quiet slam of Wren's door she gave a quiet chuckle before turning and checking the food. What she didn't notice was Dani's door, which had been open a slight bit, closing quietly.

Later that evening, once the silent, awkward meal had finished, Crow shrugged off all attempts to give help and did the clean-up alone. As he said, he had been doing nothing all day so he might as well earn his keep.

'At least someone is,' Wren snapped and strode upstairs, her door slamming too much more forcefully than earlier.

'What the void..?' he exclaimed at her abrupt departure.

Before Varla could say anything, Dani interjected sharply.

'I would say that Wren is reacting to a day spent cleaning and marketing, followed by preparing and cooking our meal, while our "housemaid" is nowhere to be seen that has annoyed our friend, but it could be more than that.' Dani said.

'Really? So, what was our "housemaid" doing all day?' Crow snapped, glaring at Varla.

'I went to try and find out about my family, to find out where they are and if they are safe,' Varla spoke quietly, her eyes downcast. 'I thought that if I knew where they were I could begin my journey to find them.'

If she had hoped that her attitude would earn her points with Crow or even Dani, she was sadly mistaken.

'Alright, well you made the decision to be our housemaid, so I suggest you do at least some of the daily chores you volunteered for. Either that or you might as well leave and go stay with those acquaintances you have been talking to. We all work together as a group and if you aren't pulling your weight then there is no reason for you to stay, is there? Haven't we had this conversation before?' Crow said, abruptly.

'Yes, we have,' Dani acknowledged, cutting through whatever Varla had begun to say. 'And while we are on the subject, just to make sure everything is out in the open, I don't class looking after the kitten as part of the daily work of a maid. It is my responsibility, and I will care for it.'

'I never meant you to misunderstand me,' Varla said, her voice sounding strangled, as if she was keeping a tight hold on her emotions. 'I was worried that the shadow kat would harm the little one, not that I wouldn't help with the care of it.'

'Really? That isn't what it sounded like earlier, but no matter. The shadow kat seems to have moved on and left the kitten in its place. I will watch over it in memory of a good friend. Thank you for your concern.' Dani's voice was cold, holding no emotion and giving no chance of Varla being able to misconstrue her words.

Varla gave a short nod and then walked with a straight spine up to the steps, disappearing around the corner. Crow opened his mouth but stopped when Dani and the kitten both shook their heads to stop him. Changing tack quickly, he began asking if the kitten needed food, if so, what? It was a good five minutes of chat about the tiny feline later that Dani gave a small sigh of relief and motioned Crow to her room.

'Alright, what is going on, blast you?' Crow asked in exasperation, once the heavy door was firmly closed.

'Varla has said or done something to upset Wren, but I don't know what. Doing the work today might have irritated our friend but I saw true hurt in her eyes, Crow. We must be even more watchful. As for the shadow kat, I saw that you didn't believe that it has left us, and you are right.' Pointing to the now sleeping kitten, she said with a grin. 'That's it!'

'What? No!' Crow almost shouted the words, and the kitten woke up and then batted at Crow's reaching hand. Although the kitten looked tiny, it was the shadow kat's strength that had Crow tumbling off the bed onto the floor. A few minutes later there was a light tap on the door and Wren popped her head around it, raising her eyebrows at the fallen Crow. Laughing at her expression, Dani explained the situation of the kitten and its reaction to Crow's disbelief. Instead of laughing at him lying sprawled on the floor as she would have done previously, Wren just commented that they should be careful about noise and left.

Dani and Crow exchanged baffled looks before he stood and, kissing her cheek, left. Feeling weary but not exhausted after her nap that afternoon, Dani read a little from the book she had taken down from the shelf before she turned out her light and settled to sleep, resting her hand over the small body of the kitten even while feeling the heavy body of the kat lying next to her. Although it was disorientating to see and feel two different sensations, it was also a comfort to her, and she slipped into slumber.

The next few days followed a similar routine for them all. Dani noticed that Wren became more and more quiet and withdrawn. Crow got even more irritated as the Leader failed to meet him to discuss Nobby's information, despite having claimed strong interest in both the information and Crow himself. Varla now spent an hour or so getting the evening meal prepared and did a little surface cleaning before she disappeared for the rest of the day. The atmosphere between them all got more and more strained until, eventually, it all exploded.

Dani woke earlier than she had been wont the rest of the week they had stayed in the house, feeling as if she had finally caught up on what she needed to be able to focus upon the next stage of her journey. Slowly at first but gaining speed as her muscles warmed up, she began moving around her room, packing as she went. Seeing the kitten staring at her, she found herself explaining to it:

'My "tugging" has started up again, really strongly, so it is time for me to get moving. I just need to speak to Wren and Crow before I leave. I don't want Varla to watch as I go, in case she tells all to her masters. You go check on Varla while I go and speak to Wren. I think it is late enough for Crow to be at the Leader's office.'

As she finished talking to the prancing kitten, Dani stepped into the main room and then stopped abruptly as she saw Wren, her back to Dani, hunched over and shaking with sobs.

'Wren! what is it?'

Raising her head and struggling to form the words, Wren was just able to cry out: 'He's gone!'

'Who? Crow? Gone where?' Dani felt completely confused, finding it impossible to understand what Wren was trying to say.

'Go a-and lo-ok in h-is room.' Wren hiccoughed, her breath coming in desperate gasps as she tried to control her breathing.

Dani ran up the steps, further evidence that she was back on top form, or close to it. Opening the door to Crow's room, she stepped inside. It looked like a whirlwind had attacked the place. Bed covers had been pulled off and left in a heap on the floor. Drawers had been pulled open and, apart from one odd sock, emptied of all their contents. The standing cupboard that had held his cloak was also empty. Bending down, Dani looked under the bed and saw a few scraps of paper which she collected.

Frowning, she left the room and went on up to Varla's room. Here, the space had been emptied out more methodically and, no matter how carefully she searched, Dani could find nothing to explain the disappearance of the supposed housemaid. Still frowning in thought Dani went back down to the main room to speak to Wren.

When she got there it was to see that the other woman had put the kettle on to boil. Although her eyes were red-rimmed and looked raw, she had stopped crying but still looked miserable. She looked up with a trace of hope on her features, only to lose it at whatever she saw on Dani's face.

'He's really gone then,' she said, a slight hitch still in her voice.

'Yes, but it isn't what it seems,' Dani replied, dropping the torn pieces of paper onto the table. 'You have been miserable from the moment we got here, tell me why.

'It doesn't matter now.'

'Yes, it does.' Dani felt more than just a little annoyed at Wren who was acting so out of character. At this thought, Dani paused before looking deeply into Wren's eyes. There, so small to almost be invisible was a slight mote in the left eye. Focusing her magik in a way she had never done before, she sent a hair thin line of energy through and into the mote. There was a sparkle of light and then Wren pulled back with a jerk.

'What are you doing? That hurt.' she demanded.

'That, my friend, was a spell. To stop you seeing the truth, I think. You have been uncharacteristically morose since we arrived here. Varla's doing in part, but also this spell. It seems to have added to your melancholy. Despite us agreeing to speak up about anything she said or did, you have been extremely quiet about her. That has allowed her to sow doubts in your mind that speaking about would have let you see the facts. You have to accept some of the blame for what has been going on; after all, you are mage-trained while I am using guesswork most of the time. Mind you, I should have been more aware of what was going on.' Dani answered.

'No, you're right, I should have said something right from the first. As to why I didn't, to begin with, it seemed that I was reading too much into things and feeling ridiculous at how I reacted. Then it seemed to get harder and harder to use my common sense. Even when I *knew* she was messing with my mind, I couldn't seem to find my way out of the mess.'

'It's about time that you just admitted that you are in love with him. Now stop prevaricating and tell all.'

With a start, a blush, followed by a startled grin, Wren began.

'The first morning, I woke up a little early. I thought I would spend time exploring the garden. As I left my room, I saw Varla leaving Crow's room. She was wearing just her underpinnings and carrying her dress and shoes. She looked up and saw me, giggled and sashayed past. Before she went up to her room, she said that Crow wanted me to do the marketing and begin the evening meal preparations as she had his permission to do other things. I intended to speak to Crow about it but, somehow, by the time he returned home, it seemed too difficult to speak about.'

'That's because you were already magiked.' Dani said. 'Did Crow say anything as she left?'

'No. Why?'

'Why? If she really had been in his bed, he would have at least walked to the door with her. I know for certain, however, that he would never sleep with her, he said she made his skin crawl.'

'Oh. Oh damn.'

'That isn't the only thing, is it? You have got more and more upset as time has gone on.'

'Yes, but now I feel like an idiot because I can see how she must have manipulated me. A day or so later, she was again leaving his room, this time wearing nothing but a wrapper. Again, she was very dishevelled and, again, she giggled. I also heard Crow say something as she was closing his door.'

'Are you sure it was Crow's voice?'

'Thinking about it now, no, I am not sure. It was a man's voice coming from his room, so I just assumed it was Crow.'

'As anyone would,' soothed Dani.

'You wouldn't,' said Wren, confidently.

'Perhaps not, but I have had a much less conventional upbringing than you.' Wren laughed out loud at the sly humour in this comment.

'Go on then, Healer, explain that one,' she challenged.

'If it is the day I am thinking of, "that one" is easy to explain, as you would know if you had listened to what we were discussing when Varla had left the house. Crow had woken late that day, after you had already gone to the market for some fish. He felt sure that he had been drugged. He told me what herbs to use, and I made him an antidote, then he stumbled off to the Leader's office just before you came back after lunchtime. He knew something had happened in his room, he even said it smelt like sex but when he checked himself, the scent was not his. We spoke about this in front of you, but you were obviously not listening. Now, tell me the rest.'

'When I left my room today, I saw Varla at his door once again. This time she was fully dressed and smirking at me. She was wearing his ring; you know the one he keeps on a chain around his neck. She told me that Crow was staying here with her permanently and, after a heated discussion, had agreed that my living in the same house as the happy couple was not ideal. If I wouldn't mind looking for alternative accommodation as soon as possible, she would help with finding me a job and some money. Then she gave me a list of things to get from the market and swept upstairs to her rooms as if she owned the place.' Wren's voice rose in indignation but as she stopped speaking she began to frown. Dani just waited.

'Why did I believe her?' Wren said in surprise. 'Crow would never have let her say any of that, in that way. Even if he really had begun a relationship with her, he would never have spoken to her

the way he did in public for the time she has been with us, all
abrupt and rude. He wouldn't have discussed my living
arrangements with her, without my knowledge or involvement.
The thing that convinced me at the time was the fact she wore his
ring.'

'His ring? You mean that ring?' Dani pointed at the centre of the
table. There was the lidded honey pot, a small salt cellar and a bud
vase holding a few sprigs of lavender. Hiding in the middle of
these was Crow's silver ring, with its obsidian stone.

'Oh.' Wren's voice sounded small and uncertain as she picked the
ring up and held it tight in her hand.

'Most of what you believed is due to the spell she used, I think,'
Dani said thoughtfully. 'I also think that the misdirection she
performed was masterly. Of course, if you had spoken out and told
us what she was doing, all of this could have been stopped.'

'I couldn't,' Wren was getting teary again. 'I felt hurt and angry
and stupid, and I couldn't say anything. If he preferred her to-to
me, then I should just accept.'

'But he didn't prefer her, she just made it seem that way,
remember that. Now the important thing is to find out where he has
gone. You stay here and pack. Not just our clothes but any food,
currency and everything else you think we might need. I will alert
Blue to get the horses ready and see if he has any idea as to where
Crow has gone. Then I am off to speak to the Leader to find out
what he knows, if anything.'

'Are you sure you will get in to see him?'

'Whisper will be going with me; of course I will get to see him.'
Dani bared her teeth in a feral grin then, grabbing some fruit and a
small waterskin, she left by the rear door, heading for the stables.

Wren spent a few minutes berating herself for being such a fool,
wiping her sore eyes carefully. She then took a few moments to do
a calming spell before she began searching internally for any more
of Varla's twisted spell work. She found another tiny fragment of
unhappiness and distrust which she carefully neutralised before she
poured a glass of cold water over her head.

Dripping and gasping a little at the cold and the release from the spell, she poured another glass of water, this time to drink and sat down at the kitchen table to catch her breath. As she did, her eyes fell upon the scraps of paper that Dani had absent-mindedly left there. Pulling them towards her, Wren turned and moved them about until what was in front of her was a message, written in a code she knew very well indeed. What she read raised her eyebrows before rage exploded from her and she ran to do as Dani had told her to do before leaving for the council chambers.

CHAPTER THIRTEEN

Walking down the path towards Blue's domain, Dani marvelled at the scene of bucolic splendour before her. The vegetables and herbs in the kitchen garden were growing well, even this late in the season, birds sang lustily and there was the droning of insects even as the bright jewel tones of butterflies and dragonflies flew about her.

Stepping into the cool dark of the stables, she stopped moving to allow her eyes to adjust. She could hear Blue humming softly, interspersed with the occasional murmur as he spoke to the horses while he cleaned some of the already highly polished tack.

Although none of them had really been out on the horses this past week, they had all got to know the young boy quite well. An orphan who had never known his mother, Blue had been happily living with his father until three years previously. That was when his father, a groom to one of the nobles, had got on a horse that was still half-wild. Blue had been told by one of the other stablemen that he had got on the horse with no problem, but something spooked the huge animal, setting it to bucking. As Amos had still been a little weak, following a fever, he had been unable to hold on and had fallen awkwardly, breaking his neck and killing himself instantly. The stableman handed over a few noons in back wages, added a tesp as a sweetener before saying that the noble had had the beast killed to make sure that it didn't kill another.

Although only ten, Blue had known that the money was barely adequate for a week's work, let alone the true wages owed. Noons were small change and, although tesps were worth much more, a single one to pay for food, lodging, schooling and other sundries would last just a few weeks, and only if the boy ate very sparingly. Seeing this, the youngster immediately left the rented house he had shared with his father, went to a cave that was out of town and stowed all his belongings there before coming back and beginning to hustle for work. Since then, he had been able to not only survive but to thrive. When he had found a purse full of tesps near to his cave a year ago, he had taken it straight to the Leader, thinking that it would be better taken there than given to a (perhaps) dishonest guard. Or even to be accused of theft.

Since that propitious day, Blue's life had turned around completely. As a reward for his honesty, the Leader made sure the youngster had plenty of work, enough to be able to afford a place in a rooming house, run by the wife of one of the guards. This had led to even more work from the guards as well as from the Leadership, so Blue was content with his life, no more so than when he had horses under his care.

Seeing Dani looking so determined as she strode towards him made him raise his eyebrows. He was used to seeing her weary or hungry, so this was a strange attitude to him. She stopped just before him where he sat and took a moment to regain her breath.

'Hello, Blue, have you seen anything of Crow today?'

Blue nodded. 'Yes, lady. He was here maybe an hour ago. He made a fuss of the horses then said that, as how you'd all left an' he was followin' on after you, I might as well take the beasts back. I tried to tell him that you weren't gone an' that the horses was his for real, but he weren't listening. He looked really sad. I didn't know what to do 'cuz after that, that Varla come out an' told me to mind my tongue an' leave. She don't pay me, so I am stayin' till either you lot or the Leader hisself tells me it's time to finish. Did I do wrong, lady?'

'No, definitely not,' was Dani's swift response. 'Varla has been causing trouble for us so you were right to ignore her. Now, I am off to see the Leader, I need you to get all the horses ready as well as the mule. Then go and see if Wren needs any help packing our things. We will be leaving as soon as possible. Have you seen the kitten anywhere?'

'Yes, lady. The shadow kat is playin' with Ladybird, second stall in.'

Dani hesitated at the frank admission that Blue knew what the kitten really was. The boy shrugged at her look.

'It showed me.'

With a smile and a quick nod, Dani went into the indicated stall and saw the "kitten" playing around in the straw by Ladybird's feet. It turned at her arrival and cocked its head. Giving it a swift summary of what had happened, Dani explained where she was going and asked if the kat would be coming with her. Standing up and shaking its fur, the kat waited until they left the stables to return to full size. A few moments of the twisting, turning and stretching, along with the hissing and yowling, soon had the shadow kat in its more familiar form. As they quickly left the garden, Blue was already getting Dazzle saddled.

The weather was bright, but a cool breeze blew which helped keep Dani cool as they marched through the streets. It didn't take long to get to the offices of the Leader, everyone who saw them coming got out of their way as swiftly as possible. Walking down the long, wood-lined corridor, Dani ignored the people determined to stop her. Most got the message and got out of the way before the kat gave its snarl. Those that didn't soon moved after it gave voice.

Once she reached the offices of the Leader she was halted by a tall, supercilious man who spoke as if to an idiot.

'You cannot bring that beast in here,' he snapped.

'Obviously I can,' Danni snapped back. 'Seeing as it is here now. I need to see the Leader immediately.'

'Impossible. There are procedures to follow. You will have to make an appointment when I know he is free. Perhaps next week?'

'No. Now.'

'Don't be ridiculous, woman. The Leader is a very important man, he cannot waste time with one such as you.'

'And what, exactly, do you mean by "One such as you"?' enquired a deep voice from the threshold of the doorway.

The secretary froze; obviously he hadn't expected his employer to hear his derogatory comment to a member of the public, especially knowing with whom she had arrived in the city. Mouth opening and closing like a startled fish, he made no sound.

'Please, come in, my lady,' the Leader said, sweeping his arm in a welcoming gesture. As she stepped inside she heard the Leader say something to his secretary but was unable to work out what it was.

Inside was a complete contrast to the dark corridor. Large glass doors opened out onto a wide terrace and let in a lot of light. Two walls were covered in bookshelves, holding hundreds of books and scrolls. Dani was so busy looking at these she almost missed seeing the man leaning casually against the wall. Before either could do more than nod, the Leader stepped into the room, shutting the door firmly behind him.

'My apologies for my now ex-secretary's rudeness, he seems to have forgotten what he was employed to do here. Now, please call me Dovas, and how may I help you?' Seating himself in a comfortable corner seat, he waved Dani to another. The shadow kat thumped down heavily onto the floor by her feet.

'A shadow kat,' mused the second man. 'Then you must either be Dani or Wren.'

'And you must be Captain Pelagro,' Dani responded. 'I am Dani and I want to ask if you have seen Crow today at all?'

Dovas looked over at Pelagro, who shook his head.

'Not since the beginning of the week,' was the captain's comment.

'And you?' Dani demanded, turning to Dovas.

'I? No, I haven't seen him since our first meeting. You were all supposed to have been told that I have been away, riding our border to the east, investigating a murder. A woman's body was found and there was worry that a Necrotic was loose. Thankfully, it was not, just a poor woman being raped and murdered by a vicious criminal. I got back less than an hour ago.'

'Wait, you haven't been here?' Dani sat up straight, confused.

'No, my dear. Didn't you get my message?' At Dani's negative response, Dovas turned to Pelago. 'Go and arrest Veltya, he has obviously been playing games with people and I want to know why.' The captain nodded and left the room. Before Dovas could begin to explain anything, Pelago was back in the room.

'He's gone and he has tried to open the safe.'

'Go and find him.' Dovas was beyond angry now. Inside the safe were important trade documents as well as certain other official documentation needed to lead the country and keep a balance between magikers and the followers of the Shining One.

'Now, tell me what has been going on, Dani. I was hoping to speak to Crow, I am sure that there is some blood connection between us as he looks so much like my brother, who had his child disappear many years ago. I wanted to go with him to a Bloodling to find out if it was more than just my imagination.'

Dani now understood Crow's cryptic comment when they were in their new residence for the first time. Taking a deep breath, she spoke quickly and concisely, detailing what had gone on, including Nobby's information, the trouble with Varla and the disappearance of Crow.

Dovas sat and listened in silence, pouring out some coffee when it was delivered and taking in all the information. When Dani finally stopped, he thought for a moment, putting all his thoughts into order.

'You were right to distrust Varla,' was his first surprising comment. 'She is a member of the Assassin's Guild, though not as one of the upper echelons. She knows a little basic spellwork and does information gathering usually. I know of her for a few reasons but mainly because she is Veltya's sister and also because I have not long been informed that she is being investigated by the Guild for various reasons I don't know the details of. I didn't realise that she had continued staying with you, I had assumed she would have gone home.'

'Home?'

'Yes, she owns a house near the lake and lives there with her brother.'

'She made us believe that she came from somewhere else and was struggling to get back home. I warn you, if she has harmed my friend I will deal harshly with her. Now, my priority is to find Crow so I will leave you to deal with your own mess.' Dani stood up as she spoke and the kat followed suit.

'Will you let me know when you find him?' asked the Leader.

'That depends on whether we catch up with him and if he wants you to know about it. For now, you have a pile of trouble on your hands that you need to clear up and we have a friend to find.'

Dovas also stood, nodding his understanding. 'I understand. You think I should have told him personally that I was not going to be here. I agree, knowing what I do now. All I ask is that you try and understand that I thought I could trust my staff, obviously I was wrong. Now, is there anything I can do to expedite your search?'

'Two things; are the horses really ours to keep? And can you send runners to find out which gate Crow left by. We shall be organising ourselves for a little time, I think, so send a messenger there telling us which way to go.'

'The horses are yours, as I told Blue. I will send someone to do the round of Gates and they will come straight to you as soon as they have the information you need,' he promised. 'I will also ask something of you. Take the boy, Blue, with you. He knows those horses and he will be of great help to you. This city isn't good for him.'

Although surprised at the request, Dani agreed even before the shadow kat gave its affirmatory grumble. Reaching into a desk drawer, Dovas removed a wooden box. Inside it was full of currency as well as a stack of promissory notes from his personal account. Counting out a large amount of coinage, he split the pile of notes in half.

'Take these, use whatever you want for whatever you need,' he said. 'Then, you can either return the rest or give them to another in need. And get yourself a new scarf for your neck, the jewels on your slave collar have broken too many threads. It's becoming very obvious to anyone who looks properly.'

Dani froze at his comment, her hand lifting guiltily to her throat, before nodding and taking the currency and notes offered. Then she left, moving past the people rushing around and through the halls of power. She headed back to the house with just a slight detour to buy herself a new neckerchief to cover the slave collar.

Getting back to the house, she saw the horses saddled, and the mule was loaded up with their goods. There seemed to be more there than Dani had expected but she didn't stop to examine anything but walked into the stone house.

There she saw Blue and Wren sitting at the table with a quick meal waiting for her arrival. She smiled in appreciation and sat down next to the stable hand. They began eating in silence until Wren got up and pulled half a loaf from its box on the kitchen chest and placed it on the table with the last of the opened butter. She began slicing it as she looked at Dani and spoke.

'Everything of Crow's has gone apart from his ring, which I found on this table, hidden among some flowers. That has confused me completely, why would Varla leave the ring here? Won't Crow demand that she wears it? Oh, and Blue has asked if he can come with us. I said yes but only provisionally. If you don't agree…'

Dani interrupted. 'Why should I disagree? I have more trust for Blue than I ever had for Varla. Let me tell you what they said at the office. Wren, what is it?'

Wren had taken three thick slices of bread and began to butter them as Dani spoke. She looked more closely at the slice she held steady, gave an exclamation of shock and disgust before running and washing her hands vigorously under the tap, using the strong soap they used for clothing and a scrubbing brush to cover every inch of flesh. After a moment, having scrubbed her hands almost raw, Wren came back to the table and threw a cloth over the bread, the butter and the knife.

'There is evil in that loaf. Everything it touches will become poisoned. The cutting board, knife, butter and dish as well as the cloth need to be burned to ash and then the ash needs to be buried deeply in sand. Anyone who touches the bread or anything it has been in contact with, needs to wash immediately. Anyone who ingests it will need help from a Healer such as you within thirty minutes to have a small chance of survival or it will be too late. I don't know *why* it was made or who it was originally intended for, but I know *who* made it. What really worries me is that there was only *half* a loaf.'

'Damn that woman.' Dani spat out, making the others jump. Neither of them had expected the usually calm woman to explode with anger as she did. Before anything else could be said there was a sharp knock on the door leading in from the street. Opening it, Wren saw the captain standing there, looking grim. He looked at the tableau at the table, including the cloth covered mound and grunted.

'More trouble? Well, we can get to that in a moment. I have been round to all the gates and have found that Crow left by the North Gate, he was travelling on foot and alone. He looked, according to my men, both upset and in a hurry. Unlike his usual self, he didn't stop to chat, just gave a nod and rushed past them.

'The idiot didn't even ask if we had gone the same way,' expostulated Wren.

'There will be time for recriminations later,' Dani said briskly. 'First we need to catch up with him and make sure he hasn't eaten any of the poisoned bread.' With this, she left the table and went up the stairs, leaving Wren to explain about the bread and take care of its disposal. The kat walked close by Dani's side, wanting to see if anything important had been left in any of the rooms.

In Varla's attic, although almost everything had been taken away earlier, Whisper led Dani to a pinch of spilled herbs, a scrap of cambric and a piece of parchment that had fallen to the floor and had slid under a table until just a small edge showed. Using her nails, Dani dragged the parchment out, put everything into a handkerchief, then left and closed the door behind herself and the silent shadow kat.

They followed the same routine in the lower-level rooms, finding a tiny cloth package hidden between the mattress and covers at the base of Wren's bed as well as something very similar in Crow's room, attached to the curtain of the window near the head of his bed. After checking out her own room, which held nothing, she took her findings out to the others.

'What are these?' she asked, interrupting whatever the small group had been discussing.

Wren looked closely, cautiously sniffed the herbs before tentatively tasting a tiny amount on the tip of her tongue. She immediately spat out what she had tasted before grabbing a glass of water and gulping it down without stopping for breath.

'The two pouches are spells, as you thought,' she said to Dani, panting just a little from the quick ingestion of water. 'One of them is for confusion and hurt, the other is for charm and malleability. I can guess which one was in which room. The herbs you picked up are part of the spell pouches, as is the material. This, however, is something I don't feel is aimed at us.' She handed the parchment over to the captain.

'What is it?' he asked as he studied the tiny writing and tried to decipher its meaning.

'It is part of a spell for controlling a person of power. Certain herbs are crushed together while the words are spoken. After a time for the spell to infuse the herbs, it is added to hot tea, a pinch at a time.'

The captain's head shot up as he recognised the full implication of Wren's words, even as she turned to Dani.

'We need to go now,' she insisted. 'I have explained what must be done with the bread. Everything else is packed and on the mule. Did you know that Varla and that bastard of a secretary are siblings? No wonder Crow wasn't getting anywhere. We should have left the bitch tied to the stake.' With this, she wrapped herself up in her travelling cloak, passed Dani's over to her and found another for Blue before heading out the back way to the horses.

Seeing the confusion on Captain Pelagro's face, Dani grinned, shook her head and patted his shoulder as she went past. Blue grabbed the last of the fruit and put them in a pouch at his waist and trotted along after the two women and the kat.

The captain stood and watched them go before he got busy; following his orders regarding the poisoned bread and then going to report to Dovas over what had happened.

By the end of the day the whole city knew that Varla and her brother were outlawed. After hearing all that had transpired and knowing that Varla had been trying to complete an unsanctioned kill, the Assassin's Guild put a price on the siblings capture, dead or alive, or for information on their whereabouts as they seemed to have completely disappeared. The rooms of the Leader were being checked for spells and all the paperwork looked into. False orders had been found and, so far, eight people who had previously been falsely imprisoned were being set for release. To say that it was chaos was a complete understatement.

Dovas cursed himself for losing sight of his own ideals and he knew he had a lot of work to do, just to get back some semblance of trust from those who mattered; the common people of the land. While he worked his way through another pile of prisoner forms, he spared a thought for the small group of people who had brought it all to light. He also prayed to his gods that the man he was sure was his nephew had survived the murder attempt by the still missing Varla. With a sigh and a shake of his head, he picked up another piece of paper to study.

CHAPTER FOURTEEN

The two women had got on Dazzle and Ladybird respectively, leaving the big stallion by unspoken consent for Crow when they caught up with him. Blue got upon Dream, caught hold of Brick's leading rein, and followed on behind. It was slow going at times, moving through the crowds attending the market. Dani noticed how many of the stall holders shouted a greeting to Wren and, when realising that she was leaving, passed along goods to help her on her travels, as well as many fond wishes to speed them safely on their way. What amazed her more was that for every one person who called after Wren, twice as many checked after the youngster. Blue was obviously a favourite with the market traders and, when they had chance to go through his gifts later, they found all manner of useful items. These included seeds for sowing three different crops, tools, a new bridle, lots of rope, oats for the horses as well as food galore. This meant that the group ate extremely well for weeks with no need of hunting except to add fresh meat to their pot.

They travelled more swiftly after they had got past the market and into the quieter, residential area. They reached the big North Gate in less than an hour. Blue checked with the guard and rode up to Wren and Dani as they waited just past the opening for him.

'Crow was walking an' he was here about an hour an' a bit ago. We ain't as far behind him as I thought,'

'We are moving more quickly than he can, even with the crowds,' Wren said. 'Once past the crowds round the gate, we will move even more swiftly. I just want to catch him before he eats that bloody bread.'

At this, they got their horses moving again. Even worried as she was, Wren couldn't help grinning when, some men having got too close, the shadow kat chose to appear, having stayed in its invisible form until then. Seeing it calmly licking its paw and flexing its considerable talons, the group decided that patting a horse, even with the added attraction of "accidentally" touching a woman, really wasn't worth it.

Moving on past this last group, they were able to move even more quickly. Whisper decided to stay visible, which made even the bravest step warily, which helped with their speed. Blue went and spoke to some of those who had set up stalls along the well-travelled route and always came back with further information on Crow's travelling direction.

Eventually, as they were heading towards a crossroads, the kat gave a loud yowl of warning. They saw a figure ahead, having gone down the left turn, stop and turn towards the noise. Even as they sped up, they saw a hand reach up and put something in his mouth.

'Nooo!' screamed Wren, kicking her heels into Ladybird's side to make the horse go faster. With the others trailing only a little behind, she raced towards Crow, who had bent over and was now vomiting.

As they came up to him, Wren was holding his upper body, even as he bent over and vomited again. Laying him down on his side, she immediately gave him water to rinse his mouth and spit out. Then, with the help of Dani, she pulled him clear of the pool of effluence and wiped his face and hands with a cloth. Then she stripped his cloak and overshirt off before piling them all in the same area as the body fluids.

Blue had stepped further away from the road and cut down a couple of saplings. As Wren put a few crushed Heal's-All leaves into some water and stroked the now unconscious Crow's throat, to persuade him to swallow the liquid, Dani placed one hand upon his chest while she placed the other on his forehead. Although Wren had seen Dani Heal before, this time seemed more urgent and more powerful. Knowing that the poison – a mushroom called Widow's Delight – almost always killed, with only a tiny minority surviving paralysed from the shoulders down, scared Wren. There was no antidote to the fungus, they both knew that Dani was Crow's only hope at ever recovering even some of his vitality.

After watching for a few moments, awestruck at seeing the black lightning flickering and flying all over Crow's body but focussed upon his throat and upper body, Blue went back to strapping poles together, to make a travelling bed for the man. Wren turned to take care of the vomit and the other items, only to find the whole mess had disappeared. Blinking her eyes, thinking she was seeing – or *not* seeing – things, she saw the kat, just sitting there.

'You got rid of that, didn't you?' She asked. After receiving a slow blink, which she took as a yes, Wren knelt and hugged the huge animal, surprising them both. 'Thank you.'

After over an hour of work, Dani gave a sigh and slumped down. Wren, who knew how Healing for just a few minutes affected the girl, was ready with a small bowl of stew. Once this was eaten, a stack of travel bread was handed over to her. Blue, Wren and Whisper dragged Crow's inert form onto the stretcher. As the horses were resaddled by the youngster, Wren checked on Crow, covered him with a heavy blanket and ensured that he was tied securely to the lashed poles. Checking that her saddle bags were filled with fruits, travel breads, cheese and other easily eaten foods, she and Blue manoeuvred the exhausted Healer up onto Ladybird with Wren climbing up behind to keep the dozing Dani safe. They followed Blue as he led them to a place he said he knew.

Although only late afternoon, Wren felt as if she had lived weeks since waking up that morning. Exhausted, she leaned her head on Dani's bony shoulder and slipped into a light snooze.

The place Blue knew of was an old-fashioned farm, almost a small village in itself that included a smithy and a water mill. They had dragged Crow into the main farmhouse that consisted of one floor and a cellar. Crow was manoeuvred into one of the rooms off the kitchen and he was laid upon his bedding roll, set by the hearth. As Blue and Wren sorted out Crow, Dani had got kindling and some wood to start a fire. Although still exhausted and starving, she knew they had to keep the patient warm, so she began hitting her flint to spark the fire into existence. Nothing happened so she tried again. And again. And again. In frustration she shouted "burn, dammit!" and the kindling was immediately aflame.

Dani reared back in shock, landing painfully on her rump. Seeing the kindling burning through, she quickly added more wood. She turned her head and saw the other two staring at her in astonishment and she scowled back.

'Don't bother asking, I have no idea.' Getting up, she staggered a little before leaving the room. Blue and Wren exchanged glances and shrugged before Blue went to help with the unloading of the rest of the supplies and Wren made supper.

Thanks to all they had been given, there was a full table of food: slices of roasted girox, ham and chicken, a soft cheese to spread and cubes of hard cheese, salad makings, eggs boiled and sliced, fresh bread, fruit of all types and water, juices, wine, mead and a fine, nutty ale. Everyone ate heartily and cleared things away. Blue seemed to know where to put everything, cupboards for crockery and a spelled cold room for perishables. There was a pump that brought water straight into the deep kitchen sink, which Wren heated with a spell, so washing up was quickly done. The women were curious about Blue's knowledge of the place but chose to wait until he was ready to tell them rather than badger him for the information. By the time everything was sorted and cleared away, Dani was white-faced and staggering, beyond exhausted. Quickly, Wren got the bedrolls ready in the room where Crow shivered, despite the heat from the fire. Within moments, Dani was snuggled down in her own blankets, Whisper laying by her side, and she was immediately fast asleep.

'Could I sleep in the stable, lady?' Blue asked, a little anxiously.

'Of course, sweetheart, if that is what you want. You are more than welcome to stay here though; you do know that don't you?' said Wren.

'Aye, lady,' Blue reassured her. 'It's just I prefer sleeping with the horses.'

'If that is what you want, go ahead. If you change your mind, you know you are welcome to come into the house anytime.' At his nod, she continued. 'Tomorrow we will begin getting everything sorted. I don't think we can leave here until Crow is well, but we need more supplies, perhaps a few beds. Maybe we can find out who this place belongs to and buy it off them. All of that is for tomorrow though. Goodnight, sweetie, and may Taynak guide your dreams.'

Kissing Blue's forehead after asking for the Goddess of children and the Protector of dreams for Her Blessing, Wren watched him walk across the yard towards the stable block. Putting a warning spell upon the front door – it would send out a high peal of noise and send a painful jolt through anyone who tried to break in – she took a quick look around the kitchen to make sure everything was sorted. She grabbed a small bowl and filled it with nuts and berries, added it along with a jug of water and three pottery mugs to a tin tray and went through to settle down for the night herself.

Blue was missing the following morning, along with Dazzle and the mule. Although worried, Wren had very little time to fret about him as, although Dani was pale faced and shaky, she was awake and able to hobble about a little, but Crow lay still, grey faced and silent with only an occasional shiver to show he still lived. The shadow kat left soon after while Wren fixed some oats and honey for breakfast for the two women.

Once Dani had eaten her fill, she gave Crow some more Healing which eased his pinched features slightly. She was unable to spend a long time on him as she had very little reserve left. Making sure she ate and drank; Wren then had her go back to bed before going and checking through the stores to make a full inventory of what they had and another list of what they would need.

It was mid-afternoon before Blue returned. The mule had a full load and Dazzle also carried a few things as well as the boy on his back. With them came a young couple on a cart loaded with household items as well as two adorable toddlers. Wren walked out to meet them, feeling baffled.

'Hi Wren,' Blue called as he rode up. Getting off Dazzle he went forward to explain what he had done. 'I been along to the nearest village over thataways, mebbe an hour away. I spoke to the headman, an' he has given us some stuff to be helping us along. We dun have to pay for it now, he sez get settled an' then if you could make up poultices an' stuff for them, that'll be payment enough.'

'For free? For how long though?' Wren was thunderstruck at the headman's generosity but worried at the price asked. Occasional free medicines she didn't mind, especially for children and nursing mothers, but she couldn't give things away for nothing forever. Especially now: there was no guarantee that Crow would ever wake up, let alone be able to work and Dani would need to be on the move as soon as she was fully fit. The fact that Varla might have guessed at her slave status meant that it wasn't safe for her to stay.

'What? No, no, lady!' Blue exclaimed. 'Not free at all. He's give us a bill an' sez if you dun mind charging just half fees for the medsins until you reckon it's all paid off, we can have the stuff right now. Plus, he sent this family to run the mill an' bakery, sez we will get locals coming from around so we can begin getting set. The missus there is also a midwife, so we can get this place working full out in a short time. An' when we do, more people will want to come.'

'You really have thought this out, Blue. How did you know there was a village there and who to talk to? They could have been hostile.'

Blue's face fell a little as he gave a deep sigh. 'This used to be my auntie's home, lady. I was staying here until we was raided, so I know a lot of them 'round here. I could have stayed in the village there when I was found after but I went to the city instead, with the soldiers that came to find the raiders, and stayed with me Da. Bin in the city ever since.'

'How old were you?' Wren asked, aware that this was the most personal information the boy had chosen to share.

'I was eight, it was my birthing day anniversary. We was having a bit of a party with the other farm workers and their kids. There was a lot of shouting outside then us kids was shoved down into the cellar an' hid behind a false wall there. We stayed there for nearly a week I reckon. Then the soldiers came an' we come out. The other kids went to the village an' you know the rest.'

Wren looked at the cart and its occupants as she digested this information. 'Do you trust them?

'Yeah, mostly. Maybe you should make sure that Dani keeps her neck covered, not cuz she will be handed over but because we dun want any Hound gettin' on her trail. I ain't told them she is a Healer either, just that we have come back, might stay but could do with some furniture and help. If I've overstepped, they can go back. They know you have to say yes.'

Wren thought for only a minute before she gave him a beaming grin. 'Yes, I say definitely yes!'

They both walked over to the cart, the family sitting there had relaxed into answering smiles when they saw her expression and understood they could stay.

The rest of the afternoon passed in a whirl of activity. Yan checked out the mill to see what was needed before it could be set to work again. He also went into the water to free the wheel from weeds which brought a skein of ducks down to land and eat the edible algae. Once he had finished checking out the mill, Yan went into the adjoining cottage and began clearing out the dust and rubbish of years.

While Yan worked out at the mill and cottage, Etla began unloading the cart of the smaller furnishings. After checking on both Crow and the sleeping Dani, making sure that Dani's collar was covered up, Wren went out to help.

By evening the main house was clean and cosy. The kitchen had a working stove with plenty of wood to last for months that Yan had salvaged from broken furniture from various dwellings and hundreds of fallen branches. Crow was settled into a big wooden framed bed with a thick mattress. He was covered in three blankets and the fire was built as high as it could safely be. Throughout the day Wren or Etla went through to check on him and, although there were no obvious changes, he seemed to find the bed easier to lie on than the floor.

Dani was woken up and was guided into another room down the passageway. Here a smaller bed had been set up and there was a fire laid out in the cleaned grate but left unlit. The Healer fell into the bed, Wren just managing to catch up a cover to lay over the still worn-out woman. A table was set at the side of the bed and later on, Wren put a platter of food there for when the exhausted Healer eventually woke up.

The evening meal had been cooked by Etla, two plump ducks roasted with cherries and served with peas and tiny potatoes cooked with mint. Wren provided a tasty cinnamon custard and even Dani ate enough, although her large appetite, even in this state, did cause Yan to raise his eyebrows, but he made no comment. There had been much laughter, mainly because of the comical actions from the twins – Alba and Brecht – with the shadow kat. Although the family had been nervous about Whisper to begin with, it didn't take long for its careful handling of the little ones to win the parents over while the two hellions delighted in riding on its back. Thankfully, by the last meal of the day, they were both yawning, tired out from both travelling and all the fun they had had.

Yan laughed when he saw this. 'I said we needed a dog to keep these two busy, looks like we need a shadow kat instead!'

Etla shook her head firmly. 'We cannot guarantee any kat being as concerned about our children as this one. Dogs are fine, as are goats, pigs, chickens, ducks and even a girox. No shadow kats!'

After the laughter had died down from this comment, there was a discussion about what Wren wanted to do with the farm. Despite not being sure they would be staying, she found herself making plans. Even after just one day, she felt sure that Yan and Etla would be perfect to carry on with the farm if Blue agreed.

It took Dani almost a week to begin gaining back the weight and energy she had lost. Once she was able, she would spend the morning exploring the various buildings, bringing anything salvageable back to the main house and to help clean things up. After the noonday meal, provided by Wren or Etla, Dani would then sit with Crow, keeping an eye on him and giving short bursts of Healing despite his still being unconscious, and to prepare the vegetables for the evening meal.

Wren would spend her time working with Blue to get a kitchen garden pegged out, dug over and cleared of stones before planting a variety of seeds and bulbs. Using her magik, Wren was able to get a few things growing, enough to supplement the larder even though it was not proper growing season. Blue worked with the horses in the early mornings then helped Wren. He also built a glass frame for some of the growing seedlings as well as preparing a field for bigger crops. Yan worked on getting the other buildings and houses repaired and ready for more families and stock that would eventually arrive, they hoped. Etla began preserving what food she could; making jams, jellies, pickles and sauces and putting them in stone jars which were then stored in the cellar; a deep cold room, dug to one side of the house, which was reached by a door within a short, covered walkway. Yan repaired the false wall in the hidden room and added bunks and a store of food, "just in case".

Whisper would spend its time playing with the children and the horses, swimming in the river and going on an occasional hunt to improve meat stores.

Crow was never left for more than a few moments. Dani watched over him the most, adding in her Healing energy whenever she felt able. Wren slept by his side every night, also popping in at random times of the day. Blue came in to tell the silent Assassin all that had been done with the horses every day before the evening meal. For a long time, Crow lay still and quiet, looking as if he were dead.

Eventually though, he did begin to show signs of recovery. Firstly, his colour became less grey, and his breathing deepened appreciably. Wren found herself crying silent tears one night when she woke up to find Crow's fingers twitching against her arm. Day by day he showed tiny signs that he was recovering.

They waited hopefully for the opening of his eyes.

CHAPTER FIFTEEN

Dani spoke to Wren one day when Yan had carried Crow outside to get some winter sun on his face and they were putting fresh sheets on his bed. After making sure that Etla was busy making some lotions for the children's dry skin, Dani closed the door to the bedroom quietly and began helping to make the bed.

'What is it?' Wren was immediately on the alert, her busy brain already making plans even before Dani spoke.

'It is time for me to go soon,' Dani spoke in a low voice, not wanting Etla to hear. 'I am getting the nudging again now that I have caught up on my sleeping and eating. Crow will continue to improve, I am sure, but I cannot say if he will walk again. I just don't know. I will leave at the end of the week, before anyone else is awake. I just wanted to let you know.'

'You are sure you must go now? You can't wait for Crow to wake up? No, of course you can't. Gods, I will miss you, Dani.' With tears in her eyes, Wren hugged the slender woman. 'Are you going to tell Blue?'

'Yes, I'll go do that in a minute. There's something else. I have been getting a bad feeling for the last day or so. Get all the weapons in the house and grab hold of Yan, Etla and the kids. Tell them to be aware that trouble is coming very soon.'

'Now?'

'Now. I will go and tell Blue about that and about me moving on.'

With that the women finished the bed making quickly then parted to make everyone aware and to get everything prepared.

Wren went straight to the kitchen where Etla was just finishing off a lotion to help an itchy rash Brecht had from falling into some stinging horsetail reeds that grew by the water. Wren explained about Dani's premonition and that she didn't know exactly when or if anything would happen. Etla gave a sharp nod before moving to the back of the house where two adjoining rooms were. After checking to see what was needed, she went trotting over to the mill cottage to collect bedding and food. As she passed him, she told Yan what was going to happen and he calmly brought Crow back indoors and settled the Assassin on a couch in the kitchen before going to join Etla, picking up the weaponry that she had collected.

Dani went over to the stables and watched Blue for a minute as he groomed Ladybird and crooned in her ear. When he noticed Dani watching he gave a huge grin which slowly dropped as he noticed her expression.

'You're leaving,' he said, full of disappointment.

'Not immediately,' answered Dani. 'Soon though.' She opened her arms, and the youth went to her willingly for a hug. After a few quiet moments he gave a great sigh before pulling away gently.

'That's not all though, is it?' he said, blue eyes searching her face.

'No, no it isn't, sweetheart.' She went on to explain the feeling of impending trouble. With a nod of acceptance, Blue gave her another quick hug before he went into the stables and passed some tools out to Dani to take back to the house. Then he led out the horses, linking all the bridles before mounting his favourite Dazzle.

'You get back to the house and get that battened down,' he said. 'I will head for the village and see what help I can get.'

Before Dani could say anything, he kicked his heels and the horse galloped off, the others trailing behind.

Shaking her head at his impetuosity, Dani retraced her steps to the house. There she found preparations almost finished. More food had been taken down to the hidden room. Later, if nothing happened before, Crow would be carried down with the two children and the shadow kat. As it had become both playmate and protector of the children, Yan and Etla were more than happy about this decision.

Once everything was sorted, food was cooked, not only for the evening meal but things that would last in case there was a siege.

Talk was strained but they were all trying to stay calm for the sake of the children. The youngsters were big eyed and solemn, very unlike their usually boisterous selves, sensing the troubled atmosphere. Dani noticed that they held onto the shadow kat and how it stayed close to them, and it struck her for the first time that she might be moving on alone. She felt a pang of grief, as strong as when she had left everyone behind in Mertam. Taking a deep breath, trying to regain her composure, she suddenly stiffened, and her eyes became fully black, with small tendrils of lightning flickering over her face and torso. She began speaking in a monotone.

'The time is close. Not as many as feared but enough. They are sly and sneaky with magiks forbidden. Be ready, be aware, be strong.' Once she had finished speaking, she gave a shudder and staggered slightly, before speaking in her normal tones. 'Quickly, we must get Crow and the children to safety. Yan, bar the rear door and windows.'

Deciding to deal with his shock at the change that had come over her later, the big man nodded his assent and rushed off, leaving Etla to carry the twins down to the safe room. Whisper followed, turning to look back at Dani for a long moment before disappearing from sight. A few minutes later Yan returned and carried Crow through and followed the group to the cellar. Crow was an awkward parcel as, although he had lost a lot of weight from the vomiting, lack of food and the coma, he was still taller than Yan. With a little manoeuvring, and quiet cursing, he was carefully laid down on to one of the mattresses and covered with some thick blankets. The twins, still subdued, sat by him and laid gentle hands on his shoulders while Whisper watched Yan leave before standing in front of the hidden door, guarding those within.

Yan got back to the kitchen in time to hear Etla speaking to Wren.

'…haps you would now like to tell us why you have hidden a magiker from us? There is no need, we live in harmony here.'

Dani gave a snort of derision before pulling off the fabric that hid her slave collar from sight. 'Using the word "harmony" doesn't fill me with any confidence, Etla. I lived in a place called Harmony where they put me in this before I even grew breasts. They took away any chance of my having children then they drugged me with a slow acting poison. The only reason I have lived so long is because I am also a Healer. Those coming here could be after me, you would just be collateral damage. Do you want me to leave?'

Etla looked at Dani, her jaw dropping slightly before she snapped out. 'Oh, don't be such an idiot! I didn't ask if you were a slave *or* a Healer, I just don't like secrets. Wait; if you are a Healer, how did you predict trouble?'

'I don't know, I don't know anything.' Dani gave a rueful shake of her head. 'And you're right, you didn't ask for specifics, and you do have every right to know. It's just, well, we weren't sure how you would react and…'

'And you expected the worst.' Etla shook her head slightly before reaching forward and giving the surprised Healer a hard hug. 'I can understand that. What I can't understand is how bad things have been for you, but I can promise that neither me nor mine will ever betray you.'

'Thank…' Dani broke off abruptly, her gaze becoming unfocused and distant. 'They're coming.'

Everyone rushed to their stations. All the windows were shuttered and barred, the back door barred and bolted. The only seemingly vulnerable place was a small side room, bare of furniture and two windows denuded of shutters that had been left slightly open, as if they had been forgotten in the rush of making everywhere safe.

Yan peered cautiously out one of the front windows, a small hole built into the shutters allowing him to see out. He had to pull back when an arrow, sent by magik, shot through the gap and broke the pane of glass. Looking down at it, they saw that there was a piece of paper tied to the shaft. Opening it and reading, Wren began laughing,

'If we give ourselves up, they will take the "slavey" back to her owner and tell them that I escaped. So, from this, I assume that they were after me or Crow originally but now Dani is the prize.

We're narrowing it down.' Yan and Etla looked confused, but Dani grinned.

'Finally! It's not all about me for once,' she said. 'So, are you going to do as they ask?'

'Nope. Not even if the she-wolf had said "please",' Wren replied. Before anything else could be said, they heard Varla's voice, shouting out to them.

'Wren? *Wren?* There is no need for this! Come out quietly and give us the slavey. We will tell the mages that we lost you and collect the reward on her. Come on, you cannot win a fight against me and the men I have with me. We can beat you in power or we can starve you out. Give up now.'

'Why? You will kill me just as you killed Crow.' Wren called back, wondering if Varla had realised that Crow hadn't died yet.

'The mages didn't want him back and he would never have let you go,' was the reply, a smug note in Varla's voice now. 'He used to be the best, you know, the one we were taught to emulate. He was supposed to be the most perfect assassin there was, and *I* killed him. All those years, all that training, and he didn't even check the food I gave him. He deserved to die; he had long got rusty, losing his skills, depending upon old glory. Now I will give you some time to discuss this, but if you don't send out the slavey, we will kill all of you. We don't need to take her back alive, just her head will do.'

Yan looked at Dani with raised brows. 'Your master sounds a right git.'

'He is exactly that,' she said with a nod.

'Well then, we can't be giving you to a git,' Yan said. 'Any ideas?'

'Hmm, I have the first glimmer of one.' Dani stepped out of the room and left the others to exchange puzzled glances. Wren began telling the older couple all that had gone on since they had met, just outside of Mertam so many weeks ago.

Fifteen minutes later, Dani came back into the room, and they stared at her in stunned silence.

Wren loved to wear flowing skirts made of a fine, gauzy material.
These she layered on until as many as eight or ten flowed about
her. Dani was wearing just one of these garments, ensuring that her
nether regions were easily seen. She was also wearing one of her
own shirts, this had been adjusted with a few tacking stitches, to
make it a *very* tight fit. She also opened the buttons a little further
than was seemly, showing the swell of her breasts as well as
allowing the obscene collar to flash in the light of the lamps. She
had snipped her hair, which had grown enough to cover her ears,
close to her scalp again, using kitchen shears and leaving a few
nicks in her scalp. To top it all off, she had raided Wren's meagre
supply and found some cosmetics, so her face was now painted
quite gaudily.

'Dani, what on Yerat have you done?' Wren spluttered.

'I have a plan,' Dani said, calmly.

'A plan. Don't you dare tell us that your plan is to give yourself
up,' Etla spoke up.

'That is exactly what I am going to do. Oh, don't be stupid,' she
snapped out in response to the shouted protests. 'Shut up and
listen, all of you. Right, now we know that Varla isn't here alone.
What we don't know is exactly what knowledge she has about us.
She may know about Yan and Etla, she may also know about
Whisper. However, she does *not* know that I am a Healer. And
what can Heal, can also kill.'

'Dani…'

'No. I won't keep letting others fight for me, I need to do this.
Varla's biggest strength is her ruthlessness, but she thinks that
emotion is a weakness. She is arrogant in thinking that she is
always right and doesn't realise is that when fear and
determination combine, the result is more ruthless than she could
ever begin to understand. Now, Wren, you need to use one of your
spells to find out how many people she has with her. She will have
at least one – the secretary, remember him? Yan, you get ready to
sneak out one of the windows and grab hold of anyone she has
with her. Etla, you get some water boiling, in case we get any

injuries that need bathing or, if anyone breaks in, just throw it at them.'

Going around the room, Dani hugged them all before she stepped out to the door. After unbarring it, she breathed in deeply, then allowing her shoulders to slump, she slowly opened the door and stepped out.

The day was now overcast, and dark clouds scurried across the sky, pushed by a fierce wind. This lifted Dani's skirt, flashing her bare legs, and more. Varla gave a quick grin before snarling a quiet command to the man who stood transfixed at the sight, by her side.

He jumped slightly before grinning, then he ran forward to catch hold of the Healer's arm and dragged her reluctant body towards the assassin.

'I knew they would send you out,' Varla gloated. 'Did you think they were your friends? Fool, everyone is always out for what is best for themselves. Now I, I mean *we*, shall get a pretty penny for you. I need to get you back to Mertam, but the principle wants you or proof of your death, so if you cause us any trouble, I only take your head. Come here. You,' She turned then to her confederate, who had shot her the glare which had caused her to change her pronoun. 'You go join the others and get in there and bring the rest out. We will have one fabulous pay-day.'

With another glare full of suspicion, the tough let go of Dani and went up to the house. Varla watched him go and, once he was out of earshot, she grinned.

'As if my brother and I would share anything with the likes of him. Now, come on, let me look at you properly.'

Varla stepped forward and grabbed hold of Dani's chin, not bothered by the slavey's hand reaching up and catching hold of her wrist. Lifting Dani's face, Varla smirked for a moment before she took in Dani's calm and steady expression. Then her smirk wavered a little before fading out completely.

'What's wrong? What are you planning, bitch?' Varla's head snapped up as a man's screams came from the shuttered farmhouse.

'You should never have tried to cause us harm,' Dani spoke quietly, barely audible over the continued yelling and cursing.

Varla gave Dani a distracted glance before looking away again, frowning at the continued noise. She let go of Dani's chin as she shouted out for information but grabbed hold of the slavey's wrist instead. Just then, the man she had sent into the house burst out of the wide-open door, screaming and cursing as he held his hand to his cheek. After a few stumbling steps his feet skidded and he collapsed, tearing his hand away and removing the skin from his face. Red, bubbling blisters were appearing all over, his lips swelling up to bursting point and his voice fading as the life dribbled out of him in the same way mucus dribbled from his mouth and nose. After a few twitches he lay still and died.

Shouting out her own curses, Varla tried to drop Dani's arm so as to be able to get closer to the stricken man. Taking two steps, she stumbled to a stop, her hand still gripped firmly. Spinning round to face the slavey, Varla found her gaze caught by a pair of charcoal grey eyes that turned darker as she stared into them in horror. Immediately, like her wrist, her gaze was stuck fast.

'What are you? Let me go,' Varla spat the words out angrily, not realising that her fear was transparently obvious.

'You should have left us alone,' Dani said, still with an eerie calm, ignoring the chaos around her. Another one of Varla's gang came running around the house, pursued by the shadow kat in its invisible form. As the man ran and screamed out in pain, slashes were appearing all over his body. More cries came from the kitchen garden as the remaining three people, including Varla's brother who was also her lover, were attacked by the defending friends.

Varla was still unable to tear her eyes away from Dani's so saw the slavey's eyes darken and turn completely black and watched with terror as the streaks of black lightning began flickering over Dani's face, arms and hands. Frantically pulling at her own hand and clawing and tearing at Dani's fingers, Varla began panicking.

'No, no, no, they didn't say you were an Abomination, they didn't say you had magik. Let me go, I will just take the mageling and you can go on your way. I won't hurt you, I promise,' she babbled.

Leaning closer, Dani lifted her free hand to cup Varla's cheek, the black lightning making Varla blink rapidly and shake her head to ease her dazzled eyes.

'No,' Dani said, her voice still low and soothing. 'No, you won't hurt me, but you won't have the mageling either. Tell me all you know, and I promise you a quick death, if you don't tell me all I want to know, then I will make it as slow and as painful as I can.'

Varla gave a shout of frustration and continued pulling and tearing at Dani, turning and ducking her head to shake the hands off herself. Nothing worked, Dani didn't move or even get knocked off balance.

Varla gave a shriek as she felt crippling pain run through the hand caught in Dani's iron grip. It felt as if every bone was breaking and snapping. Even as she wailed in agony the bones seemed to grind down even finer. Finally able to break the gaze between them, Varla looked down and then abruptly turned her head and vomited.

Instead of the slender and shapely hand with its long fingers tipped with delicately coloured nails, what she saw was a lump of misshapen meat, raw and beginning to rot.

'What are you?' she moaned. 'Just what the void are you?'

'I am the woman who was minding my own business until you decided to play games. Now are you going to talk? Or should the pain continue?'

Again, Varla howled in pain as her wrist broke with an audible snap.

'What do you need to know,' she finally managed to say through gritted teeth.

'Who were you after?'

'The mageling, Wren,' Varla had stopped screaming but each word seemed forced out as she waited for…*something*.

'Who set the contract? I want all the details.'

'They said that they felt her magik being used, they knew she wasn't really mad, just play-acting all these years. Ow, stop, it hurts,' she squealed in pain, feeling the bones break and crumble in her wrist. Her mind became so full of it, she no longer heard the questions, just screamed and screamed.

Suddenly, like a cool, refreshing breeze, the pain dwindled away, to be almost non-existent. Varla turned her tear-stained face, still with Dani's hand touching her cheek gently, to stare at the slavey with hope.

'Is that it? Are we done? I didn't know that you were an Abomination, I swear. I will say you died, I will even leave the mageling, just, please, let me go.' Varla hated hearing herself beg but she wasn't so bothered she would stop. As soon as this bitch let her go, she would pay a herb witch for poultices and healing draughts. Then she would hunt this bitch down and kill her a little at a time. Staring into the slavey's face, she waited for a weakening that she could then take advantage of.

Instead, there was the implacable stare. The woman, still cupping her hand to Varla's cheek and tenderly holding the crushed meat that used to be a hand, tilted forward slightly and sniffed at the Assassin before shaking her head sadly.

'Don't you realise that I can smell your lies? You have no intention of letting any of us live. You want the kudos of killing a mage, the best Assassin of your age and an enslaved magiker. You don't seem to realise that you died the instant you began trying to cause my friends harm. How many have you killed?'

'W-what?' Varla struggled to keep up with the slavey's words. 'How many? Why do you want to know?' Then she screamed as her ulna and radius began to crack and splinter before beginning to snap and break.

'Answer me,' Dani barked, rage colouring her voice. 'How many kills do you have?'

'F-forty-o-one, stop, please, please stop!' Her voice was losing any power it had had, her screams becoming grating whispers of sound.

The pain had her dropping to her knees, but the slavey's hands stayed glued to her.

'I will pay you back, every smidge of pain you caused your victims and their families, whether physical or emotional.'

Then Varla found that what had been done before was much less than what was happening now. She found enough energy to scream again but not for long as she lost her voice completely when her facial bones began to break in the same way that her arm bones had. She tried to black out, she begged for mercy but there was none to be found. As each bone broke, she felt the snapping and tearing of nerves, tendons and muscles, the screams she could no longer express built up within her until she began praying for death.

Suddenly the hands that had not moved from wrist or cheek, lifted from Varla's flesh and the Assassin felt only a little relief, the pain being so huge it stopped her mind from understanding the next words Dani said.

'You think you will be left to die now, your bones crumbled to dust. And if I were a better person, perhaps that would be true. But you have a little more to endure. This is for us, the last ones you tried to hurt. Oh, and Crow lives. And your brother doesn't.'

With that last parting shot, Dani turned and walked away, leaving Varla in such a broken mess, she was unable to express any of her shock and hurt at losing the one person whom she loved, the one she had been enduring the pain for, whom she had been expecting to rescue her.

Thinking to just wait and die alone, she wasn't prepared for the agonising bite as teeth closed over and pulled at her flesh, opening up the skin bag to the tenderised meat within. Her last views of the world was of a wild sow and her piglets climbing over her and biting into her body. The sow breathed a sickening odour into Varla's face as it studied her. Then its jaws shot forward and bit her face off and Varla felt her life, at last, leave her.

CHAPTER SIXTEEN

The next few days were spent in cleaning up the mess caused by the short but violent fight. Varla's body was never found but Dani assured them that the female was dead, and no-one argued with her, especially as her face held such an expression none of them had seen on her before.

Blue had returned with eleven men, including the village constable. Near to the farm, they saw a wild pig disappearing into the underbrush and a huge bloodstain on the ground but no body. The other raiders had been tied up and basic nursing done on their wounds. The man who had lost half his face and the use of one eye to burns from the boiling water thrown at him was covered with an old horse blanket and the one who had been attacked by the shadow kat was already breathing his last.

Varla's brother had been captured, trying to sneak into the house through the small windows in the side room. As his feet had touched the floor, his body had spasmed as he set off a spell Wren had put in place. Now he scowled at the last member of the gang who was spilling his guts, telling the constable everything he knew. Despite the glares from Veltya, the traitor wouldn't shut up and he, himself, had been gagged and tied firmly. Then Wren whispered in his ear that Varla was dead, and Veltya screamed out his pain before collapsing, losing all interest in what was going on around him. He stayed in this stupor for a week, right up until the hangman's noose tightened around his throat. Then he moaned her name as his neck snapped.

Dani's name wasn't mentioned by anyone. Wren had worked hard on the bandits, smudging every memory of the Healer and, as she had already moved on from the farm, no-one ever connected her to the troubles there. Nothing could prevent the story of the fight from flashing over the countryside though.

Crow woke slowly and lay still, allowing his senses to absorb all that was happening around him. By flexing his fingers, he knew he was lying on a sheet. By the comfort his body felt, despite the aches he felt in his muscles, he could tell he was on a proper mattress. He could hear birds singing, the sound of horses running in a field and Blue's cheerful cursing faint in the distance. Nearer at hand was the muffled sound of pots and pans being moved around and an unknown female voice singing. His mouth was dry and had a sour taste, making him long for a cool drink. It took a few moments to be able to pry his eyes open and, at first, he couldn't see anything through the tears caused by the brightness of the day. As his sight cleared, he could see a white ceiling and, turning his head a little, white walls. These weren't the same as the place they had been staying though. Why wasn't he there? Then he gave a grunt of pain as a sharp spike drove through his mind. Something he needed to remember, something…

He froze as the door to the strange room burst open and Wren, *his* Wren, rushed in with a cry of gladness.

'Crow! Oh, my Crow, you're awake at long last.' With that, she fell over him, hugging and weeping into his neck. Not one to lose an opportunity, even in this state, Crow lifted rusty arms to hug her back, annoyed that he couldn't seem to grip any tighter.

After a few moments, Wren sat up and wiped her eyes. Crow tried reaching up to touch her cheek but, annoyingly, his arms wouldn't stretch far enough. He felt an edge of panic, what was wrong with him? Was he sick? Stupid man, he was in a bed in daylight, of course he was sick. If he could only remember what had happened. Without meaning to, he let out a frustrated growl which made Wren grin.

'Oh, so the growly Crow is back. Now I know you are going to be well' Crow frowned at her, confused at the comment but before he could say anything, the door flew open and Blue fell through, almost dropping the jug he held.

Tutting, Wren jumped up and fussed about a little while Blue leaned in and hugged Crow, shedding a few tears of his own. Then Wren was there with a glass of fresh juice and a hollow reed, bent slightly, so that he could sip the cool, refreshing liquid that soothed his parched throat.

'What happened?' His voice was rusty and faint, fading out towards the end of the second word but the other two in the room seemed to understand him. Wren began to tell him about their first meeting as he sipped the juice again, but he gave a short nod to indicate he remembered that bit. So next she spoke about meeting Dani, and he twitched again. Through the next few minutes Wren spoke a few words, got a twitch before moving forward a little in her narrative.

Eventually she spoke of the day he had been seen running away from the house. When no twitch came, Wren began filling him in on all that had happened since. Hearing of his poisoning by Varla made him growl again but, other than that, he made no sound. Blue sat by, putting in a few words every now and then, holding on to Crow's hand as if afraid to let go.

'So, that is the whole story. Dani gave you a final burst of healing and assured us both that you would fully recover but that you must go slowly to begin with in trying to gain your strength.'

'She's gone?' Crow felt sorrow spike through him at the thought of the Healer no longer being around.

'Yes, she left as soon as she had given you your final boost after the fight, even before Blue got back with help. She said it was more than time. Strangely, she didn't seem tired, despite your Healing. She seemed to think it was because of the way she killed Varla.'

'It just might be. After all, not only was she protecting herself, but she was defending us all, including children.' Crow finished with a huge yawn.

'Right, we have kept you awake too long. Go back to sleep and I will bring up some broth later.' Wren said but was unsure of how much of this Crow had heard as a soft snore was her only response.

Both Wren and Blue crept out of the room, leaving the door ajar. The youth turned and flung his arms around Wren, sobbing out his relief. She stood there and held him tight, stroking her hand down his back. When his convulsive cries had lessened, Wren tilted his chin up.

'You go out the back way, sweetheart, and wash your face by the pump. Then go spend time with the horses. I'll call you in when it is time to eat, and you can feed Crow his broth.' She winked and gave a wicked grin. 'He won't yell as much at you as he would at me for treating him like the invalid he is.'

With an answering grin, albeit slightly watery, Blue skipped off. As soon as he was out of sight, Wren fell against the wall, shuddering with the emotions coursing through her. As she calmed down she remembered Dani's parting words.

'When he wakes up, stop wasting time. This shows you how lives can change in an instant. You might have lost him before ever telling him how you feel. Don't let pride or fear stop you speaking out.' With this admonition, Dani had hugged her and slipped away.

Over time, Crow was awake more and more. He began to understand Dani's frustration with her need to rest and felt more sympathy for her than he had done previously. Yan helped him every day, carrying him outside and moving his limbs with him, to build up muscles that were butter soft. Crow found himself liking the miller, with his sly humour and his strength. He found himself nominated to keep the twins busy while the others went about their work, which in itself, was the hardest job of all, although he loved the time he spent with the bright, inquisitive duo.

One lunchtime, a few weeks after Dani's departure, everyone sat around a large table outdoors, eating soup and chatting. Crow was finding that he was more able to control his body and although he was still extremely weak, was slowly beginning to build up a little muscle. He looked up from his bowl when he heard Blue call his name.

'Crow? Why did you leave Drintoth without telling anyone? And in such a hurry?'

Crow smiled ruefully. 'Varla told me that Wren, that they, had both gone. That Dani and she had become irritated with waiting and had left to find the Healer's next portal. I was stunned and went straight off after them. I even left most of my belongings behind. Remember that the next time you think I don't care.' He winked at Wren, and she blushed a little before frowning in remembrance.

'Your room was empty, Crow. There was nothing there apart from a sock. Oh, and your ring.' The ring was now on a chain that was settled around Wren's throat, and she had no intention of returning it to him. 'That bawd must have been much better with spells than the Guild realised. She was certainly remarkably able at sowing confusion. I believed her, even when I should have known better. Next time, I will definitely speak up.'

Crow raised his brows in horror, making the twins giggle. '*Next* time? Are you mad? I can see I will have to keep an eye on you, to try and keep you out of trouble!'

Everyone at the table burst into laughter at this, drowning out Wren's giggling protests that she wasn't the one who had been taken in by a pretty face. With the laughter, the happy shouts from the twins and the barking from the young hound Crow had got Blue to purchase for the twins, it was some time before they noticed a man, covered in road dust, riding slowly up to them. The silence fell quickly as they all stared, even the twins becoming quiet.

'Pelago? Is that you?' Crow was astonished to see the young Captain and was quick to invite him to step down off his horse and accept some refreshment.

'I won't say no to some of that tea and maybe some cake in a moment Crow, but for now, Dovas is waiting a little way off, wanting to know if he is welcome to come and visit. He has things he needs to discuss.'

There was a short silence, as they all waited to see what Crow would say. He took a few moments to think it over before giving a sharp nod of his head in acquiescence. Pelago raised a bugle to his lips and blew a series of melodic bursts before swinging his leg over his horse, seating himself on a chair and accepting a mug of hot tea.

Within fifteen or so minutes, there was the sound of many hooves, the creaking of wagons and voices. Crow looked to Wren in confusion, and she shrugged her shoulders before slipping her hand into his.

Dovas rode up in a small dogcart pulled by a white mule, behind him were three produce carts, each pulled by a girox. Tied to the rear of the last cart were two young horses, a beautiful charcoal grey mare and a deep chested bay stallion. These were followed by a unit of soldiers, all in uniform. The convoy came to a stop and Dovas gestured, asking for permission to step down. Crow nodded curtly, a little confused about it all, and the older man climbed down slowly, and headed to where Crow and the others sat. Etla murmured to Yan, and they went to their protesting children and gathered them up before heading into the house.

Crow didn't say anything, he just watched the Leader calmly.

Dovas sat down where Wren gestured and gave out a sigh of relief.

'That dogcart travels fast, children, but it rattles my bones.' Turning to Blue, he asked after the youngster. Although Blue was a little guarded in his responses, it was obvious to them all that he liked the man.

'I see that I have nothing to worry about, you look to be in the best of health. As do you, Wren, m'dear. I can't say the same for Crow though, he looks extremely peaky.' Dovas spoke quietly, examining each of them closely.

'That is what happens when you are poisoned, die and have to make your slow way back to life,' Wren snapped out, annoyed at the perceived insult to her friend.

'Poisoned? Die? What are you talking about?' Dovas was aghast. Very little information regarding the details of the fight had filtered back to Drintoth, most of the information travelling the other way across the kingdom, towards the smaller villages to make them aware of Dani's presence and to help her if they could. Crow gave

a nod to Wren, and she explained to Dovas all that had happened
since they had left the town.

'Ah, the information regarding Veltya must be in one of the
dispatch boxes I haven't yet had a chance to work my way
through. All I knew is that Dani came to me and shouted at my
wasting all your time before she ran off. I had heard that Blue had
returned to his farm from a traveller that you had given a night's
lodging to so decided to come and see for myself what was going
on.'

There was a brief silence as they all thought about the chaos that
Varla and her brother had caused. Then Blue shook off the
memories and looked at the carts, the soldiers setting up some fires
and unharnessing the beasts as well as unsaddling their own
mounts.

Eyes wide with interest he blurted out, 'What's going on?'

Dovas smiled at the eager lad. 'I knew you wouldn't be able to
resist asking for long. This is the result of your years working for
the town of Drintoth. I was originally waiting until you had
reached your majority at fourteen next year, before I handed over
all the gems that you have earned but refused to accept for the
work you have done for many of us. However, as you seem to have
settled here, I thought goods would be more useful than pretty
pieces of crystal. I have your land-deed here, that gives you this
farm and the six hundred acres surrounding it. The first cart is full
of seed for the fields, fruit tree saplings and various other useful
things, including new tools. The second cart holds household
furnishings, to enable you to fill every room in every household,
plus the linens, crockery and silverware needed also. In the last
cart are items for the various workplaces. Leather for harnesses
and the metal fastenings. Base metals, coal, hammers and bellows
for the smith's and various other things. Anything you don't want;
we will take back with us and credit you with their worth. There
are also writs for pigs, cattle and a couple of half-grown girox, if
you want them. Again, what you don't want, we will take back and
credit you with whatever is needed.'

There was a stunned silence before Blue said, 'And the horses?'

Dovas gave a huge laugh which set off the others. 'I know your ambitions, son, I have known them for years. The horses are yours. Both young, only trained for a walking rein, so you have the chance to train them up properly before you breed them. If you are smart about it, which I am sure you will be, you will be able to become known as both a trainer and breeder of fine horses in the future. What do you say?'

The youngster sat immobile, his eyes wide with pleasure. 'Really?'

At the Leader's nod, the boy shot out of his seat and ran to the horses, still tied to the last cart. Halfway there, he skidded to a halt, turned on his heel and ran back, pausing only to give Dovas a huge, neck choking hug, before turning again and running full tilt to the cart. Crow watched with the others as Blue checked out the two beasts, stroking and murmuring to them quietly and calmly, showing none of his excitement of just a few seconds previously, before leading them off to the stables.

Turning to Wren, Crow grinned. 'We are going to need bigger stables.'

'We have timber to help build them.' Dovas said, his eyes still on the happy youngster.

Crow turned to him, raising his brows in question.

'I wasn't exaggerating, all that we have provided is what he, himself, has earned. In the town, he would only accept a small payment on what he was owed for each job. Enough to provide a roof over his head and regular meals. He paid Pelagro's landlady to allow him to sleep in the stables and fed at her table or at the barracks. He didn't want to worry about being robbed so, every time his wealth began to get too much, he would hand it over to the captain or me, to keep safe for him. He has always worked damned hard for very little and deserves his full rights now. And all we have brought with us? There is plenty more we still have.'

'And what about Wren and I? What do we deserve?'

'Well, I ask that you keep watch over Blue, help him where he needs it and stay as his family. It is obvious that he cares deeply about you both and that is wonderful as he has been alone much too long. We would all have done much more for him, but he only let us in so far. You two, however, he loves unconditionally.'

'You know,' mused Crow. 'If you had come here, full of demands that I meet your brother, I would have baulked at the idea. As, however, you just want us to do what we already intended, you can send a message to the Bloodlings that they may test my blood. If it matches your brother, we will see where it takes us. Whatever the future, I am no longer the child he knew. If I am his child. Each step, therefore, must be taken carefully.'

Dovas looked at Crow, surprise and a deeper emotion crossing his features. He had to swallow two or three times before he could speak. 'Thank you, Crow, more than I can say.'

There was a pause as he got himself under control then he clapped his hands and began bellowing out orders, getting the soldiers moving. Some went to check storage facilities, others to the other houses. A couple checked the smithy while two went with Yan to check on the mill.

Crow heaved a great sigh and squeezed Wren's hand gently. 'Are you ready for the next part of our lives, love?'

'*Our* lives, Crow?'

'Aye. Our lives. Where you go, so do I. Tell me if you don't want this.'

'Don't want it? Crow, this is my dream. A home, with a boy I adore, and a life full of doings. It is perfect.'

'And me, love? Do I belong in your dream?'

With a laugh and a shake of her head for his foolishness, Wren replied. 'You, you idiot, are the central point of my dream. Without you, all would be ashes.' Bending over she kissed him lightly on the lips and whispered against them. 'So, get your arse into gear and stop lazing about. Our boy and our home need a strong back to keep everything moving.'

With a shout of laughter, Crow pulled Wren into his lap and they watched the bucolic scene with pleasure. Even as they sighed with satisfaction at Blue joyfully grooming one of his new horses in the field, both the ex-Assassin and the ex-Pick-pocket sent thoughts of hope to their distant friend, hoping that Dani would also find what she was seeking.

CHAPTER SEVENTEEN

Dani had jogged away from the farm, freshly bathed and wearing clean clothing that included a thick scarf that covered her slave collar completely, and a pack full of provisions. She didn't allow herself to feel any of the emotions that were trying to break free at having to leave behind her friends, including the huge kat as it had been playing with the children when she left. She just focused upon where her "tugging" took her.

She was surprised with how much energy she had now, especially considering just how much using her power usually drained her. When she had killed Pandam, her normal exhaustion had hit harder and stronger than usual but the result of taking Varla's life was almost the opposite in every way. As she moved forward at a steady pace along the roadside, she thought about the circumstances leading up to both incidents and concluded that the killing of Pandam had been fuelled by just fear for her own skin, whereas with Varla, there was real dislike of the woman but also fear of what she might do to the others. The Assassin's sly actions, her way of trying to drive wedges of discontent between the small group had fed Dani's dislike, but the fear was built of knowing just how much the woman was hiding and the vitriolic way she had had of speaking to Wren, especially. So when Dani had loosed her energy at Varla, intending the Assassin's death, she did so driven by the need to protect others, especially the children. This attitude of protection seemed to feed Dani all the energy she needed, rather than draining it away from her.

Whatever the reason might be, she didn't currently feel tired or have any need to stop and rest although she did make sure to eat regularly through the rest of the day.

As evening came but before it got too dark, Dani set up her camp. Her bedroll was laid out, a fire was blazing away in a small fire pit, and she had some food Etla had prepared heating up.

As Dani looked up at the darkening sky, a few stars beginning to peep out and shine brightly through the deep indigo twilight, it suddenly hit her that she was finally, absolutely and completely alone. She gave a muffled cry of both shock and loss, before dropping her head onto her folded arms and beginning to sob loudly, as the deep pain of all that loss seemed to fill her every pore.

Sam. Bili, Mr Poole, Luke, Rook, Jasper and the Twins who were now back in Bisra. Then there was Neera, Captain Poole, Zutana and the others she had cared about on the ship sailing over the oceans. On Mertam there had been Mallie and Brim, then Nobby, Gilly Flower, Fox and Vixen. Loss upon loss. Each one a huge blow to her, each one held hidden deep within as the need to move grew to become a complete obsession with her. This last loss though, oh gods, this last was almost beyond bearing. Blue, who she could see as an older Bili, full of the joy of life despite knowing the pain of living. Crow, so strong and so free with his knowledge, whom she would never know if he walked again. Wren, so much a sister to a lost and uneducated slavey. Who taught Dani about things she needed to know on a personal level, things that no-one had seen fit to teach her.

And lastly, lastly there was Whisper. A true friend and protector who had been with her through thick and thin since being on the Mertam docks. This latter loss made Dani wish for Numb and wonder if it was such a bad thing to use, if it would keep this excruciating pain away.

Her sobbing got more and more wild, until she could hardly draw breath and her coat sleeves were soaked with tears and mucus. Using a large square of cloth, donated by Nobby, she blew her nose again and again, and tried to dry her eyes. Every time she managed to calm herself down though, she would have a memory surface of someone that she had had to leave behind, and her sorrow would begin again.

Eventually, her face felt swollen and raw, her eyes just tiny slits, and her cheeks felt grazed from the scrubbing she had done as she had dried them again and again. Ripping off her coat, she dropped her head again, and wondered if she could live any more. Was feeling this pain worth staying alive for, even if her "tugging" told her she wasn't wherever she needed to be yet?

Feeling worn out and aching from the crying jag and all the emotions she couldn't control she moved the food away from the flames and lay down on her bedroll to rest. Surprisingly, she quickly nodded off, despite the occasional sob or hiccough that still wracked her body periodically.

Waking up to a warmer, sunnier day than there had been in weeks it seemed, helped Dani's mood a little. Sitting up with a sore face and eyes that still couldn't open properly, she looked around the small camp and froze, stunned at what she was seeing and afraid to move for a moment, in case she was dreaming.

Then she leaped across the fire, almost singeing her shirt tails on the way, before throwing her arms around the shadow kat. It sat regally still and tall, on the other side of the fire, glaring at the girl for leaving it behind.

'I'm sorry, Whisper, my love! I thought you wanted to stay with the children. I didn't want to force you to come with me.' Her voice trailed off as she hugged and kissed the great beast again and again. After a while, Whisper unbent enough to lick the side of her sore face, from chin to forehead, which started her giggling even as she let out a series of "ow, ow, ow," that sounded steadily higher at the contact with the kat's rough tongue.

Feeling much happier, and still with that extra energy pulsing around in her, Dani prepared breakfast for herself. While it heated through, she went and washed her face. It was most uncomfortable, very tight, sore and scratchy. After hissing in pain as the water hit a few raw patches, she reached into her pack and removed a small tin of unguent. Emotions rose a little as she remembered using this on Bili when he had become sunburnt one day on the ship. Swallowing convulsively for a moment, she twisted off the top of the faintly minty smelling stuff and dabbed a little of it onto the worst bits of her face. Immediately the cooling ointment soothed her pains, although her heart still felt sore.

After she had eaten a substantial breakfast, she quickly cooked up some travellers bread, adding various fillings of meat, cheese and vegetables. These would keep her going all day.

Throwing some soil over the dying flames of the fire put it out completely. Dani moved about, replacing stones, branches and anything else she had inadvertently moved while there in the clearing. Rolling up her bedding, she strapped it on top of her knapsack. Making a sling of an old shirt, she sat her little bits of bread within and got ready to move out. Whisper eyed her carefully, gave a huff of satisfaction and walked a little way in front.

This day's journey was an education for the slavey. Without the distraction of the others, she was able to look around her with both wonder and pleasure. There were also times of shock and wariness, such as when they moved past a tree and heard a slight rasping sound. Turning her head, Dani gasped as she came eye to forked tongue with a Barrier snake. Although very venomous, this snake was actually all for an easy life, so on hearing Whisper's warning growl, it gave another warning hiss and slid back into its hole at the base of the tree.

'Oh, wow,' Dani breathed. Although it had scared her, she had been able to take in its beauty. From the brown, gold and copper patterning in its scales to the beautiful emerald shade of its elliptical eyes and the dark brown of its questing tongue.

They continued moving quickly through the undergrowth. Dani following her internal tug while Whisper did its best to guide her around obstacles in her path.

By the time they stopped for a mid-day meal, Dani found herself back to her usual lower levels of energy. She wasn't exhausted by any means, but she knew that she would sleep well that night because of how far she had travelled already. Now the high level of energy had dissipated, her pace would now be a lot slower. She was pleased to find that her sense of loss was now easier to handle, although still sharp at times, and she still missed every one of her lost friends like crazy, but she wasn't anywhere near to incapacitation as she had been the evening before.

Pulling on her pack, adding a few more filled bread pockets to her improvised sling, she led the way past a small orchard, protected from the road with a short stone wall. Lying on it, sunning himself, was a black and white feline gentleman. As Dani walked past, this cat took it upon himself to purr and look winsome. Dani, having little knowledge of the independent nature of small felines, put out a hand and stroked along his back. With a hiss of indignation, the contrary creature sprang up and slapped out with sharp claws. Before he connected with the startled Healer though, Whisper raised its huge head from sniffing the base of the wall, causing the small cat to roll over in shock before promptly falling off the further side.

Dani burst out laughing, unable to stop as Whisper turned to her with a quizzical look on its face. She bent over, laughing even harder, when the cat finished scrambling back up the wall, and gave her the exact same look of enquiry as his bigger cousin, including the tilt of his head.

Finally, after a few moments of laughter, Dani straightened with a smile. Her emotions were now settled and her sorrow, although still there, was at an understandable level. She had originally taken this journey on to find a place where she could die as a free woman instead of a slavey. She would much rather do so without causing any of her friends the pain of watching her die.

'Thank you,' she told the bemused cat. 'You have helped me, even with your fiendishly sneakiness. Here.'

Reaching into her sling, she pulled out some pieces of fish from one of her bits of travelling bread and laid them on the wall. The cat sniffed them suspiciously, then making a chirruping noise, he settled down to eat. Risking her fingers, Dani gave the soft coat a few strokes, which he loftily ignored, before she turned and walked away.

It took a few more days for Dani to reach the next portal as she had tried following the pulling sensation in an almost straight line. This had meant she needed to backtrack a mile or so on one occasion, to a faint crossroads to take the right fork there, which led her directly to a small town, built around the magikal travelling device.

All the way there, she had been conscious of the feeling of being followed but when she turned around, she could never spot anything. Whisper never acted wary, it just stalked along, monarch of all it surveyed. The nearer they got to the village, the fainter the shadow kat became until, from one step to the next, it completely faded from view.

Hearing a chirrup of shock, Dani whipped her head around in time to catch sight of the black and white cat staring at the spot Whisper had faded from. A low purr from the empty space had the young cat run to Dani, climb her like a tree and settle on the top of the bedroll.

'What on Yerat is going on?' she hissed at the kat. All she got was a loud grumble that moved away from her into the village. With a snort of irritation, Dani followed, the cat making himself very comfortable by turning in circles and plopping himself down. Then, crossing his front paws, he stared out at his subjects.

Charlie moved away from the portal connected to Mertam, heading off in the direction his instincts pointed. He grinned to himself as he heard the voices calling behind him as he went in a different direction to what he had been advised to take. Knowing that the portal gnomes had lied to him but that they wouldn't be able to leave their magikal charge, he kept moving steadily through the wild country.

At his first sight of the huge, twisted sculpture that could have been an old-world dwelling of some sort, he gasped before going on alert. This was the sort of place he would expect to be attacked by bandits or even, perhaps, Necrotics. Moving closer to the building, he was stunned at its height but also (just like Dani if he had but known) at the number of scraps that could have been scavenged and re-used. Metal, glass, chunks of building materials and also rare plastic littered the ground. What also surprised him was the relatively few patches of Black Mýste around, and what was there was easily avoided.

He also let his instincts guide him through the huge space, the scent of fear and determination directing his steps. He sensed the chase and followed the emotions through and upwards until reaching the broken doorway the group had run through. Again, the scents were his guide, and he descended the rusty, broken things carefully, not able to resist a sigh of relief when he safely reached the ground without mishap.

Moving more swiftly, now he was outside again, it was no time at all until he arrived at the place of battle. The bodies, just meat to the animals around, had mostly been eaten, although three or four of them had been studiously ignored.

Moving closer to the bones, clothing and weapons, Charlie was quickly able to establish the fact that the rotting remains of the bigger pile of partial corpses were not Necrotic and further examination told him that these were probably the remains of Eaters, which the wildlife had enjoyed to the utmost, while the almost untouched portions that had been dragged away were the last of those who had turned or were in the process of becoming Necrotic and losing their humanity.

While staring at the two groups, one of Eaters and one of Necrotics, he struggled to think of which one was the most inhuman. After checking things out thoroughly, he also found the signs of a gnome having checked the area before, more than once in the last few days. Seeing this, Charlie nodded to himself. No point in him trying to see if there was anything to scavenge. Anything remotely useful to him would have been taken already by them.

Sniffing the air, he stiffened before he turned slowly and looked straight into the eyes of a wood gnome, partially absorbed within a young beech tree. The gnome's lower legs were firmly encased within the trunk while his upper body leaned out at a twisted angle, eyes firmly fixed on the Hunter.

Charlie raised his hands slowly and the gnome watched him, face expressionless and without moving. Then, lowering the short bow that had held an arrow fixed and aimed directly between the Hunter's eyes, the wood gnome pulled free of the trunk, patting it affectionately as he came away with a slight "pop". Facing the taller man, he gave a short nod and spoke.

'My sweet lady wishes speech with you, or you be dead already. Come, come, follow now.'

Slightly bemused, Charlie kept his hands clear of his weapons and did as he was told, without saying a word.

CHAPTER EIGHTEEN

Walking into the small inn alone was a little daunting for Dani. Hesitating for a moment to gather her courage, she eventually stepped through the heavy wooden door, with a little bump of encouragement from Whisper. At her stumbling entrance, all sound stopped, and she felt as though every eye was fixated on her. Before she could gather her wits to try and laugh her embarrassment off, the plump, smiling woman behind the waist high plank of polished wood, waved at her enthusiastically.

'Come in, my dear, and be welcome! You'll forgive us staring, my love, but you seem to be growing a cat from your head. Do that often, do you?'

At that comment Dani began laughing. She could feel the bony front paws of the black and white cat resting on her scalp as he surveyed his kingdom. Considering just how small he was – especially compared to Whisper – this little scrap was completely unaware of being outclassed.

Still grinning, Dani replied. 'A cat, you say? Phew! That's a relief, I was beginning to worry about the size of the lice here!'

A roar of appreciation filled the room at this sally, and everyone turned back to their conversations, drinks and food, after sending smiles and nods of appreciation her way.

Dani went over to the bar, and people stepped out of her way with friendly nods. One or two even petted the cat, which set him purring loudly. Once she stood at the bar, the woman reached over and removed the cat carefully from Dani's shoulder and fussed over him while she asked Dani what she wanted. Explaining that she would like food, drink and a bed for the night, followed by a journey through the portal the following day, the woman beamed.

'That will be fine, my lovely. Now, my name is Hella, you can stay in here or go through to the dining room. We have roast girox with hazelnuts, stuffing, little roasted potatoes and some cauliflower in a cheese sauce. Will that be alright? There's also a cherry crumble for pudding.' Still chattering, Hella turned round and stepped through a curtain, still holding the cat. When she came back – without the cat – she came around the plank of wood to lead Dani into a cosy room set with six or seven tables. A few of these were occupied and the customers looked up and nodded acknowledgement to them both before turning back to their heaped plates.

Dani settled at a chair near the window, gave her order then leant back and relaxed. Although tired, she wasn't as worn out as she had been these last few months. She also found that her emotions were now more under control, making things so much easier for her to cope with.

When her food arrived, she was amazed at how full her plate was but happily ate her way steadily through it all. The dessert that followed was wonderful; sweet, crunchy and chewy, flavour bursting over her tongue. Eventually, after realising she couldn't manage another mouthful, she leant back, replete, and sipped on her mulled cider, contentedly.

Partway through her meal she had felt Whisper slip away, presumably to hunt its own food. Hella came through and seeing that the Healer had finished her meal, escorted Dani to her room. It was bright and cheery, with a small fire to chase away the slight damp in the air. When she checked, she found that her sheets were white linen and smelt of lavender. Pushed halfway down the mattress, nestled underneath the blankets, was a heated brick wrapped in towelling, that warmed the whole bed up wonderfully. After washing herself with the warm, scented water provided, Dani put on some nightwear before slipping into bed and opened one of her books to read.

An hour or so later, there was a tap on the door and Hella stepped in at Dani's call. In the Innkeeper's hand was a tray which held a selection of small cakes, some sweet pastries and a cup of something that steamed delightfully.

'Ooh, I hope that I haven't disturbed you, my love. I like to provide a night-time drink and a few snacks to everyone, just in case. I sometimes find myself needing a bit of a nibble in the middle of the night. Here you go.'

She settled the tray on a side table, within easy reach of Dani. Feeling a little awkward, the Healer asked about payment. Hella looked at her carefully.

'Well now, that all depends on who you are, dear. A friend of ours, he asked me to keep an eye out for a female. She would be grey eyed and brown haired, a bit too skinny and be wearing a scarf or something similar, tied around her throat. Are you her?'

'I think so, if you are speaking about Neera.'

'Ha! The very man himself!' Hella clapped her hands in delight. 'He says you are a magiker but didn't say what sort. No matter, there is only a small charge, just to cover food and fuel.'

'Hmmm, in that case I might have to leave by the window, considering how much food I have eaten,' Dani laughed.

Hella joined in with her merriment and then left the Healer to enjoy her hot drink and her snacks in peace.

After finishing her drink, a smooth, milky concoction, and eating two of the pastries, Dani read to chapter's end before asking the fey lantern to quieten down and snuggled down under the covers. A few hours later, she half awoke as a heavy shape thumped down next to her on the bed and began loudly purring. She only realised that it was the black and white tom once Whisper had returned from hunting and objected to the little cat trying to usurp its position. The almost silent hisses only stopped when Dani whispered that both animals would have to leave if they didn't shush. With identical grunts of disgust, the two disparate felines settled down and fell asleep quickly, becoming curled into each other.

After a heartening breakfast, Dani found that her travelling clothes from the previous days had been washed, dried and mended. She was given a large pack of food to take with her and she made her goodbyes to Hella. The Innkeeper had refused to accept any payment, so Dani had placed a gem by the side of her bed, covered with her morning teacup. Pleased with herself, the Healer stepped out with a gnome to go to the travel portals.

She was surprised, once she reached the stone circles, to be warned that the next land she was travelling to would be completely different to anything she had known before. Taking off her coat, as advised, she shivered in the cold. Whisper allowed itself to reappear, causing the gnomes to fall about comically, in shock and then to refuse any payment, and so the young woman and the shadow kat stepped through the shimmering circle of multi-coloured lights together. Just before they disappeared, Dani flicked another gem through the portal, giggling as she did so as she saw the frustration on the gnomes faces. She was determined to make sure that those that helped her did not lose out on the various transactions they made on her behalf. She was so very grateful that Neera had put out the word that she was travelling, but Dani was determined not to get used to others paying for her, especially when she had plenty of the various currencies, gems and gold left over from what she had been given, way back at the beginning.

Once through the portal, Dani's jaw dropped in utter astonishment at what she saw. The grinning gnomes that helped her down the steps from the landing plate obviously enjoyed her amazed expression. The shadow kat seemed to ignore the strange, new landscape and just walked steadily in front of the gawking woman.

They had arrived in a place so different to any that Dani had seen before that she struggled to accept everything her eyes took in. She felt as if she had shrunk down to the size of an ant as the foliage, apart from the field grasses, all grew so high here. The flowers, weeds and fungi were huge. Trees disappeared high above the clouds, some of the various plants grew perhaps five or six feet in height while others seem to be as tall as twenty or thirty feet high. Every shade of green, brown, yellow and purple rioted in front of her very eyes. The sun shone so brightly through the foliage that some plants seemed to actually glow.

The heat was a shock too. It was so thick and muggy that breathing took a little bit of effort and the air felt almost moist as she took it into her lungs. Her thick, winter shirt was immediately wringing wet, not just with sweat but the damp heat.

'Ok, lads,' the lead gnome said, after a minute or two. 'That's enough laughing. I dun wanna upset t'kat, even if you do.'

At the timely reminder, the others straightened their faces, although Dani laughed and shook her head in amusement at their solemn visages and eyes full of humour. Then she waited for instructions on how to tackle the road forward.

'Alright, missy, which is the way you are heading?'

Thinking a moment, allowing the "tug" to guide her, she turned in a slow circle and pointed to the North.

'There, that's where I need to head to.' The gnomes frowned at each other before the lead gnome's brow cleared and he gave a grunt of understanding.

'Aah, we don't use that one much, seeing as where it goes to,' he said. 'It's still manned both ends though, so you will be alright. You are going to be going through a good chunk of the island though, so go into the room over there and strip yersen down to your thinnest clothing, or you'll be passing out before you know it.'

Giving a nod of thanks, Dani headed over to a small hut that had been pointed out to her and did as she had been advised. The gnomes themselves wore loose, sleeveless shifts of a fine linen, embroidered with bright colours at neck and hem. Open sandals were on their broad feet and most of them wore wide straw hats too.

Looking through her clothing, Dani managed to put together something a little similar to the gnomes' apparel. Sam's shirt, brought with her as a reminder, was slipped on, turning the sleeves up. It reached down way past her knees, and she slipped her belt and knife around her waist. Under the shirt she wore loose under things for modesty's sake. She left off her trews and, apart from changing the thick scarf around her throat to something flimsier, that was all she wore. On her feet was her only set of footwear, the boots she always wore but there was nothing she could do about them.

Feeling very under-dressed she hesitated with her hand on the door handle. Then she breathed in deeply, gave herself a nod of encouragement, and stepped out into the heat and the sun.

As soon as she was outside, any embarrassment she had felt regarding her apparel disappeared. She was still very hot; the atmosphere was still heavy, but her clothing was no longer weighing her down. The gnomes made no comments regarding her unconventional attire, just nodded in approval at her more sensible clothing.

One of them stepped forward to hand over a large bottle and a piece of soft wool and showed her how to cover her exposed flesh with the soothing, scented lotion. He also handed her one of the broad brimmed straw hats they all wore, and Dani felt the relief of the shade that now covered her eyes and the back of her neck. The kat looked her up and down before giving her a huff of amusement and lay down to bask in the bright sunshine.

After a few words of warning regarding the need to drink lots more water and what plants in particular to avoid, the small group of gnomes waved the two adventurers off with smiles, water and more food. Dani was pleased with herself for having had the foresight to place some gold dust within the changing hut.

Dani's pack felt heavy with the water, clothing and food but she was so much fitter now than she had been just a few months ago, so didn't feel the strain very much. Even though she knew she was dying – the Numb drug, or lack of it, would see to that – she actually felt better in herself every day. Even the exhaustion and hunger that reared up was more manageable, not nearly as debilitating as it had been. In fact, ever since she had drawn Varla's life force from her, both things were much less of an issue. She slept well but not as if she was unconscious and although she still liked a good meal, she ate much less than she had originally needed just to function.

Smiling, Dani followed the kat down a slight path, the green fronds of certain plants towering over them both. Making sure to drink plenty as well as to rest and eat every hour or so, she found that they still covered a decent amount of ground before nightfall.

Whisper found them a place to camp, close by a stream. It also snagged a couple of fish from the fast-flowing water. Dani made a small fire to cook hers and to make fresh travel breads. She also emptied out her pack, to see what food stuffs she still had, and to fold things a little more neatly.

'Dammit, Whisper! Did you do this?' The Healer looked wide eyed at the small gems and gold dust sitting on top of her cloak. The very gems and gold that she had been happily leaving in hidden places for those that had helped her for little or no payment. The kat just raised its brows in inquiry before going back to enjoy its fish. She still looked at the beast, suspicious of its attitude, before she sighed in defeat and repacked everything again. Unless she was prepared to retrace her steps to leave the payments again, with no guarantee that they would stay where they were put, there was nothing she could do.

After she had sorted out her pack, she ate much of the tasty fish, which had been deboned and covered in a herby crust. The little that was left over she popped into more of her favourite travel breads, ready for the next day. She filled some other of the simple pockets of cooked dough with shredded duck and a last few with vegetables and cheese, until she had fifteen or so of the tiny bites of food for the following day's walk.

Once the food had all cooked through, Dani gratefully swept dirt over the low flames of the fire, stamping down on the patches of smoke until it was safely out. Although the sky now looked like the black fur of a blind mole, spotted with early morning dew, the heat still remained. The damp muggy weight of the air did eventually lighten up a little as the night drew on, however, and a few times Dani could have sworn she even felt a cooling breeze slide across her features. She rolled her cloak up into a pillow before laying down and she sighed in contentment at the sound of the rushing stream as it sped past, the faint droning of insects from far away and the purring snores from the huge shadow kat at her side.

She was still smiling as she drifted off to sleep.

CHAPTER NINETEEN

For the next day or so, Dani followed the direction her instincts guided her. The kat was able to pick out pathways and trails invisible to her eyes through the strange foliage that her own eyes couldn't spot. This was a big help, especially as she was busy trying to absorb the new species of life she saw around her.

Some insects flew by, shockingly quick on wings that beat so fast they were invisible. Others flew past, high in the sky but were so huge they blocked the light for a few seconds every time they passed. Large, trundling bugs went by her at a rolling walk, their brood following in single file behind. Whenever this happened, Dani would take time to drink and eat a little, sharing both with the kat as the trundle bugs had offspring of at least a hundred or more so took time to move past on their journey.

Birds were also present, again in widely differing sizes. All were highly decorative, with feathers of every colour of the rainbow, and more besides. Some had long, sharp beaks and a delicate song, others had strong curved beaks and a harsh croak. Some ate the offerings from various plants, others snapped up the smaller insects and a few even captured and ate their fellow avians and smaller mammals.

The plants were as mixed as the bird and insect life. Tall plants with broad leaves held onto the water, allowing one to drink deeply if one thirsted. Smaller plants had tender shoots that were tasty when set within the travel bread. Bright flowers burst into life from plants of verdant green that attracted and absorbed insects, mammals and birds alike.

The animals were difficult to see close up. Overhead were bipeds, strange little beasts that chattered away and enjoyed throwing hard fruits down on the luckless Healer if she got too close to their trees. There were also hints of big cats – just a shadow moving here, foliage rocking back into place there. Dani never caught sight of these, but she found their large footprints. She showed one to Whisper, exclaiming at its size. The shadow kat looked at her and sniffed in disdain, before placing its own foot over the print, completely obliterating it. She laughed out loud at this, conceding that it was much bigger than any other cat around. Her head turned from one side to another constantly as Dani tried to take in everything that was happening around her. She was grateful to the trundlebugs for not only did she get time to eat and drink, but she also had time to let her thoughts settle.

The further away from the portal and closer to the middle of the island they went, the more space between each group of growing things became. The ground was very uneven, and Dani found herself hiking up large, steep hills that the kat danced up easily, or stumbling down the other side, legs pumping frantically as she tried not to fall over her feet and land ignominiously upon her face. The fact that the kat managed to slide down with grace and ease annoyed her immensely, especially when it went past, waving its thick tail, with a smug look upon its face.

As they moved up an easier slope that there had been for a while, Dani found herself berating the kat for being so cocksure. It ignored what she was saying but picked up speed, swaying its hips exaggeratedly from side to side.

'Now you are just being rude!' she called out, grinning at its rear end.

As she watched it closely, she saw when it stiffened and dropped to the ground before it stalked forward to peep over the hill. Following its lead, Dani dropped down and scuttled much less elegantly up beside it.

Down below lay a small village. In the centre of it huddled a group of strange old magikal beings that were being hugged tightly by a slightly larger group of frightened children. Surrounding this group were angry horsemen, all in the livery of the Shining One. With them was a Mage, dressed in gaudy robes, waving his hands about and shouting at one particular elder. As Dani watched in horror, the Mage swung a sturdy cane high in the air and lashed it down with all his force at the being, who collapsed like a felled tree. The horsemen joined in by attacking the group, shouting and kicking out with pointed boots and wrenching around their mounts heads, tugging the reins and punishing the horses mouths, causing the animals screams to join in the cacophony. A few moments of this chaos: of shouting, of kicked up dust, of screaming children, horses and wailing adults, the yelling of men and the cursing from the Mage, all finished when the Mage flung up his hands and spoke a curse in very dramatic tones, swept his horse around and gestured his escort to follow him. The group of horsemen left after a few extra kicks, falling in behind the haughty Mage in a double line. The onlookers saw two of the horsemen at the end of the line both drop packages even as they disappeared out of the village.

Before the end of the horsemen had fully left, Dani went down the steep slope, leaving the kat to follow. She didn't try running, just planted her feet and slid down at great speed, the kat easily catching up and allowing her to grab onto its fur to stop her pitching forward.

Not stopping to think, the Healer hurled her way through the protective group who surrounded their fallen comrade. The kat gave a quiet growl which warned some of the angry mob to step back in shock. Skidding to a halt, Dani dropped to her knees and clasped the two frail claw-like hands and sent her magik flowing down her arms into the unconscious female.

The crowd watched in complete silence as she began to glow, her hands sending out a light so bright, it made the onlookers squint. Because of the brightness of the light, many thought that the flashes of black lightning that began to flow from her fingers and the darkness of her eyes were just optical illusions but then realised that they were truly seeing the dark slashes.

After almost ten minutes, the still figure on the ground began to stir, giving a moan of pain. Dani pushed her back down, gently, when the older creature tried to rise. Another minute or so, and the Healer sat back on her heels, allowing the elder to sit up slowly. Although her face was covered in dried blood, the broken cheekbone, jaw and eye socket were back to their proper shapes. Her left eye was still a little bloodshot but was no longer hanging down her cheek. One of her people came through the crowd and handed her a wet cloth while another went and got both Healer and patient a much-needed drink.

As the elder got to her feet, she looked at Dani, who was now drooping a little with weariness.

'Thank you, my dear,' she spoke in gentle tones, her voice a little cracked with age. 'It has been many years since one such as you travelled our lands. Hail and welcome, Healer. You are now Friend to the Zylphas.'

'Zylphas?' Dani asked, curious despite her tiredness.

'Yes, my dear. We are a breed of magiker that the One religion does not allow to be seen because we look too alien to humans. So, I am not surprised that you have not heard of us. I am Casella, granddaughter of our Sect's Elder. I invite you and your kat to come and stay with us until you are back up to your full strength.'

'I had just been thinking how I was feeling less exhausted than I used to, but that might have just been wishful thinking. I would appreciate staying with you for a short time, just until I get back to normal, but I will need to leave once I am fine.'

'Perfect.' Casella smiled before clapping her hands and directing the villagers towards certain chores.

Whisper arrived back at Dani's side, having gone to pick up her pack that had been left behind up the slope in her mad dash. She popped three of the bread pockets into her mouth, one after the other, to calm her raging hunger. She also drank water to slake her intense thirst. All the while, she watched in amazement as those around her went from one small green hut to another, clearing out crockery, furniture, pots and pans, bedding and anything else within. Three large carts were pulled up into the open space in the centre of the village and were soon piled high, each with a different cargo. The first held the furnishings from the houses, the second carried anything extra plus tools, food and seeds. The last carried wooden crates filled with eating fowls, pets and had a long wooden pole rearing from the back, to which were tied goats, sheep and other animals Dani couldn't name. Two of the younger ones collected the parcels that had been deliberately dropped.

The whole exercise took less than two hours and Dani had managed to recover a little of her energy. The kat sat purring smugly as many of the villagers petted it as they went past. Dani found herself confused as she looked from the spry and flexible elders to the slow and creaky youngsters.

Casella saw her puzzled face and laughed. 'Come and sit with me, my lovely, I will explain all.'

Sitting in the last cart, full of the animals who contentedly munched on their preferred foods, Casella waited until the last person left the village astride a trundle bug, similar but much larger than the ones Dani had watched earlier. Then the village elder raised her hands and muttered a string of words too low for Dani to hear, despite her close proximity. The Healer's jaw dropped as the whole village gave a shudder and then kept shaking. The huts, so solid just a moment before, all collapsed at the same time, throwing up dust, leaves and debris. Casella looked over and smiled at Dani's amazement, waiting so the Healer saw it all.

After the huts fell, green seemed to flow over the rubble. All different verdant shades of plant life grew and spread in moments. It was as if nature exploded into action. The deep well at the side of the central meeting place crumbled in on itself, the stones separating and rolling away from each other. Thatch fell to the ground and was smothered by ground hugging ferns and bracken. In the time it took for Dani to breathe in and out slowly twenty-five times, the whole area became overgrown and covered in the thick foliage that was everywhere.

Catching the lead cart driver's eye, Casella gave a nod, and he led the way forward.

'Now, we have a bit of a journey ahead, my lovely, so ask your questions whenever you are ready. It will help the time pass more quickly,' she said kindly.

'Well, apart from the shock of seeing a village disappear, please explain why your elders run about and do handsprings while your youngsters step slowly and drag their feet? The younger they are, the worse they seem.'

'Well, to begin with, Zylphas are connected to the Earth. We worship Her and Her gifts to us. With this worship, we find that we grow food that is tastier and freer from pests than much that is grown and sold by others. Our magik allows us to build our villages out of the natural materials available, everything changing shape and size to become whatever is needed. Once we have finished with an area or we need to move on, we remove our magic and return everything back to its natural state.

'Now for our people. You look around and see young things who walk like the old, and old ones who run and jump around. When we are born, we hatch from eggs grown from a dying body. We are born looking, in the eyes of humans at least, very old, with small, twisted bodies, wrinkled and fragile. As our time moves on, we slowly begin to lose the stiffness of "age", becoming straighter, stronger and quicker of movement. Then age keeps coming and we grow smaller, less confident upon our feet, less able to communicate. Eventually, we are carried into our temple, laid upon a bed of herbs and our bodies begin to decay. Once our bodies have fragmented, we leave behind eggs that contain new life. And so the cycle continues.'

'Wait a moment,' Dani gaped. 'You mean the elders that I am looking at are *younger* than the others?'

'Exactly, my dear,' smiled the Zylpha, happy the Healer understood.

Dani mulled things over for a short while, amazed at how things had been abruptly turned on its head. Then another question that had been nagging her for months occurred to her.

'Just one other question, why do so many of you speak Bisran?'

'Bisran? What is that?' Casella frowned, confused as to what Dani meant.

'The language, Bisran. What we are speaking.'

'But my dear, you are speaking the language of the Zylphas, which I own is strange as we rarely share even a few words in our language with outsiders, let alone the whole thing.'

Dani frowned; she had assumed that everyone on her travels had spoken Bisran. Yet, even as she had that thought, common sense told her that she had travelled too far from Bisra for any common language connection.

'So how is it that I understand you?' she asked.

'I think, that as a Healer, you have the ability to understand all the languages as you need to be able to communicate with the ones you heal. You don't have to have learned; you just *know*. It might be one of your magikal skills. As is not seeing the differences between various beings.'

Dani frowned even harder at the latter comment. 'What differences?'

'Exactly,' laughed Casella. 'Look more closely at me, girl.'

They rode along quietly for a few moments before Dani gave a startled grunt. Satisfied, Casella nodded her head at the Healer. 'So, you have seen the differences now.'

The differences the Zylpha was speaking about were now blatantly obvious to Dani, making her wonder how she hadn't noticed before. Skin of a pale green, faceted eyes set into a triangular shaped face. Long legs that had joints that bent the opposite way to a human's and arms that ended in a double pincer. There was a thick carapace covering Casella's back which, later, Dani would see open up to show beautiful diaphanous wings. The Zylpha was taller than Dani, taller even than Sam had been and, although strange looking, she held her own beauty.

Looking around at the others, Dani saw skin of all shades of blue, green and a combination of both colours. Their heights varied but most were taller than Dani, who was still bubbling over with questions. Before she could ask anything else though, her face split into a huge yawn and Casella grinned at her.

'Enough now, my peach. You step into the back and cuddle up to one of those sacks. It sounds as if your body needs rest, even if you don't think it does.'

Dani gave a tired grin before yawning again. Taking the advice of the Zylpha, she crawled into the back of the cart, wriggled around to get comfortable between a crate of what looked like horned conies and a trio of sleepy goat kids. After another yawn, faithfully copied by all who saw her, she snuggled up against one of the kids and fell deeply asleep between one breath and the next. Casella exchanged a glance with the shadow kat before concentrating on following the cart in front.

When the carts entered the hidden Zylpha compound, the surge of magik caused Dani to murmur in her sleep but she didn't awaken. Casella pointed to a few of her friends who all hurried away to get a room ready before coming back and carrying the sleeping Healer gently away. Casella hurried to her grandmother's chambers to explain everything that had happened, carrying one of the WANTED posters showing the Healer's face that had been in the parcels dropped at the village.

Dani was woken up by the faint sound of a gong, reverberating through her sleep. Yawning and stretching, it took her a moment to recognise that there was very little familiar to her in this room. White plaster walls with no windows, a side table holding both ewer and bowl. There looked to be a smaller chamber which led off the main room, and Dani hoped for some kind of water closet. She was thrilled to find that she was right.

As she finished washing her face and hands from the ewer after relieving herself, the thick curtaining that covered the opening to her chamber was pushed aside and the shadow kat stalked in. Seeing Dani up and about, it turned around with a huffing noise and left. While Dani dried off her hands, chuckling at its antics, the kat came back, leading a tiny sprite of a Zylpha with it.

Dani knew that, in the reverse way of the Zylphas, this youngster was actually much more elderly than she seemed. The Healer was proved right when the young female introduced herself as Casella's grandmother, Phaemal. After checking that Dani wanted to go with her, the Zylpha Elder took the Healer's hand and led her out to the communal room, which was set up with tables and chairs, plates and cutlery. Huge cauldrons of food were being carried to the tables and the exciting tang of spices wafted across Dani's senses.

Very little was said as everyone settled themselves and then filled their plates. Before taking a bite, Phaemal spoke a ritual blessing, asking her Goddess for Her blessing and giving thanks for the feast, and everyone else joined in with the responses. Dani, not knowing the ritual, said her own words which seemed to please them all.

Taking her first bite, tasting the flavours that exploded in her mouth, she couldn't help but give a moan of pleasure. After that wordless comment on the exquisite cuisine, she dug into the small bowls of all the different foods set before her. It seemed that as soon as one dish or plate was finished, another took its place. As each dish only held a small amount, Dani was able to taste a large variety of tastes without becoming bloated or over full. Eventually, she was fully satisfied, and she lay down her spoon, even as others continued to eat.

She gazed around the room, fascinated by what she saw. As more and more of the Zylphas finished their food, the noise level rose. Soon, plates and dishes were piled at the end of the tables before being collected by the younger Zylphas, who tottered away with tall piles of wooden crockery. Dani met Phaemal's eye as she looked around and blushed with embarrassment while stammering out her apologies for her rudeness at staring around her.

'Don't be silly, child,' Phaemal said with a smile. 'Let your curiosity shine. It is a great compliment that you are interested in us.'

'Oh, I am,' grinned back Dani. 'I have seen so much on my journey that is wonderful but nothing as much as the Zylpha.'

'Well said,' Phaemal was delighted at this woman. 'You still need to regain a little energy, so we won't discuss anything serious this evening. Now is the time for tales and music, songs to send you to sleep. Tomorrow is soon enough for the rest.'

There followed a delightful evening for Dani. There were tales about the history of the Zylphas, which answered many of her questions about this strange race. Haunting songs and melodies relaxed and soothed them all, with even the kat putting off its evening hunting to stay and listen. When Dani eventually left to find her sleeping chamber, there were many others still happily listening and singing along. The harmonies sent Dani into a deep sleep, where she still heard the voices blending beautifully in her dreams.

CHAPTER TWENTY

While Dani stayed with the Zylphas, all of her meals were taken in the communal hall. In between meals, the room was full of Zylphas spinning, weaving, knitting and crocheting, using the thread that they harvested. Dani was fascinated with the whole process of harvest to cloth so happily went along with a group to cut down the fast-growing grasses the thread came from. She carried armfuls of the stuff to a cauldron, there to soak in a heavy brine mixture to remove insects and other impurities. Someone went back every half an hour or so to stir the mixture. After a week of soaking, the grasses were removed and hung over long poles to dry out a little. While still slightly damp, the fronds were taken down and stamped on before going into various dye vats. Then they were dried out a little again before being taken and spun gently on a wheel. Eventually, the Zylphas spun the fronds into a delicate, but hardy thread, using it to make clothing, bags and lengths of brightly covered material. Seeing and learning the process used muscles that Dani didn't know she had and she found that she could only do a small amount compared to the eldest and the youngest magikers.

One morning just having finished tidying her room and waving off Whisper as it went hunting, Dani headed towards the hall. She was a little surprised at the distracted air that everyone wore and the fact that the looms and needles weren't clacking. Before she could say anything, Phaemal came rushing over to her and caught her hands.

'Thank goodness you are here, my sweetheart,' the Elder said, breathing heavily. 'Do you remember Pols? He was at the village when you saved Casella.'

'Yes,' Dani answered quickly. 'Yes, I know Pols, is he sick? Can I do anything?'

'No, no, my lovely,' Phaemal soothed. 'Not sick, just very close to returning Home. He has asked if you would like to see our Ending and Beginning, but you can say no, of course.'

'I would be honoured, Elder,' Dani replied, formally. She knew what a great gift she was being offered here. The Zylphas were a very private people, knowing how their appearance put others off. Dani knew that she was one of the very few outsiders who would ever see this ceremony.

There followed a morning of preparation. A ritual bath for all the celebrants, and beautiful new robes were brought for Dani. She gasped when she saw them as they were the finest things she had ever seen. They were of a gorgeous bright red, embroidered over in gold. Looking closely, she was able to see that the embroidery showed the birth/death/rebirth ceremony in exquisite detail. Thanking Casella profusely for bringing them, Dani slipped the robes over her head. Once she had them on, she noticed just how light the material was, considering how much of it layered her body. She also saw pieces of diaphanous material, stiffly hanging behind her, that resembled the wings of the Zylphas. A twisted gold headpiece sat on top of her short curls, and at the request of Pols, she removed her scarf, allowing everyone to see her slave collar.

Walking back into the Hall in her finery, she thought she heard an exclamation of dismay. She didn't have any chance to look for who had made the sound as she was soon surrounded by Zylphas, fussing over her and making incremental changes to her robes and her headwear. She didn't feel too much of a spectacle because, even though Zylphas as a whole wore very little clothing as a rule, now they all wore robes and headwear in the red and gold fabric. After a few moments of general fussing, Phaemal gave a low call, stopping all the chatter at once. Gesturing to Dani to stand by her side, the Elder gave another of those low calls.

Dani felt shivers run down her spine as, across the hall, another voice took up the wordless sound but in a slightly different key. Another, then another, then another, until everyone there sang the wordless harmony. She found herself joining in the cry, her voice sounding completely different to the crowd but somehow managing to harmonise beautifully. She felt her hands grasped by the people standing either side of her and the crowd opened up. She saw a male Zylpha, of middle age, walking slowly down the aisle between the two groups of beings, carrying a bundle wrapped in the same cloth that they were all wearing.

As the male came closer, Dani saw that he was holding a tiny infant. Faceted eyes that seemed too big for the small body smiled up at her and then slowly closed. As the male left the hall, everyone turned and flowed behind, Dani settled between Phaemal and Casella. As they walked in slow procession, the wordless tune continued, echoing off the walls as they headed out of the main building towards another, a distance away.

Entering into the birthing building came as a surprise. Narrow passages allowed a maximum of three to walk side by side, almost half the width within the main hall. When they stepped into the large open space at the centre, it was almost as humid and hot as outside rather than the cooler atmosphere of the communal hall. Holes in the roof allowed light to come in and there were no doors or windows, allowing what little breeze there was to try and flow through.

The tall male, whom Dani learned later was called Wiltner and was Pols' son, carried his father over to a long, low stone basin, padded with pillows. Laying his father down in it, he leaned forward and whispered a few words, impossible to hear over the song. Then he stepped back, taking the wrappings with him, leaving the naked "baby" lying on the cool stone, his head resting on a soft pillow.

The song began to build in volume, the power inherent in it sending goosebumps along Dani's flesh. The sound became more and more powerful and there was a buildup of magik within the cave-like room. Lights began to spark and fly from the shallow basin upwards and across to where eight or ten eggs sat in a bed of sand. These eggs were of various sizes, some just a few inches, others as tall as two feet. Their colours were as varied as their size, ranging from blue to green and all shades between. The sparks rising from Pols seemed to flow thicker and faster, along with the humming of the crowd of onlookers. Then there was an explosion of light that blew everyone backwards and Dani knew no more.

It was only a few minutes later when Dani came to, and she took her time to let her head settle and stop spinning. When things had settled, she looked around to see what the others were doing and saw most of the Zylphas moving over to where the eggs lay. Dani decided she could wait a few minutes for that visit and, instead, she went over to the shallow basin where Pols had lain. Inside the basin there was no trace of Pols at all but, seated on the pillow, was an egg. It was the size of the palm of Dani's hand and was a rich blue. Hearing a slight cough, she turned her head and saw Casella standing by her, with a huge smile on her face, surprising Dani a little.

Using the swaddling cloth that Pols had been carried in, Casella gently picked up the egg and, seeming to echo Wiltner's journey from the hall, walked towards where the other eggs lay, between two columns of humming Zylphas. She nodded to Dani to help her lay the egg in its slight indentation in the warm sand. Although Casella held the cloth around the soft, waxen egg, Dani caught the shell with her finger and felt a slight tingle. From the open eyed stare from Casella, Dani realised she had also felt something. As the Healer opened her mouth to apologise, Phaemal's granddaughter gave a minute shake of her head and finished laying the cloth around the egg. Then she led Dani over to the others and they both gazed at the new-born but elderly looking man who now lay back in Wiltner's arms, wrapped in more cloth. This Zylpha was a gorgeous deep turquoise in colour, his hair sparse and white on his wrinkled scalp. He grinned up at Dani, flashing toothless gums at her before giving a delicate little burp and nodding off to sleep.

'You have done us great honour, Dani,' Wiltner said, his voice a low rumble. 'My father has been greatly blessed.'

'It is I who have been blessed, Wiltner,' Dani responded. 'This is a moving and emotional ceremony which holds much joy. So strange to think that humans only think of loss rather than gain.'

'Aah, but that is because, like most magikers, we think of life as a cycle. There is our first birth, where we live in joy with others of our kind. Then, when it is time, our bodies go to our Mother. Our essence stays with Her until it is time to be reborn, while what is left over becomes the soft covering of new life. There is no loss. Although I will miss my father's presence, I know he is giving energy to another.'

Dani felt her eyes widen as she realised that the waxy covering on the new egg she had helped to carry was literally what was left of the physical body of Pols. For a split second she wondered if she should be unnerved by the knowledge but then just shrugged it off. This was the way that Zylphas held their loved ones in memory and, as far as Dani was concerned, it was a much better choice than huge pits where the ordinary people who were nearly dead were thrown and Black Mýste was allowed to feed, or the huge stone buildings that held the affluent dead of the Shining One.

Going back to the communal hall, people broke up into groups to laugh, chat and sing in celebration. Reaching the hall, there was a great meal waiting for them and Wiltner lay his new relative in a supportive hammock and there was feasting for the rest of the day.

What Pols' family didn't want of his personal belongings were laid out on tables in the hall, for anyone to go and take if they needed. The new child was brought several items to help in their growth and development and the whole time was a mixture of joy and a little sorrow but no real sense of loss. Dani really enjoyed herself, now able to join in many of the songs, knowing what emotions to display when stories unfolded thanks to the many that had been told on previous evenings. What she couldn't do though, was ignore the growing "tugging" sensation that told her it was time to move on, as well as the sense of unease that had begun when she had heard that stifled gasp earlier in the day.

As she sat there, enjoying a tale of derring-do, she made the decision to move on before the mid-day meal the following day. She looked over at Phaemal and saw that she was looking back at her. Once their gazes met, Dani got up and made her way over to the Elder.

'Sit by me, Dani, my child,' Phaemal said, smiling at the Healer. 'You are ready to leave us, yes?'

Dani wasn't surprised at Phaemal's quick understanding. Both had known that the Healer's stay was only temporary and she had already been here longer than she had expected to be. She had no regrets about staying though, especially the amazing experience of the death and rebirth she had seen today. Talking to Wiltner she had found out that the new egg would now stay with the rest, growing among its brethren. When it was time, an old one would die, and the energy of the death and physical changes needed to make a new egg would magikally melt the wax like covering on another. Inside would be a fully grown "old" person who would then, over about a year, slowly grow younger until it was time to repeat the cycle. For now, though, there would be a week of feasting to celebrate new life before things got back to normal.

Dani was able to express all her gratitude for the comfortable stay as well as the insight and help the Zylphas had given. Phaemal laughed.

'You are a Healer, young one, so this has been our pleasure. It is wonderful that you have recovered so quickly from your weariness and, if it were possible, we would love you to stay longer. I don't think that you realise just how much of your magik that you have sent out over the last few days. Those suffering from pain or fevers have all improved in health. Everyone has felt more industrious and able to achieve certain goals. Pols wanted you to be a part of his Change for many reasons but one of these was because you eased the pain and twisting in his limbs, something that had caused him many problems. Casella says she felt a slight zip of energy when you touched the new egg?'

'Yes, although it wasn't done deliberately.'

'Of course, it wasn't. It will be interesting to know what will happen when it hatches. I will have gone through my own Change by the time we find out, so Casella is looking forward to being the one who knows. When you do find your home, don't forget to send us a message about where you are. You are one of our Friends and your memory will be long remembered in our songs and stories.'

'I will let you know as soon as I can. You do remember that I am trying to find a place to die though, don't you?'

'I remember. I also know that when it comes to Healing magik, nothing can be assumed. And with *untrained* Healing magik, even less can be expected. Don't write yourself off just yet. You have lived so much longer than expected, what is to say you don't have even longer?'

Dani gave a wry smile. 'I would love it if you were right, Phaemal, but I feel a deep weariness in my bones that no matter what I do, how much I eat or rest, I cannot dispel. I am slowing down and, eventually, just won't be able to continue. If I find my place first, I will get someone to send a message. In fact, wherever I am when it catches up on me, I will send a message.'

'Knowing you have a connection to Neera, I think all you will need to do is to speak your news out loud, as the slightest breeze will take it directly to him. Now, do you want to dance? Or is it time to go to your room?'

'My room, I think. I want to make sure everything is mended, clean and packed.'

'Good idea. Don't try leaving any of those gems or gold around though, we will only return them!'

Looking into Phaemal's laughing eyes, Dani grinned in return.

'Blast, you caught me. I would like to buy some clothing though.'

'We will discuss that tomorrow. Go now, I have dancing to do.'

With another grin at the Elder's back as she ran off with a whoop of joy, Dani went back to her chambers. On her bed sprawled the shadow kat, glaring fixedly at her, making Dani laugh ruefully.

'I wasn't thinking of going without you,' she said. 'I have explained until I am blue in the face why I did so before. Now I am going to sort my pack out, bathe and make sure all is ready for the morning because I would prefer to be gone by the mid-day meal if we can manage that. The tugging isn't very strong at the moment, but it won't be long before the pressure builds up and becomes painful, if I don't begin moving quickly enough. So, you go hunting and I *promise* not to sneak away.' The latter was said in response to the kat's less than trusting look.

Once Whisper had reluctantly left, with many a backward glance, Dani repaired any of her torn clothing and stitched a few thin straps to her knapsack. She thought about hiding a few gems around her chamber before reluctantly deciding against it, not wanting to offend the Zylphas after all their help. Then she had a relaxing bath, washing her cap of curly hair. Despite being shorn close to the scalp when tricking Varla, it had already grown thick enough to cover her scalp in curls. Dani knew from previous experience, that as her hair grew, the curls would loosen, becoming bigger and bouncier. She idly wondered if she would live long enough for it to touch her shoulders but quickly shrugged that thought away. From now on, she refused to dwell on when she might die but she would concentrate on one foot in front of the other.

Once in bed, she opted to go straight to sleep rather than read, thereby missing Casella's quick peep in and the heavy sigh from Whisper as it jumped up on the bed next to her where it collapsed in feigned exhaustion.

CHAPTER TWENTY ONE

Dani wasn't able to leave as early as she had hoped but she had no complaints to make about the situation. When she had gone to get breakfast, the hall was full, which was unusual as there were no fixed mealtimes, Zylphas going for food whenever they were hungry. After piling her plate high with food, the cooks then handed over a large packet of travel breads, fruit and meat that she could eat as she travelled.

Wiltner came to her with a pack almost twice the size of the now battered one she had had since leaving the ship, yet it was much lighter than hers. Then a stream of people that she had helped, knowingly or unknowingly, followed with various items. Clothing thin enough for the tropical climate was packed away neatly in her new carrier, with a pair of knee-length trews and a cool tunic put on one side for her to change into before she left. Spices, herbs, flour and other foodstuffs were also brought and packed away. Then someone had the bright idea to unpack her old carry sack and they realised that they needed to unpack her new knapsack so as to pack the books, Sam's items as well as the other bits and pieces Dani didn't want to part with.

While they all laughed about this, Dani was led away to bathe again and to dress herself in the new clothing. The fabric was so light and airy she almost felt chilly in the magikally cool air of the hall. When she got back to the main room, her pack was full and two male Zylphas stood by it.

'Dani, we will miss you so much, but we will also remember you in our songs,' Phaemal spoke solemnly as the whole room quietened down to listen. 'We have added clothing, foodstuffs and some medicines to your pack. It has been magiked a little so won't weigh you down. It might even be a little lighter than your old bag. Now let me introduce you, this is Bertal, and this is Pob, two of our best trackers. They will guide you to your destination and keep you safe from harm.'

Dani looked at the two males by her side. Bertal was young, a deep blue face that was full of wrinkles, his double clawed hands trembling a little where they held onto his spear. Pob was more of a turquoise which made his dark, faceted eyes glow out of his face. His face and hands were less wrinkled and firmer fleshed than Bertal's, but Dani saw certain similarities in their features.

'You are related?' she asked them.

'Yes, Lady,' Bertal replied. 'Pob is my sire, my egg was made from his sire.' That gave Dani a clue on how family lines were sorted.

'Is it your wish to come with me? I don't want anyone being forced to come along with me, I don't know how far I am travelling or where I will end up.' Dani felt a little uncomfortable at the thought of these two being made to go too far away from their home.

'It is our wish,' Bertal said, even as Pob gave a brief nod. 'We have not been forced to offer our services to you. We want to make sure you are able to travel in safety.'

Seeing that she wasn't going to be able to leave without this pair as escort, Dani gave a nod of acquiescence to them and those around her surged forward to say their personal goodbyes.

Despite a pleading glance at Phaemal, this continued for most of the morning. Before she left Dani was handed a full plate of food to eat as Whisper joined her to eat its own plateful. Once the food had gone, the two guides stood and led her away from the hall, down a twisting passage and out into the heat. The move was done so swiftly and so smoothly that they were away before anyone noticed or could cause any more delay.

After only taking a dozen or so steps away from the Zylpha compound, Bertal told Dani to look behind her. When she did so, she felt her jaw drop in astonishment. Even as she watched, plants grew and intertwined together, not only covering the entrance to the compound but beginning to hide it completely. The beginning of the pathway was covered in ground covering plants, hiding their first steps of the next part of the Healer's journey. A moment or so later, there was no evidence of the compound at all. With a sense of wonder, Dani looked at her two companions.

'How will you get back?' she asked, a little anxiously.

'Don't worry, lass,' Bertal answered. 'We can always find the right pathway home.'

With that, the four beings walked away from the Zylphas, not knowing if any of them would return.

Dani had forgotten just how hot and humid it was outside the cool air of the hall. Her new clothing helped to keep her cooler than she had been in Sam's shirt, but the air was heavy and damp. She was glad that the two males were with her as they found pathways between the huge trees and the other massive foliage as well as the smaller things that grew only to trip her up, or that is what it felt like. They stopped more frequently than Dani would have thought to do, making sure that everyone ate a little and drank a lot each time they did.

By evening, even the shadow kat was showing fatigue. Bertal found them a place to camp and Pob started a small cooking fire. Dani opened her pack to remove some of the foodstuffs and gave a gasp at the flash of red and gold from further in her bag. Setting her jaw, she removed all the various meats, cheeses, flour, spices etc that had been put in there – twice as much as she remembered receiving – and took them over to Pob, who set about putting cubes of meat, vegetables and fruit onto some thin metal sticks before putting a covered bowl of mixed cheeses into the fire's embers.

Once she had done this, she marched back over to her knapsack and began unpacking the whole thing. Her precious gifts from the ship were still there; the male clothing from Lady Constance, the gems and gold she had tried so hard to repay kindnesses with but always seemed to find their way back to her, her tool wallet had been refilled and the needles and fishhooks sharpened, her map of some of the world was still there but now had further places she had travelled drawn in fine detail making her gasp in delight, her books were all safely tucked in at the bottom of the sack, giving it a firm base to stand on. The gifts and clothing had filled her old bag, but in this much larger one, she found lengths of fabric in various colours. There was a long pouch for her to sleep in, as thin as gossamer to keep her cool in the heat but would also be warm when it got cold. Another book, full of the stories told by the Zylphas every evening, had been added along with more clothing. Her weaponry had been sharpened and her holsters and belts oiled and polished. Lastly, were three narrow lengths of heavier fabrics, in shades of brown, to wrap around her throat and completely cover her slave collar.

Feeling overwhelmed, Dani untied the material that she wore around her throat and was beginning to fray and wrapped one of the new scarves in its place. This fabric, although thicker, was nonetheless a lot cooler to wear. If a few tears at the generosity showed to her fell, neither of the males commented on it.

Sitting around the fire as the light dimmed, Bertal finally asked about what was to happen next. Dani, listening to the whining of invisible insects as they hit the opaque covering over the three sets of bedding, thought about where she needed to go and how urgent it felt.

'Right, so, I was a slavey, as you know so I am not expecting to live very much longer. I know that I am some kind of magikal miracle, but I cannot allow myself to hope to live. If I get that hope in my head, it will freeze me every time I am tired or ill, which happens often.

'I have a compulsion that is tugging me in that direction,' she pointed out where she was being guided. 'I feel it is important that I get there, the sooner, the better. Unfortunately, I need to balance speed with plenty of breaks for rest and food. When I first met Casella I had just killed a woman who was threatening my friends. This gave me a lot of energy and an ability to move faster and rest less. Spending time with you was necessary and a pleasure but it means that my energies have faded back to my old levels, maybe even a little bit less. If we have to stop before I reach where I want to go, I would like you to set me under a tree, so that my being can become one with the earth again.' Finishing what she was saying, the Healer shrugged and ate more of the meat off her skewer before taking a long drink of the cooling fruit juice Bertal had made earlier.

'Alright, Lady,' Bertal said. 'I know there is a portal over there, it is only a small one and unmanned but we won't have any trouble going through it with a kat.'

'What about you males coming back though?' Dani said, worriedly.

'Don't fret, lass,' he grinned. 'It is manned on the other side. No-one thought to man this side as us Zylphas rarely leave our lands, but we do travel further into the FreeLands occasionally, although usually by boat. We will stay with you as long as you need us.'

'What about your Change?' Dani asked. 'I know you are young, Bertal, but your sire isn't. What if we are travelling so long that his time draws close?'

'I can speak for myself, lass,' said Pob, virtually the only thing he had said all day. 'There is another song Bertal can sing if I reach my time away from home. I may not pass on my essence, but it would harm my spirit more if my honour was besmirched by leaving you while you needed us.'

'Huh,' Dani said, disgruntled. 'You do know we will be having this discussion again, don't you?'

Both Zylphas laughed but didn't make a verbal response. Instead, they began packing away all the foodstuffs as they were no longer needed, put out the fire and washed hands and faces. Dani followed suit, making sure that her knapsack was tightly sealed before shuffling into her pouch, laying her head on the strangely comfortable pack and fell into a deep sleep.

The two males exchanged a wry glance before getting into their own sleep sacks.

'Do you think we will win this argument, Pob?' asked Bertal.

'No,' grunted Pob and there was silence from the three until morning, apart from Pob's loud snores.

◄◆►

It took another four days to walk through the huge and heavy foliage. When it began, at last, to disappear Dani thought her eyes were playing tricks on her. Huge trees slowly became shorter and thinner, as did all the other growing things. The animals and insects also began to change, certain things being seen less and others beginning to be noticed. The kat brought a fowl back that was only a little bigger than a goose Dani had seen, which provided lots of meat for the four of them. It still only made a meal and snacks though as Dani was already needing more fuel to keep moving even as she walked less.

Coming out of the overwhelming forest of huge growths seemed to ease some of the intense heat. After walking a little way further on, Dani's hair that had lain flat against her head soaked with sweat since leaving the compound, began to dry and resume a little of its bounce. Bertal kept an eye out and the next time they stopped, made sure that it was by a stream. It was a little early for a complete halt, but Pob agreed that they could stop early and still reach the portal by mid-afternoon the following day.

Using the time wisely, a larger fire than usual was built and then, one by one, they went and bathed before washing their clothes and putting on fresh ones. Dani had been impressed at how the Zylphas fabric managed to slick off the sweat and body odour as they were worn but she was even more impressed with how quickly and easily they became clean. Taking a fresh set of clothing with her, she walked over to a dip in the stream bank, shaded by heavy bush. Once she had washed and dried, she dressed in her new clothes before bending and scrubbing the ones she had worn before. Leaving her things to dry over the bushes, she went back to the fire with a slight shiver. Combing her clean hair by the fire ensured it dried quickly and, not much later than usual, they ate and settled down to sleep.

Dani slept, that is. The two male Zylphas shared a worried look. The bathing had done a little to restore Dani's flagging energy, but

209

she had already lost some of the weight she had gained when staying at the compound. Although she was setting the pace and only slowing down marginally, Bertal determined to slow it down further and agreed with Pob that they should look to trying to stop near running water or even ponds every time, just to try and help a little. Taking a last walk around, Bertal collected herbs and fresh vegetables for the following day. He piled up some more fuel for the fire and slid into his sack to go to sleep.

Pob nodded his thanks to the shadow kat as it arrived and dropped a young goat at his feet. Working quickly, Pob gutted and skinned the small animal, giving the offal to the land as an offering. The kat took the head away as its portion and crunched happily away, out of sight. Pob then wrapped some slabs of meat in certain leaves and buried them deep in the fire's base. On a large frame over the fire, he laid other pieces of meat as well as more that was cut into chunks in a cooking pot of water, herbs and vegetables. Then, satisfied that these would all cook gently through the night, he went to his sleep sack and joined his companions in slumber.

Dani woke up to the most wonderful scents, her stomach rumbling loudly. Bertal laughed at the noise, carefully not mentioning that his own stomach had sounded even louder when he had woken. Pob shook his head at both of them, sending them off to bathe while he put the finishing touches to breakfast.

By the time the other two returned, they had plates full of thin slices of meat, slices of red and yellow vegetables, a cooked egg each and some pieces of travel bread. Dani kept an eye on more of the cooking bread while Pob went and washed, then they all ate until satisfied. The rest of the meat was either stuffed into travel breads or wrapped in the large leaves and the cooking pot had a lid firmly set on it so that they could carry it to eat later.

Making sure that the area was left clean and free from as much of their presence as possible, they left and began the last leg of the journey to the portal.

Both Zylphas had noticed that Dani was still tired, despite her longer night's sleep. They didn't know human skin tones well enough to recognise the greyness that was beginning to bleed into the flesh of her face and hands. They did notice the way her skin was beginning to swell underneath her eyes though, as well as her occasional stumble as she walked.

Even so, despite Dani's slower pace, they still reached the portal in daylight. This one was almost invisible to the naked eye, just noticeable from the corner of the eye but disappearing when faced head on. Looking at Whisper, Pob gave his chin a jerk in the portal's direction. Giving a huge put-up-on sigh, the kat moved until Dani rested a hand on his ruff. Bertal held onto her pack and Pob held on to his and they marched through into a new land.

CHAPTER TWENTY TWO

The heat immediately dropped as they stepped through the flicker of energy. Instead of the heavy, moist atmosphere in the land of the Zylphas, it was fresh and even a little chilly. Before Dani could reach into her pack for a jacket, the clothing she was wearing seemed to become thicker and soon warmed her up. It seemed that the Zylpha material could regulate itself in both hot and cold temperatures.

They were on a scrub of grassland and the gnomes at this side of the portal scrambled at the unexpected arrival of the four, rushing to make sure the small group were alright after travelling through the portal without professional help. The gnomes all muttered and glared at the shadow kat, obviously not seeing it as a professional. The huge kat eventually gave a yawn of disdain, showing off its yellowed fangs and the gnomes shut up very quickly.

When they demanded to know where the group were going, Dani pretended not to understand what was being said while the Zylphas spoke about trade in their own tongue. The gnomes understood perhaps one word in three, but they knew what the word trade meant so began threatening, and demanding, a bribe. Eventually, after a suitable payment from Pob, the shadow kat was allowed to lead them away.

This was a good job as they had only just got out of hearing range when Dani exploded in anger.

‘They are a disgrace,’ she stormed. ‘Did you see their clothes? Even though they didn’t expect us to come through, they had no reason to be so slovenly. I have met many of these portal keepers in my travels from over half of Yerat and I have never met a bunch of them so awful. And they were so rude to you, why?’

‘Calm down, little one,’ Bertal grinned. ‘They thought you did not understand what they were saying so spoke at us as they usually would. Some gnomes can be prejudiced against those who don’t look like 'em. Don't you be worrying about it, I ain't. What is important is that they aren't. Important, that is, and the bribe was easily affordable. Don't waste your anger on something so trivial, lass, save the emotion for something much more worthy.'

Dani stalked off, muttering under her breath, and the two males followed meekly behind, making sure to hide their curiously triangular smiles. Unlike the other portals, this one didn't have a town grown around it, so they hiked just under two miles before finding an inn. When she saw the dilapidated state of the building, Dani gave a growl of frustration that would have done the shadow kat proud. Whisper shot a startled look at her and the Zylphas moved to open the door, trying to muffle their laughter. Dani walked past them, snarling as she went. 'I can *hear* you, you know!'

At this, the high-pitched laughter exploded out of the Zylphas with an *ee-ee-ee* and everyone in the tavern turned around at the sound. Seeing strange magikers, the scowling man behind the counter thrust his thumb towards a door set in the side of the room. Pob led the way, followed by Dani and Bertal, the shadow kat moving behind, invisible to all.

'You freaks can go in there, but you can leave the woman with us.' The comment came from a huge, black bearded man, who moved forward to block Dani's egress. Before he could grab her arm, as he intended, however, a low growl echoed around the room, seeming to come from every direction.

'What the…?' the drinker spluttered as he was pushed back hard enough to slam against the bar.

The kat slowly became visible and the men; who had moved aggressively to take Dani by force, now tripped over themselves to get back against the bar and act disinterested. They were also determined to disassociate themselves from the original speaker but needn't have worried as Dani and the Zylphas ignored them all and walked though into the magikers part of the inn. Whisper waited a moment, snarled at the crowd again then turned away and followed its friends through to the other room.

Looking around her at the room set for magikers, Dani was dismayed. She was used to the disguises that magik gave to both people and places, but this broken down area was not an illusion but lack of care or interest. She looked at Bertal and Pob, expecting them to shrug off the state of the room as normal, but she saw her own dislike echoed in their features as well as some surprise and a lot of worry.

'Is it always like this here?' she asked. Both Zylphas shook their heads emphatically.

'No, never before has this place been unwelcoming to magikers. It has never felt as angry. I think we need to leave as soon as we can, without eating or drinking anything they try to give us. Whisper? Can you get us out of here without them knowing?' Pob spoke in a low tone and with some urgency. The kat gave a nod of its heavy head, grabbed hold of Dani's hand carefully. Bertal and Pob held onto her shoulders, one each side, and they saw the room fading away, just as the door began opening to the barkeep holding a crossbow. By the time the bandit had entered the room fully, followed by some of his cutthroats, the place was completely empty. The thugs scratched their heads in frustration and worry at the lost victims.

Dani and her friends were transported far enough away by the kat that only a faint shimmer of light glowed from the inn. Leading the way, the kat headed away over some fields to the side of a small stream. There they set up a camp without a fire. Luckily they had plenty of cooked meat and vegetables, travel breads, cheese and fruits to last for the next day or two. The sleeping pouches meant that, even though the weather was a lot cooler than before, they were all cosy enough not to need an open fire. There was no conversation between any of them as they ate and settled down. Bertal had tried to sort out a watch rota but a snort from the kat decided them against it. As Dani's eyes closed in exhaustion the last thing she saw was the kat, sprawled by the fire, head up with eyes and ears alert to all sound and movement.

They all slept restlessly, even Dani, so all woke early the following morning feeling heavy eyed. The lack of fire was felt as it was a chilly and windy start to the day, so they ate and packed as quickly as possible before setting off in the direction Dani's intuition guided them. The two Zylphas used personal magik to look a little more human, although their skin colour was still a little unusual. The kat took its invisible form and Dani made sure to wear a hat pulled down low as well as a jacket done up at her neck, covering the scarf that hid her slave collar.

The road they followed was well travelled and, despite the disguises, the males were obviously magikers of some sort. The people moving in the opposite direction sometimes stopped and stepped off the roadway completely to avoid the small group, sneering as they went past. Others made various signs to ward off evil, many not seen by Dani since Bisra. A few spat at the ground when seeing the group. After an hour of this, Pob led them off the road when it was clear in both directions, taking them away from the concentrated hate.

Stepping down through an empty ditch and through a gap in the thick hedge meant they were out of sight of the road when a clattering of hooves and the jingling of bits had them realising that they had left the main drag just in time. Peeping through some leaves, Dani saw a group of liveried horsemen going rapidly past, with patches denoting that they belonged to the Prefecture of the Shining One. Stifling her gasp, she moved her head down slowly, so as not to catch anyone's interest. Bertal widened his eyes in query, but she shook her head and kept quiet and still until the riders had gone past and the sound had faded off into the distance.

'What is wrong?' Bertal hissed, once the sound had died away.

'The Army of the Shining One,' Dani gasped, struggling to draw in an easy breath. 'I had thought I was safe here in the FreeLands, I never expected to see any of them again.'

Bertal and Pob exchanged glances, confused.

'You shouldn't be seeing them here, lass.' Pob said. 'The last time I came through here, I was about Bertal's age and there were no Shining One adherents here. I have no idea what has happened in the meantime.'

There was a rustle of sound behind them, and they all whirled around, shocked that anything could have got close to them without Whisper's intervention or warning. Their shock wasn't lessened when they saw a group of winged humanoids there. Some hovered on their varied coloured wings, some stood in seeming casual poses. What made Dani's eyes bug out was seeing two of the creatures riding around on Whisper's back. Each being stood at various heights up to four feet tall, varying a little each side of that mark. Dani had seen other beings like these, admittedly a lot taller, on her travels so felt inclined to trust them, especially seeing how the kat was reacting. The Zylphas weren't quite as sanguine, however.

'What do you want, puck,' Bertal demanded, losing his human visage.

'Why, nuttin' from ye, sor,' said the puck standing directly in front of Dani. Sweeping his hat off and bowing low at her, he continued. 'If this is the Healer who we've all bin hearing about though, well, I would be welcoming ye and takin' ye somewheres safe away from them Shining idjits.'

'You tricksters like to cause trouble,' Bertal grumbled. 'How do we know we can trust you?'

'Again, *you* can't be trusting us, sor, but the lady has our promise of safe passage. My life is forfeit if I be lyin'.'

At that, both Zylphas relaxed. Dani stood, looking confusedly from one group to the other.

'Would someone like to let me know what is going on?' she asked, mildly.

'That we will do, lady, but let us be leaving this place first. Too many sets of spyin' eyes 'n' ears around here, for my likin'.'

'Yes, and most of them are yours and your kinsmen,' Bertal continued with his grumbling.

'Enough, Bertal,' Dani said, then turning to the puck, asked his name.

'I am known as Felse; I am the son of the head man of our pack.
Word of your arrival has come before you. We have been watchin'
the roadway for a couple of weeks to try and get you before the
damn Shiners do. Before we carry on with the conversation, I
suggest we leave here quick foot.'

With that, he flew upwards a short distance in the air, spun around
and led the group over the fields to a copse of trees away in the
distance. As they got closer, Dani saw the shimmering air that told
her of a magik shield. Once they stepped through the covering
magik, she realised the place it covered was much bigger than
expected, and homes were built into the above branches of the
living trees. More of the pucks came fluttering down from the trees
to greet the strangers. Whisper was petted and stroked by everyone
it went past and Dani found herself grinning at the way it preened.
The Zylphas weren't as happy as the strutting kat, but much of
their wariness had lessened.

As they got closer to the centre of the group of trees, an older puck
stepped forward. He was still a small man; his wings held very
little sheen, his hair grew in three tufts; one at the top of his
forehead and the others just above each of his sharply pointed ears.
He grinned broadly at them all in greeting, his three fingered hands
folded over his paunch.

'Welcome, welcome,' he boomed out, making them all jump. 'My
name is Feldor, and I am headman here. We were told you were
coming this way and thought we had better meet up with you, to
prevent any problems with those Shining folk. It's good to see that
you met up with my son. Come in, have something to drink and
rest a little before we eat.'

Dani looked at the two Zylphas and saw their nod of agreement.
Accepting the invitation with a smile, she then followed the
headman to an open platform, and he began turning the wheel to
take the non-flyers up to the homes level. Even though Whisper
chose to make its own way up, there was still a bit of weight on the
moving platform, but Feldor made short and easy work of the
journey.

Once above, the group went into a meeting room, large enough for them to sit comfortably. Large jugs of fruit juices and water were brought, along with hot tea and biscuits, and they all relaxed at last.

'The platform and the tree houses remind me of my friend, Nobby,' Dani broke the comfortable silence.

'The wood gnome?' inquired the puck. 'He's a good fellow, and a distant relative. So you've met him, have you?'

'I have,' Dani replied. 'I wasn't able to stay as long as I wanted though.'

'We've heard much about your journey and will gladly provide any help or goods you need while you are in our lands. You must be careful though, some o' them Shiners aren't nice.'

'No, they aren't.' Dani left a brief pause. 'So, what are you going to do about it?'

'Do? What do you mean? We don't need to do anything; they'll soon move on.'

'Move on? You must be joking! The Shiners, as you call them, don't move on unless somewhere is made too dangerous or cost-effective to stay. Believe me, they will not easily leave a place they want to keep, they will just bring more people over, a few at a time. When they feel they have enough of their own people here, they will begin making rules against magikers to keep humans "safe", adding more and more until they begin to completely oppress you. Eventually, in a much shorter time than you would think possible, they will have taken over and all the magikers who live here will be enslaved or dead.'

'Come now, pet, it can't be that bad.' Feldor started to say.

'She speaks truth, Da, we been tryin' to tell ye but ye ain't been lisnin' to us.' Felse spoke up. 'Widder Clangeene has been told by her new landlord that she mustn't be feeding and caring for the grindylows that live in the Barth river as flows by her house. Ma Clangeene has seen over fifteen generations of grindylows born and bred, hand fed more than a few of them over the years and buried more than a fair few more. She's now been told she has to stop doing anything with 'em or she will get a huge fine that will end up with her place being forfeit. If'n she carries on after that, she'll be sent to the Punishment Square.'

'What?!?' If Feldor's voice had been loud before, it boomed even louder now. 'Who do these foreigners think they are? *This* is one of the FreeLands, not one of their consortium or compendium thingies.'

Feldor sat silently for a moment, brooding, thinking hard and making plans. Then he looked up and gave his son a quick nod. 'You, my boyo, I want you to go round our pack here and ask everyone if they have any information about these Shiners. Send messages out to all the magikers, land wide. Tell them we will meet at the Stone Circle at midnight, bringing anyone who has been affected by these invaders. Let them know that the Healer is her, then we shall see. Go, now, son, as quick as you can.'

Felse left hurriedly and the time until the main meal was taken up with chats about the journey so far, questions about what Bisra was like for magikers etc. The food, when it arrived, was glorious with plenty to choose from as there were a variety of dishes set out, all with different things to eat. Each time a plate cleared; it was replaced with a full one. As the whole village came to eat, the talk became more general and new information was exchanged between them all.

After the evening meal, Dani found herself beginning to droop. A few minutes later she was led into a multi-bedded sleeping chamber where she gratefully curled up on the short bed offered and was asleep before the door shut. Whisper had followed her in and laid himself down on the bed next to hers at first but eventually had to get off and lie on the floor because of the shortness of it.

While Dani slept, Feldor questioned the Zylphas more, wanting to know her health and needs. He was also told the story of how the Zylphas had met Dani and that there had been Shiners there too. Realising just how close the bigoted people were made both groups of people frown.

'It looks like we need to get ourselves a better communication system and *use* it.' Feldor said. 'Though I am not sure how or in what way.'

'Ask Dani when she wakes up,' Bertal suggested. 'She has a good grasp of what's going on, she knows lots of different magikers, including an Air Elemental and a Water one. She has also met lots of portal gnomes. Believe me, most folk like her, she has an open heart and shares what she can.'

'She in't perfect, like out of a story,' Pob said, unexpectedly. 'She is stubborn, and she has a temper. She will also give you her last breath. She is a bit of an innocent about some things and not innocent enough about others. She's always quick to offer help but gets confused if help is offered to her. She doesn't realise just how many folks like her, and that's the truth.'

Feldor rubbed his chin and nodded. 'I have already felt her charm, but also her sincerity. What we can help with, gentlemen, we will.'

After this, the conversation turned more general as pucks began arriving with various messages from all over the land.

Dani woke feeling a little more refreshed, the dull aches she had begun to feel all over her body had faded back to an ignorable twinge. After she had washed her face and made her way to the hall, she was offered some fruit she had never seen before and enjoyed the tart but refreshing taste. Once she had drank some water and was more aware of her surroundings, Feldor came to lead them to the Stone Circle.

The way lay over a few fields that sank lower and lower so subtly into the earth, everyone was below the horizon and hidden very quickly from the sight of casual travellers. As they moved along, the pucks sang, danced and flew about in dizzying ways. Although it was a solemn occasion, none of them acted seriously and Dani worried that they didn't understand the seriousness of the situation.

That was until she heard a fluting whistle. As soon as this was heard, all the flyers dropped to the ground. Bertal caught Dani's arm and tugged her down, where he and Pob watched for whatever the problem was. The pucks moved quickly and formed a wide circle, facing outwards and Feldor murmured some words before flinging his arms wide. Once he did that, Dani saw the shimmer before her eyes that she had seen at the copse and knew they were now unseeable by the naked, unmagikal eye.

The group all seemed to be holding their breath when they saw someone riding a shaggy horse from the direction of the portal then go behind a pile of rocks close by. A few minutes later, another man rode up from a different direction and also went behind the stones, which were obviously more of a disguise then they looked as the two men, as well as their horses were hidden from the road and the footpaths. Neither one seemed to care that their voices carried in the night silence and so the magikers heard every word.

'Well, do you have anything for me, Gixt?' One man said, his accent polished.

'Oh yes, yer 'oner,' a rougher voice answered. 'I'm finking vat girl you wus after wus at ve inn a couple o'days ago. 'Er was with them beasty bugs from uvver there,' here the listeners imagined him waving in the Zylpha Island's general direction. 'Dunno wat 'appened vo. Jeg pointed 'em to the room, vey went in, but wen Jeg went in a few minutes later, vey wusn't vere. Gone. Poof.'

'Did you see a collar?'

'No, no collar, sur, but her wus wearin' a scarf 'round 'er neck an' had one o'vey big shadow kat killers wus wiv 'er, like yer sed wud be.'

'And you lost her, you fool? I don't know why I should pay you, idiot.' The first man's tone was icy cold, but the second man was not cowed.

''Ere now, dun be 'asty. Ifn I 'adn't come 'ere an' told yer, yer wudn't know 'er wus 'ere, now wud yer? Besides, You need me to pass yer messages onto the others an' stuff. Can't do it wivout me, can yer?' His voice held both confidence and arrogance, but it didn't last long.

There was a flash of bright light immediately followed by a hoarse scream, then a deep silence.

'You damn fool,' the cold voice snapped out. 'Did you really think I would only have *one* of you thugs passing messages?'

There were a few grunts and muffled curses before the man who had arrived last rode out from behind the rocks, leading the other horse which now held a body. The wind blew hard enough to open the rider's coat and they all saw the badge, denoting a mage's personal messenger, although Dani was the only one to understand the significance of it.

There weren't only the Prefecture's soldiers here, but at least one mage too. This meant that there would be far more of the fanatics of the Shining One hidden within the ordinary people than she had first assumed. Trouble was definitely here.

Charlie had left Nobby and Gilly Flower with mutual respect. He now had a much clearer idea of why Willoughby wanted the girl back. A Healer, by the gods! He had heard of them - who hadn't? - but there hadn't been one in his life. He also realised that the two magikers he had just left held more secrets about this missing girl than they had shared openly, but that was ok. He would find her and ask her what she wanted to do. Nobby had mentioned that she was travelling away from her Lord, not just because she hated him but also because she was dying.

Charlie knew other Hunters and other Blood Hounds that worked for mages on a regular basis. His work with the Army had circumvented this option where he was concerned, which he was very grateful for. He had known of a few children taken to the Mage Academy for training but something about what they went through seemed to change even the easiest, happy-go-lucky youngster into a dangerous person, only interested in their own wants.

All Charlie wanted was money. Not even someone else's but his own pay. Was this too much to ask? If it hadn't been for the machinations of his ex-commander, he would never have taken the job in the first place.

Thankfully, now that he knew Willoughby had lied and used magik when making the contract, it was no longer binding and there was leeway in how he responded. He still intended to find the missing Healer but instead of automatically returning her to her Lord, he would be able to ask her if she wanted to go. If she said no, not even a Lord who had been mage-trained could demand recompense and Charlie would happily forgo any extras or bonuses promised just to finish with the whole mess.

His plan now was to find the girl, find out her wishes then go back to Mertam and collect his fee from the Guild. When he gave Willoughby either the girl or her decision, perhaps he would be lucky enough to see the woman in the yellow dress again.

Whistling cheerfully, Charlie stepped out, more than ready to finish this job and then find the lady in yellow.

CHAPTER TWENTY THREE

The magikal folk moved out again, once the scouts following behind the mage gave the signal to allow them to move. This time though, they made very little noise, speaking in whispers or flying quietly up and down the line with messages. There were scouts moving ahead but also, set in a protective ring around the group, warriors and bowmen who kept a wary eye out for trouble.

It took a little time for them all to reach what looked like a small group of ruined buildings and rubble. There was a narrow gap between two huge stone slabs that had a monstrous male and female stone figure carved either side of the opening. These stood about fifteen feet tall with heads that looked similar to a shadow kat, but which sat upon muscular human bodies. A scabbard holding a large, curved blade was carved hanging from one hip while on the opposite side was a tall spear with a heavy blade held upright by strong, muscular arms.

Dani stepped closer to look at the marvellous etchings that were carved decoratively into both the weapons and clothing. She stumbled back with a cry as the statues slammed their fists to their chests and dropped to one knee in a smooth movement, ending with them both offering up their spears to her in supplication. Dani heard a gasp from behind even as she stood frozen in front of the kneeling guards, afraid to move.

'Well, lass,' Feldor said, awed. 'I haven't seen the Guardians reacting like that for more years than I can count. T'is a great honour for you, girlie. Place yer hand on their shoulder an' thank 'em for their service. They and their kin have been cursed to stand yere fer centuries, protecting every being that asks for their help, unable to say no.'

Dani turned and acknowledged Feldor's words before she turned back and walked forward. She stepped between the two kneeling

Guardians and laid a hand on either shoulder beside her. Bowing her head, she whispered her thanks for their long, brave service and then asked for the blessing of their gods and/or goddesses. Those watching, who hadn't seen it before, were surprised to see Dani's signature black lightning shoot and fizz from her body and hands and run and play over the two cursed magikers. With mouths open in shock, the crowd saw that as the lightning ran over the stone bodies, the surface began to crackle and make explosive snapping sounds. Crevices ran across the Guardians bodies, weapons and clothing until, with a bright explosion of light, the statues exploded.

Eventually, after quite a few minutes of blinking and wiping stone dust and tears from their eyes, the group of magikers could see enough to have shouts of amazement echoing up and down the line. There, on either side of Dani, knelt two living beings. Instead of bodies and heads made of stone, these were now flesh and blood and fur. The kilts around their hips were of a heavy cloth while the scabbards were of tooled leather. The spears had metal blades, decorated with runes and scrolls etched into the silver blade with a thin copper wire attached firmly to gilly tree shafts.

The Guardians stood and looked down on themselves in dazed surprise. Then they looked at each other, amazed at their true aspects showing for the first time in living memory. They both crashed down onto their knees again, tears of emotion running down their faces. Many in the crowd joined them on their knees even as cheers and congratulations showered down upon them and the Healer.

Dani stood awkwardly, not knowing how to respond. The Zylphas and Feldor were among the first to notice and moved forward to usher her through the narrow stone entrance. Feldor stopped to ask if the two giants would keep watch for danger and both creatures gave a solemn nod of acquiescence.

'I'll send out scouts around the Circle, to help,' he continued. The Guardians both shook their heads and stood. One closed her bright orange eyes for a few seconds before both of them made their salute, smashing heavy fists to chests twice. Crashes could be heard from all around the sacred Circle and Feldor gaped.

'Well, I'll be…she's awoken *all* of ye?' He struggled to imagine the power it would have taken to wake up the fifty-eight Guardians, scattered around to protect the magik place.

The silent giants tilted their heads, not quite agreeing. The head puck stood and thought before giving a quick nod to let them know he understood the differences between what he thought had happened and what actually had.

'Yer mean she asked your goddesses for their blessin' an' they heard?' he asked.

Again, there was a long look followed by a slow nod. With that, Feldor scurried to catch up to Dani and the rest, patting one strongly muscled knee as he went past, which was as high as he could reach.

As the line of magikers went through the entrance, they gawped at the Guardians. Instead of being carved from rock and looking virtually the same, there were now more obvious differences between them.

The one to the left who had responded to Feldor's comment regarding scouts, had a striped head with large, orange eyes. There was a broad ruff of orange and cream striped fur coming from the top of her scalp, down over her shoulders and a narrow stripe down the centre of her back that disappeared into her kilt. A tail appeared from a slit in the kilt material, waving about in pleasure. Pointed ears sat either side of the strip of fur on her head, pointed with wisps of fur growing from the extreme tips to make her seem even taller. Long, white whiskers completed the cat part of the picture. From the neck down there was a tanned and heavily muscled body with a double row of nipples – six in total - narrow hips wrapped in a vibrant blue cloth and strong legs that led down to clawed toes. Wrists and ankles were supported by beaten silver cuffs and a heavy torc lay flat around her throat and upper chest.

Both Guardians had a flat muzzled face with a split upper lip that allowed deadly fangs to flash whenever they drank, ate or washed themselves with their tongues.

Her partner's fur was of black and white patches although body shape and musculature was very similar. His eyes were of a vivid blue. His kilt was a vibrant red, denoting that he was from a different family than his partner. His decorative cuffs were of beaten leather and he had only two nipples on his broad chest. He found himself wondering if the goddess's blessing would mean they could now breed again as a people. He flicked his glance sideways at his partner, catching her glance as she did the same. Both faced forward again and smiled almost imperceptibly, satisfied. Even if no kits were forthcoming, they were both interested enough in each other to try. They stood still, alert to every sound and movement, linked to their squadron through their mind magik and trying to get used to having the use of their senses again after more than two hundred years.

Around the Stone Circle, protecting those within, especially the Healer who had broken the curse that had kept the Guardians frozen in their stone bodies, there was exultation. The Guardians were all connected, mind to mind, so could feel each other's emotions and rejoice. Not only in their own release from their personal stone prison, where they were still able to see and hear but were trapped, but in everyone else's release and pleasure. Many minds were thinking of pleasure – of sex, of hunting, of the taste of blood bursting into the mouth – but their vigilance didn't waver.

As Dani arrived at the arena, she stared around her, awed by the size of the area she was standing in. There was a large depression in the earth that Felse had led her to, the head puck's son preening at his important role. On three sides there rose staggered tiers of grassy steps, allowing all size and shape of magiker to be able to see those below.

As she looked around her, she saw all types of beings arriving and quickly settling down. Most looked at least vaguely bipedal and humanoid, but not all. Some flew or crawled instead of walking.

Those who walked moved on two legs, or four or more. The Healer found herself stunned at how many different types of magikers lived in this one land, never having seen so many different types in one place before. As the last of them came in – a group of graceful human and animal hybrids – Feldor nodded to his son, who flew off and sat with a mixed group of magikers sitting a little behind Dani and the head puck.

There was a lot of chatting and comments being made, even a few challenges being sounded out. Dani wondered how they would be able to get the crowd's attention when a tall man moved to stand by her, raised a curled ram's horn, and blew a long note followed by three shorter ones. As the first note had died, there had been a wave of magik flowing across the huge arena. By the end of the last note, everyone was silent and focused upon the tall man.

'We gather today at the behest of Feldor, King of Triksies, and first among his people. Are there any here who deny his right to speak?' Although he spoke in a normal tone, it was obvious that everyone could hear everything he said. He waited for an answer and when none came, nodded to Feldor and stepped back to stand behind where both Feldor and Dani stood.

'Well met, all o' ye. I have some troublin' news we all need to hear, not just here though, but all over the FreeLands. Before we work out how to send the information out though, there's something else we need to speak of first.

'About a year ago, we started getting a few of them Shiners coming over yere. I dint think much of it, I figured they'd stay a bit, hate the way we wus, then go.' There were murmurs of agreement from all directions.

'Thing is,' Feldor continued, his voice clear to everyone there. 'Thing is, I wus wrong. An' all o' yu's bin thinkin' the same's also wrong.' The murmurs from the steps became louder, irritation making the tone sharper. A short blow on the ram's horn shut everyone up and they sat down, many crossing their arms in annoyance.

'Aye, that's made all on yer angry, or most of yer. But I'ma gonna let you lissen to summan who knows better than we what these Shiners is like. Thissun,' he drew Dani forward, holding her arm gently. 'Thissun is Dani, she's the Healer we's all bin told about on the wind. She int happy at all with how we's sat back so be prepared for a drubbin'. Before her starts though, I got summat to say that might get you all to lissen to her.'

Dani, looking around the stadium, wasn't so sure. There were a lot of disgruntled faces, even some sneers cast in her direction. It was obvious that Feldor could see the attitudes because when he spoke again, his voice had lost a lot of his easy-going attitude and had become sharper and more precise.

'Right. We all know Neera, or of him at least, an' we all promised to keep an eye out fer his friend. This is her. She's good people, even better, she's a true Healer...' Feldor's voice was drowned out completely with the shouts, comments, shock and disbelief. Before he could say more, the ram's horn blew a double note and a second or so later there was a double "*thump*" that shook the ground. Two Guardians that Dani hadn't seen before had leapt over the barrier that hid the Stone Circle and landed on one knee, facing the crowd and staying protectively just in front of her. They slowly stood and, as they did so, all sound died out as the crowd realised that these were not the stone beings but the living Guardians. The male was black and white but with a different pattern of markings to the one at the entrance. His eyes were of a dark brown that looked coldly at those seated. The female was pure black of skin, fur and eyes, beautiful to look at, even to one not of her race. They stood either side of Dani but slightly in front of her, obviously ready to protect her from any in the audience that might want to cause her harm.

There was a stunned silence before noise erupted. Questions, cries of delight, shock and other unexplainable reactions made the air shudder with sound. The Master of Ceremonies allowed it to continue for a few minutes before raising his horn and giving a blow on it.

Gradually everyone calmed down. Standing at the back was a group of hybrids, part human and part animal. One seemed to be their spokesman, he stood tall with a stag's body and antlers rising high from his head.

'We need no more proof that this woman is who she says she is. The prophecy speaks of her.' His voice boomed out, silencing even the quietest murmur. There were nods of agreement from most of the crowd and the Triksies took careful note of those who abstained.

'H-hello,' Dani's voice was low and hesitant but through the magik, all heard her. Catching the eye of a small, wrinkled crone-like figure, who nodded at her and smiled sweetly, Dani felt her confidence soar.

'For most of your enemies, your attitude of sitting back and waiting is laudable, but it just won't work with the Shiners, as you call them. These people are patient and sly. Those that aren't fanatics who will do anything they are told, are power-hungry despots who will kill or order their minions to kill, any in their way. Not just fighters but the young, the old and the pregnant. According to the people who preach to their congregations, *anyone* with magik is an abomination unless they are mages. Anyone who doesn't look human is also an Abomination, including their own young who are damaged at birth.'

There were shocked cries at this. Many magikers had problems reproducing, which made them treasure their own young and the young of others. Even those who had no problems gaining children knew each child was to be loved and protected. Dani waited for the noise to die down again. Then she took a deep breath and unwrapped the scarf from her neck, baring the golden filigree choker with its brilliant gems flashing in the sun. There were calls of confusion and puzzlement. She held up her hand and spoke again.

'I was in an orphanage, a place where children without parents were sent to live together. There wasn't much food, we wore our clothing until we outgrew it, or it fell to pieces. I had my first new set of clothes when I hit puberty.' She saw the confusion in many faces and paused to think how to explain it. Feldor was able to do so for her.

'Ahh, she'm thinkin' of when our kiddoes reach the betwixt stage o' growth. Yer knows, the bit between youngling an' grow'd.' Rapid nods signalled understanding.

'Sort of,' Dani continued. 'For me, it was nearer to being a child than a grown up. My breasts were just beginning to bud, so I was separated from the mixed group of youngsters and made to sleep in a separate wing with the others at my level. When we girls began our first menses, we were taken to bathe, one at a time, in a huge bath, with oils and bubbles. I actually thought I was being given something because I was special.' She gave a short laugh, unable to keep the bitterness out of it. Taking a deep breath, she continued.

'After the bath, a woman came in and cut my hair. She shaved my scalp, saying it was because I had head lice. I was given a huge meal, a tasty fruity drink unlike anything I had tasted before and dressed in beautiful clothing, all ruffles low neckline and a short skirt with a split up the side. Then, the woman who had cut my hair put paint on my face and on my nails before sending me through to the warden. As I turned away from her I saw an expression I didn't understand then. Now I do. It was a mixture of sympathy and contempt.' A glass of water appeared before Dani, whose voice had begun to croak slightly. She gratefully swallowed the cool, clean liquid, revelling in the way it filled her parched body with moisture.

'The warden looked me up and down, sniffed in annoyance at the scars I wore, I had been found under rubble as a toddler. He took me to a coach with closed curtains, sat me inside, locked the door and walked away. I never saw him again.

'The coach moved off and travelled for, perhaps, ten miles. I was let out and a man wearing a red and orange striped robe looked me up and down, glared at the scars before walking me out to a place similar to this. In the centre was a platform, just high enough to make sure that all were able to see who stood there. Then I was led to the back of a short line of children. We were taken up onto the stage, one by one and the men – for it was only men there – began to offer prices on us. Pretty girls and boys went for the highest prices, those with the biggest muscles went next. The rest of us trickled down in price, depending upon what was needed. I was one of the last to be bought. The man who became my "Master", Lord Willoughby, was the only one bidding for me, so he got a real bargain.' Dani paused again. This was harder than she had expected it to be. She felt so far away from that poor, scared girl, shivering in the heat as a hundred men or more ogled her before dismissing her but she remembered the fear making her want to vomit as her body shivered. She drank a little more water and breathed deeply. When she felt ready, she began speaking again.

'I found out later that the prettiest were taken to private houses or brothels, to be used for sex. The muscular ones were taken to the mines, where they perhaps lasted a year. Those who weren't bought were given to the mages of the Shining One. They were experimented on and when they died, blood, flesh and bone were used in spells by the mages. Nothing was wasted.'

'What about you?' Someone called out from the higher seats, voice choked with either anger, tears or a little of both.

'Well, my Master was looking ahead. I was the perfect age for his son to learn his sexual skills on and, when I began dying, I could be used in his own experiments. He had trained to be a mage.' She had to stop speaking as the curses and cries drowned her out. It took a few moments for the crowd to calm down and Dani hurried to finish.

'Not much more now, and believe me, there is a reason for telling you all of this sordid tale. When I was given to Willoughby, he took me straight to the local physician. There I was given my first dose of a drug called Numb. Numb does what it sounds, your senses and emotions are completely numbed. It is addictive from the first dose. After perhaps five years, it kills. Everyone. No exception. While I was succumbing to this first dose of one drug, they gave me another, operated and removed my reproductive organs. This was to make sure that I didn't breed. They also fitted my slave collar.' Ignoring the distress now, she ploughed on.

'So, to the point of the story. If the Shiners decide to settle somewhere, they take it over. From what I have learned from two wonderful men, it starts in the same way. They settle, a few at a time. More move in. For every one or two Shiners that you see there are twenty more that you don't. The fact that they are bold enough already to speak of a Punishment Square means they feel they have enough people here to take you over. They are just biding their time for more of their men to arrive. They have started spreading rumours about magikers to people who aren't magik. Those that disagree with what is said begin to have bad luck and accidents. Those who are isolated – magiker or not – disappear. Eventually, usually within a year, the land you all call home will no longer be yours. I know, it happened to Cryllek, my own home. It no longer exists.'

Dani stopped talking, her own emotions overwhelming her. Felse stood and led her to a seat while Feldor told the Widder's story and called out for more. The next few hours were filled with different stories of the Shiners atrocities that had been going on all over and they all finally began to understand just how insidious the invaders were. There was a break for food and drink, people wandering about in groups or singly as they tried to digest the information along with the food.

Eventually Dani stood with Feldor again, waiting for quiet.

'Any questions?' Feldor asked. A small bear-like creature stood up. Dani had to bite her lip to make sure she didn't offend it. The trouble was, it was so cute. Fur of a rich red, white muzzle, ears, tummy and paws with a black nose, eyes and stripe from forehead to tail end. When it spoke, she realised that it was female, and her tone was both apologetic and determined.

'You say that you were scarred, but I see none. You say the drugs kill after five years, yet excuse me, you are no youngling. You still wear the slave collar around your neck. It's pretty and shiny, I grant you but…' The den mother stopped talking when she saw Dani nodding and smiling.

'Good questions, all.' Dani said. 'I will take them in the order you asked. I am not really sure why I don't have scars anymore, but I think it *might* be because of Healing. I still have some on my body which I don't mind a few of you seeing. Since I found my gift, which was only as I began my escape from the Shiners, everything I know, I have learned through trial and error more than knowledge. I was, well, *am* the longest surviving user of Numb. Again, I think it is the Healing gift. Although mostly dormant while I was fed the drug for twenty years or so, I think the gift kept me alive. I don't expect it to always do so though. Once off the drug, the brain begins to bleed. Eventually, my gift will not be strong enough to fight anymore. Lastly, my collar. The catch is sealed both magikally and mechanically. Unless you are able to manipulate the catch in exactly the right way, it will explode, killing me and whoever tries to help me. As I am dying anyway, I am content just to wear the scarf. Do those answers satisfy?'

'Yes, my dear, they do. I would like to see those scars you still have though.' Cutting through the discontented rumbling, she continued. 'Feldor spoke of spreading the message of the danger of the Shiners. If we are able to say we have seen proof of what the Healer has said, there will be less arguing.'

There was a split second's silence and then Feldor began laughing his booming laugh. 'Aah, and doesn't she have the right of it?' he crowed in delight. 'Magikers bein' whut we are, arguin' is in our blood! Good on you, Minty, for using the common sense the rest of us left at home!'

With this, the whole stadium burst into laughter, the first lightening of atmosphere and shards of hope filling the space.

'Right, now, lissen! We need ideas. One, how do we get rid of these land thieves? And how do we let other FreeLands know of their treachery?'

The whole audience began moving about, changing places and speaking to those they would usually avoid. The talk went on, and the sky began to lighten as still they discussed all they had heard.

CHAPTER TWENTY FOUR

Dani slept poorly and felt as if she had only just fallen into a proper deep sleep when Minty came and gently shook her awake. Taking the yawning Healer by the hand, the Taramag bear led her to a bathing hole. There Dani stripped off and Minty plus half a dozen others, saw the scars she had spoken about, although they were mainly on her back and thighs now. Although much healed to what they were, it was obvious that they had once been deeper, more plentiful and horrifying. There were no gasps of shock, but teeth and fangs were bared and claws flashed with anger. They managed to get themselves under control with a struggle so when Dani finally turned around, all she saw were slight frowns and headshakes of sorrow.

Going back into the wide space of the arena, Dani saw food laid out on grass, stones and tables. Drinks stood to one side, and everyone helped themselves to anything there. Once she had filled her plate, she went and sprawled on the grass near Feldor. The Head puck looked tired but triumphant. He had slept a little but had spent the rest of the time moving among the throng. He was able to bring clarity to confusion, stop arguments before they started, clear up any discontent and more. For all of his jokey ways, most here respected him and the fairness of his actions, especially since becoming the Headman.

Eventually everyone had finished eating and then tidied away the debris. Feldor again stood in the centre of the clearing and asked, to begin with, for any ideas on how to spread news of the danger of the Shiners to the other FreeLands.

Many ideas came forth. Those that travelled from one place to another promised to spread the word to those they met. Others said they would go to the docks and speak to those who sailed the seas, especially the Water Elementals. Others promised to run over the land, warning all those who dwelled there to be careful.

As each of them stepped forward with an idea, Dani looked more and more puzzled. Eventually, Felse spoke up.

'Whut's up, lassie?'

'Well, all your ideas are laudable but none of you have said the one I expected you to.'

'Oh yes?' said Felse. 'And whut wud that be?'

'Well, how did you all hear about me?'

There was a stunned silence before Felse shook his head in self-disgust. 'Oh, bloody stars, we must tell the air!'

There were puzzled looks until Dani explained about Neera, the Air Elemental who would always be waiting to hear from her and about her.

'If I go somewhere a little quieter and call his name three times, he will listen. Then I just need to explain everything to him, and he will make sure that the news spreads. You should still pass on information your way too. Rather tell too many than not enough.' There were chuckles from all sides, but they quietened down quickly.

'Right now, lads,' Feldor grinned. 'Now we have been put in our places an' feel like idjuts, let's get some plans sorted on how to get rid of the pestilential Shiners, shall we?'

As ideas were called out, Dani realised that the spectators who had been sitting in separate groups when they had first arrived, were now more intermingled. Youngsters from various species were playing together and being watched over by carers from all races. She smiled to herself, if nothing else, the Shining One's followers had pulled the whole land together, healing the rifts that had grown from such disparate beings sharing a fixed amount of land. No matter how long the peace lasted, at least everyone here would remember when it happened.

She left the group to go and sit near one of the Guardians. After asking permission, she leaned back against a tree, breathed in and out slowly three times and then began to speak.

'Neera, hear me. Neera, Hear Me! NEERA! HEAR! ME! It is me, Dani. I still live for now, but I need your help. The followers of the Shining One are trying to take over the FreeLands. They arrive slowly and then sneak more and more people in over time. They stir up discontent, set one species against the other and let more of their own come. Slowly they begin to take over the land, killing or enslaving those who live on the edge of groups. Eventually, all magikers are put to death, their screams of agony used in spells for mages.

'Spread the news to all the FreeLands. Join together, watch out for strangers, guard your borders. Now is not the time for petty disputes between yourselves, it is time to fight for your lives! I love you all and miss you. Take care.' With the last words, she slumped down, overwhelmed by the sense of loss she always felt when she thought about her friends from the ship and those she had lost on the way. Wiping her eyes, she sniffed and thanked the black headed Guardian for her company and went back to the planning session.

After another few hours of talking, the magikers began breaking up into smaller groups. These groups would move around the land, going to where the biggest influx of strangers were. Luckily, this was an area of approximately twenty square miles, so no one had to travel too far. Guardians split up between fighting groups, staying with their partner. Dani noticed that each fighting group was made up of different races who had different skills, which should mean that all mage magik should be neutralised.

She noticed that smaller groups of between five and ten left as soon as they were ready. She raised an eye at Feldor, wondering where they were off to.

'They are off to find any who live on the fringes and bring them here to safety. Half the Guardians will be staying to protect the Circle and all those within, we will all bring food for them and the magik will hide the ones who can't fight. That way, there will be survivors both young and old, in case we die.'

Dani shivered at the reminder of how dangerous this enterprise was. Although they all laughed and chattered as they got themselves organised, there was an underlying seriousness to them that only showed slightly.

Bertal and Pom came over, now wearing their own guise, which was a relief to her. Dani was able to see that both were ageing, which worried her. They sat beside her, bending their strange, elongated limbs back on themselves.

'We will be going with the group that will cleanse the portal and the inn. What will you be doing, lassie?' Bertal said.

'I will stay here as the wounded will be brought here for healing and medicine,' She sounded calm, even to her own ears but then she spoiled it by grabbing Pob's claw feverishly. 'You will be careful, won't you? You must be, I don't know your death songs.'

Pob pulled her to him in an awkward hug. 'We will do our very best to stay safe, lassie. I think that Whisper is coming with us, he really did not like the way we were treated when we arrived. With the Guardians flashing messages back and forth, we will all attack at the same time, so they will find organising any defence difficult. Be easy in your mind, little one. We will be moving on with you very soon.'

Dani's smile of encouragement was watery at best, as she waved to everyone as they left. Four of the Guardians stayed with her in the arena, along with many of the youngsters and elderly as well as herbalists, potion makers, spell weavers etc, all getting prepared for the first casualties to arrive after battle commenced.

Among the older generation of healers was the plump, apple cheeked woman who had given Dani courage to speak. The Healer went over to talk with her and found herself smiling back at the old woman who greeted her with a broad grin.

'Hello, my lassie. T'was a good thing yer did, speakin' out. ''Specially when I knows just how nervous you was. You did well though, really well.'

'Thank you. I am Danielle, known as Dani. May I know who you are?'

'I am Nelly, I have lived 'round yere for most o' my long life. It does me good to know that not only are the magikers talking to each other again but also ready to fight together for their land. Now I got some advice for yer. When the patients start to arrive, you will be tempted to rush in an' try an' help everyone, I'm askin' yer not to. Let the other medicine folk play their part, helpin' out where they can. Only when there's folk who can't be helped by conventional stuff should you step in. Or you may use up all your magik an' hurt yersen just when you are needed most.'

Thinking this over, Dani gave a nod, knowing that it was sound advice that she needed to hear. This wasn't all about her being the only one to be able to do the work, but being part of a team where they each had a part to play. Suddenly, one of the others called over to her.

'Oy! Dani! Come an' get some coffee. We will all be working flat out soon enough, let's relax while we can.'

Dani waved to acknowledge that she had heard, then turned back to offer her arm to Nelly. To her consternation, the plump, smiling woman wasn't there. Despite standing close to a close growing cluster of shrubs, bushes and trees, somehow Nelly had disappeared without a sound.

Dani turned thoughtfully to the fire, where she was handed a steaming mug of a milky liquid which tasted nothing like the thin, watery stuff she had drunk before. This stuff was rich and tasty, fragrant with a pinch of spices. Sipping slowly, she savoured every mouthful.

'Have you seen that lady I was talking to?' she began, stopping when she saw the group around her exchanging puzzled looks. 'What?'

'When do you mean, Dani?' asked Albas, a herbalist who had provided lots of blood clotting powder and other items, suitable for minor wounds.

'When you called me a few minutes ago,' Dani replied. 'I was talking to an elderly woman called Nelly, but she seems to have disappeared. I wanted to get her a drink of this, but I can't see her now.' The complete silence that greeted Dani's remarks brought her eyes back to the little group around her. They sat, wide-eyed at her words until, eventually, Albas shook his head at her.

'You weren't talking to anyone, lass,' Albas said. 'We just thought you needed a few minutes to yourself, so we left you until the coffee was ready. When we called you over, you looked a bit dazed, but we put that down to having worked yourself to pieces, setting up the tents and stuff.'

'That's crazy.' Dani spluttered in indignation. 'I was just talking to her, right over there.' As she spoke, she stood up and stalked over to where she had been standing. There, in the mud, were the blurred marks of her boots, still recognisable. Blinking, she realised that her boot marks – and *only* her boot marks - were so close to the shrubbery, there was no way that anyone, especially not a plump, elderly woman, could have stood there too. Going back, she sat down and shook her head.

'I am sorry for saying that it was crazy. I swear, though, I was talking to a woman called Nelly.'

Again, there was an exchange of looks, then Albas asked her to describe the woman. Once more, there was that exchange between them, making Dani's temper rise and get ready to blow.

Seeing her eyes flashing with temper, Albas immediately tried to calm her down. 'Now lass, stop with yer temper tantrums. We are all a bit surprised. See, Nella is our Goddess of the Green Places. Legend says that she appears as an elderly woman with a loving smile when the land is in danger. The fact yer saw her and she spoke to yer, means you and us, is real blessed.'

Dani wasn't sure what to say. She thought that a casual conversation with a Goddess to be extremely unlikely, but this group of people seemed so sincere in their beliefs. She heard a melodious whistle and her head whipped up. There was Nelly, in the centre of the arena, but instead of a short, stumpy woman, she stood taller and wore a beautiful green gown, with a wreath of herbs in her hair. It was obvious that everyone else could see her too as conversations died out and people froze in place as they saw her. Nodding and smiling at all who stared, Nella spun around like a whirlwind, sweeping her arms out. Petals seemed to flow from her hands and the spinning form got smaller and smaller until she disappeared with an audible "*pop*". Those who ran over to check what flowers had been thrown down were soon shouting for joy and relief.

Many of the herbs and medicines had been in short supply, each medical practitioner keeping on hand just enough for a handful of patients at a time. They had already begun trying to work out what wounds would be treated first. The Goddess's bounty had thrown down so many that they could now help hundreds more. Another shout of glee came from the tents. These structures had no walls but an overhead canopy and a few beds only. Now they could see that not only was every tent full of beds with linen and plenty extra, but there was a fully operational operating theatre too. Dani's jaw dropped further and further as she noticed a large metal bin, piled high with fuel, ready to use as a furnace. Miles of clean linen, already rolled into bandages. Gallons of clean water appeared as a new puddle that grew and grew until it was deep enough to be able to use it to boil, clean wounds, linens etc.

As different beings danced in gratitude, arms raised in prayer, Dani took a few moments of quiet to send up her own deeply felt thanks. A light breeze blew the scent of apple blossom past and felt like a gentle hand patting her cheek.

With almost everyone running hither and yon, checking up on equipment and supplies, there were only a few who began the main meal. Even here the bounty continued as fresh vegetables, game and fruit along with herbs and spices sat by the cooking fires. Gradually, as the aroma of the food cooking spread around the camp, they calmed down and began helping each other again, as they had before.

Spooning in a mouthful of venison stew, with chopped vegetables and cherries, Dani enjoyed the explosion of flavours. She wasn't surprised in the least when she found that the pot of stew, enough for perhaps ten people, managed to feed ten times that number, including the huge Guardians. Only when the last person was full, the pot was empty.

As the evening rolled in and the skies darkened, someone began humming a tune. A few notes later, someone began to sing and before long, everyone was joining in. Song after song, all gentle and sweet, filled the evening with the sounds of joy, hope and determination to do their best. Dani went and lay down in her tube bed, listening to the songs as she drifted off to sleep, knowing that this might be the last good rest she would get for a while.

Across the land of Pertrept, the magikers moved as quickly as they could. Many realised that there was deeper magik happening as they all seemed to arrive where they needed to be at the same time, no matter how far away they had started. The Guardians sent mind messages back and forth between themselves and were unconcerned about this so the rest of the magikers shrugged their shoulders and followed their lead.

Each group had a specific job to do, so they began to make ready. The first group, no bigger than fireflies, had volunteered to move through each residence in towns, villages and hamlets, looking for evidence of followers of the Shining One or any mage magic. If they found any evidence they were to mark the places and the people. If, however, they felt that those within had no connection to the plotting, a different magical rune was to be put upon them.

As this group left their mark at one place before rushing to the next abode, the others prepared themselves for the starting signal. No-one was exactly sure what this would be but the grindylows had assured them that they would know when it happened. The smile that showed off the razor sharp teeth of the grindylows made many of the bigger magikers grateful to not have ever tangled with these small, frog-like creatures.

CHAPTER TWENTY FIVE

As dawn began to light the sky, the new people who had taken over the large mill by the Widder Clangeene's farm began to prepare for the day. The millstones were brushed clean, windows were open to disperse any of the tiny particles of flour dust hanging about. The water wheel machinery was greased well, and the brakes removed. None of the very few survivors ever managed to work out what happened next. Or if they did, they didn't say.

What was known was that the young workers, not quite slaves but definitely not respected employees, were led away by harmless looking magikers. Triksies, using all the magikal skills they had, cast fascination spells upon the workers, who followed them out of immediate danger. Then, some of the stronger hybrids barred the closed doors of the mill. The grindylows had mentioned that these huge wooden doors were always opened last of all, to make sure that no one got there too early to disturb his workday. Inside the mill, the tiny gremlins, bigger brownies and other fae gleefully went about disabling machinery and fraying sacks of flour waiting to be collected. Flying up, they sprinkled the dust in the air slowly, adding a bit more, then a little extra, to the layers already there.

The hopper on the upper floor had grease poured slowly down it, and any other sacks near it were opened if they were full of flour and then the young brownies, grindylows, fae and hobs began playing in them. Flour was thrown about, danced upon, wings blew it in all directions. Only a few adult brownies kept the flow of the ground up wheat from floating down in such quantities, even the owner couldn't ignore.

The mill owner, a slovenly man who happily watched all the others do the work as he scratched at his belly, hawked and spat out a glob of mucus, just missing one of the grindylows, if he had but known it. Then, one of the biggest grindylows, still just the size of a woman's hand, jumped onto the open window and let out a loud fart. The mill owner looked up, stunned at both sight and sound of

the strange creature. When he saw the deep green, algae covered
being, with popping eyes and a wet skin, dancing and pulling faces
and letting rip with some of the foulest smelling explosions anyone
had ever smelt, he roared with rage. The grindylow flipped
backwards off the sill, allowing the window to slam shut behind
him, to land with a quiet "*plop*" into the mill pond.

Running past the wheel mechanism, still screaming with anger, the
mill owner's braces got caught on a lever – with the help of a
brownie - which set the stones turning. *Somehow*, as the wheels
turned, a fragment of flint – this time it was a grindylow who did
the deed - found its way between the millstones, right at the edge
of the moving stones. The turning stones chapped against the flint
which then made sparks. These sparks, although not many, were
enough to catch the hundreds of thousands of fine flour dust
particles, causing them to explode with a huge *BOOM!* that was
magikally heard all over the land.

Nothing was left of the mill owner, but most of his downtrodden
workers had escaped harm. Those with Shining One marks had
further calamities though. One or two seemed to have run off and
disappeared, although their trousers could be later found padding
more than one grindylow nest. Another ran straight into the arms
of a huge beast which, although it didn't kill him, frightened him
out of his wits, which never returned. All he ever said was
"antlers".

The true mayhem began, almost immediately.

Servants disappeared from homes and businesses, some never to be
seen again. Shops had goods ruined, cloth nibbled on, flour, salt
and sugar urinated on other foods partially eaten or stolen.
Buildings cracked, split and collapsed; certain Shiners found
themselves being grabbed, pinched, slapped and punched by
unseen hands as they twisted and turned, trying to escape the
stinging pain. Regimented gardens that were full of mage magik
and spells to stay neat were suddenly ripped up and flowers, shrubs
and other things were shredded, and the ground opened up. Water
stopped flowing, or flowed too quickly, damaging land and
buildings. The most worrying thing for most of the Shiners though

was, apart from many missing servants and children, every shrine and temple dedicated to their god, Kintrelle, either collapsed in on itself or was smashed with heavy objects.

The worst retaliation was left to the portal, inn and the mage house.

As the explosion of the mill echoed around them, the slovenly gnomes ran from their bunkhouse, pulling on as much assorted items of grubby clothing that was at hand. As they spilled out, they shouted and pushed at each other, trying to get answers to questions that no-one knew. Suddenly there was another, albeit much quieter - "*boom*" and the portal keepers spun around.

Behind them was a line of magikers. There were hybrids, pucks, hobs and many more. The line began to grow, and the gnomes turned with it until they realised that they were actually surrounded. The foreman gulped a little before he raised his hands placatingly.

'Well, lads,' he wheedled. 'What's going on a'here?'

'We have a few questions, boyo,' said Feldor. 'Why have you allowed yersens to become such a mess? I thought you gnomes were 'specially chosen a'cos a'yourn smart dress and pleasant attitudes. Your bosses really buggered that up, din they?'

'What!?!' roared the foreman, aghast at being spoken to by what he considered a lesser being. 'How dare ye talk aboot us like that? We can cause a bloody ruckus for yer, don't you know? We can get the portals all closed down an' stop a' yer buggers travlin' anywhere.'

'Really, Derkesh?' The foreman felt his heart sink into his boots as he heard the voice coming from behind him. Turning his head, he closed his eyes in horror even as his mouth opened and closed soundlessly as he tried to think of something to say to Bletham, his ultimate boss and controller of the portals, to excuse his actions. After a short pause to gather his few wits, he opened his mouth again to say something, he knew not what, but Bletham held up one warty, clawed hand and slowly looked about himself.

As Bletham took in the state of the portal landing area, he began to frown. He moved forward to check out the gnomes and his expression grew even darker. Still, without speaking, he stepped over to the changing hut. By the time he came back to where his employees stood, he looked thunderous. He noticed that they now looked rather hang-dog and even more untidy, arising from the scuffles caused by the gnomes trying to escape the circle of magikers. Turning, he looked at Feldor and nodded.

'Thank you, Feldor, my friend. I am so glad you insisted I came without warning. We inspected just a month or so ago and this place was thriving with plants, it was clean and polished, and all uniforms were worn with pride. Yet now I see what lay under the mage glamour.' Derkesh gave a start, which he tried to disguise with a cough.

'You seem surprised to know that your bought glamour has its own distinctive scent. All magik has a scent, you fool, as you should have remembered. The mage magik smell is different, more subtle to what you are used to, but it is there, so you conned yourself.' Bletham glared at the small group of terrified gnomes, some now snivelling shamelessly, before he turned to Feldor. 'Leave it with me, my friend, I will sort this out. I will be taking this sorry lot back home and getting a group together to come here and clean up and get everything nice and polished again. This lot won't be coming back, ever. In fact, I think they will be working nothing but body waste jobs for the foreseeable future.'

With that, he gave Feldor a friendly wink before freezing the gnomes with a spell, grabbing onto the foreman and then they all disappeared.

Those left behind felt not only breathless but also disappointed at not having had a fight. Feldor laughed aloud when he heard their grumbles.

'Don't yer be worritin', lads,' he cried, chuckling as he did so. 'We still got the joys of the inn to come!' With a roar, the rest joined in the laughter before it died down and they began moving quickly, but silently, towards the inn.

Whisper had joined this group, without their knowledge, as it had kept to its invisible form. As they got closer to the inn though, it became visible from one step to another. This caused some muttered surprised curses that soon died down to grins and nods.

The shadow kat projected itself in its invisible form, into the inn, checking out who was there. Slipping unseen into the bar room, it saw Jeg, the innkeeper, standing behind the thick wooden table, complaining that Gixt had gone and disappeared, leaving heavy debts behind.

'I wunt 'ave let him 'ave any credit, dun care wut that mage fella said, iffen I'da known 'e wud've runned off.' The man said, angrily. 'It's alright tellin' us we's workin' for the Shinin' One, but I needs more brass than empty promises provide.' He glared around the room at his fellow drinkers. Not all of them met his eye though, not wanting to be caught speaking badly about men who were known use every part of the body for torture, death spells and other disturbing magik.

Seeing their reluctance to speak or even acknowledge the truth of his statement, Jeg sneered at them, his lip curling up at their cowardice. He spat into a spittoon, kept near his feet. 'Feeble, the lot of ya. And wut do ya think that bloody bangin' was? You think that one o' they mages buggered up a spell?'

Before he could say anything else, the door opened with a flourish and a tall man stepped in. He wore the gaudy robes of a priest but without the ridiculous head gear. Although still invisible, Whisper slipped deeper into the shadows, not knowing if the newcomer could sense it.

'Aah, innkeeper Jeg, how nice to see you,' the mage drawled laconically. 'I have spoken with my fellow mages and would like it if you would spread the word that we will begin squeezing this land three days from now. Get all frailer members of your families away if you have to, barricade your doors against Abominations and sit tight until, or unless, we call for your input.'

Jeg's eyes had been moving rapidly from one side to another and he spoke quickly. 'Wut about spies an' that? They could tell the Abominations wut's goin' on.'

'What about them? And which Abominations would they tell? Now, don't be foolish, man, just make sure to spread the word. Oh, and that *bangin'*, as you call it, was nothing to do with a spell going wrong.'

Jeg gave a shaky affirmation to the man's comments, and, with another sneer, the mage swung around, ready to leave. Before he did so, he turned back abruptly to stare in the dark corner where Whisper had been a split second before. That canny kat though, had managed to teleport out as soon as it had heard what was said.

No-one spoke for five minutes or more after the mage had finally stalked out. Jeg eventually broke the silence and told the crowd to pass on the message the mage had just given. Every man there gave a grunt or nod of acknowledgement and used the news as an excuse to drink up and go home to begin doing what had been advised.

Whisper appeared next to one of the Guardians and, touching his leg, managed to convey the information, mind to mind. When Feldor was shown through the same skill what had just happened, he made a split second plan.

'Right, lads an' lasses, listen up. I want some Triksies, Fly-By-Nights and others who can stay hidden, followin' every one o' they that leaves the pub there. Follow them home. Check everyone out, not forgetting to mark those that are Shiners. Through the night, we's goin' ta nick ev'ryone who int with 'em and get 'em safe. Then we will round up the Shiners after, bring 'em here an' we will 'ave a play!'

There were dances of glee and everyone scattered. Feldor, a grey tabby Guardian and Whisper stayed behind at the inn. They had a plan of their own to follow through on.

Many different mages had gone through the land, spreading the word about their attack in three days so, all through the night, men - and a few women - scuttled about, collecting family, friends and more of the Shining One's followers. Small groups began leaving homes to head for the marina, to be able to get boats to other lands. A few groups arrived at the portal, hoping to use that, but it was dark and empty, so they eventually left, cursing the unreliable gnomes.

Near to dawn the first non-Shiners began arriving at the arena. Many were scared and confused, some were angry whilst a very few were nonchalant. Dani found herself telling stories and playing games with the youngsters while some of the older magikers explained the situation to the older humans. The horrified outcry let all the magikers know that these people, at least, hated all they heard.

One plump woman stepped forward with tears pouring down her cheeks. 'I knew something was goin' on,' she sobbed. 'I used to 'ave an old willer tree by the bottom of my garden. Little folk used to play an' swing in its branches of an evening, and there was a Lady that lived within wot wud come out an' sing in the night. A week ago, I 'erd a screaming an' wen I went out, I found the tree dead and black, like it 'ad bin struck by lightnin'. But there was no storm that night, not even rain. I tried tellin' one o' they new mages aboot it, 'opin' 'e would offer to find out 'oo did it. He just laughed an' told me to be careful who I mixed with.' She turned to the others and shouted at them. 'An' all you lot wunt b'lieve me an' now we's 'avin' to 'ide from the buggers!' She buried her face in her hands as she sobbed loudly. Two ladies who wore short frocks covered in leaves and embroidery, came forward and gathered the woman in their arms, leading her gently away.

As her sobs faded in the distance, a strong looking farmer stepped forward. 'I have always been proud to live in the FreeLands. I was born here but travelled the world on a ship. I saw lots of places that were like here, a few that were just for magikers and many that were lands of the Shiners. I was glad to be living in a place where we got on and laughed, drank and played, side-by-side. I was shocked to come back and find we was living in separate groups, which we'd never done before. Now I will fight by the side of those the Shiners call "abominations" cuz if they are evil, I am too.'

There were cheers when he had finished speaking, then the newcomers crowded forward, asking to be put to work. The big man came and stood by Dani, smiling at the hustle and bustle around them.

'Now this is like old times,' he beamed. 'Let's hope it continues.'

'It will if you don't forget,' said Dani, smiling gently. Then her face slackened a little, her eyes flooding with obsidian. When she spoke, her voice was deeper than before.

'Ged, you will keep this land, and others, free of corruption. You will go to other places and spread the news of our success. In doing so, you will find your heart's desire. When the Hunter finds you, tell him of me.'

There was a short pause, then Dani staggered a little, putting the palm of her hand against her forehead. 'Damn, I hate it when I do that!' She turned and looked at the man next to her, her eyes back to their clear grey as she took in his stunned expression.

'Oh dear, I hope I didn't say anything upsetting?'

'No, no, you didn't,' he said, still surprised at the words and dramatic change in her demeanour. 'What you said has helped me decide something that I have been turning over in my mind for weeks. I just didn't expect anyone else to be able to do that, especially someone I have only just met.'

'Neither did I!' Dani said with a grin as she trotted off to see what they wanted by the fires.

Through the night, male and female Shiners had been dragged from their homes and taken to the inn. Although a big building, it filled rapidly and more kept coming. Feldor kicked himself for not recognising sooner all the strangers that had filtered in locally over the last few months. What upset him the most was seeing a few faces he recognised though, not all of them human.

'Nick? What on Yerat is yer doin' with this bunch o' bastards?' Turning to Felse, he raised an enquiring brow.

Felse scowled at the ghoul before answering his father. 'I 'eard 'im plotting with a couple of 'is men about c'llectin' bodies fer the mages. What type, where from an' if they shud still be kickin'.'

'Well, I niver did like you, you two-faced dung eater.' Feldor scowled. Stepping aside from the glaring ghoul, he raised his voice and shouted for the amassed crowd to shut up. As his voice was magikally enhanced, it echoed around the inn and the surrounding crowd.

As soon as they had all shut up, Feldor gave a nod of satisfaction. 'Right, you buggers,' he continued, lowering his voice but using magik to make sure everyone still heard him. 'You came sneakin' in 'ere, to try an' overthrow us. To enslave us. To use us in your mages weird hexperryments. Well, we ain't goin' to take it lyin' down so's you now has a choice. You can leave yere an' niver come back, or you fight us, one on one, and when yer defeated, you leave and niver come back.'

'That ain't fair.' An anonymous voice yelled from the rear of the crowd. 'You lot can use magik agin us, we's only got our fists.'

'Ain't my fault you ain't got power, you stinkin' pile o' crap. An' you gotcher mages, ain't yer? Where are they at? I wonder why they's left yer to deal with this all on yer own?'

There was a low rumble as the prisoners realised that Feldor was right, in the whole crowd, there was not one mage to be seen. The rumble grew louder and louder, finally being understood to be cries from those wanting to know where the mages were.

Again, Feldor raised his voice through magik. 'Enough! They ain't 'ere, they are all holed up in their tower, leavin' you lot to cope by yersens. Now, which of yer is stayin' to fight an' which of yer is going down to the 'arbour to get boats out of yere?'

There was a period of quiet, everyone trying to avoid the gaze of those around them. Suddenly, from inside the inn, Jeg yelled that he was coming out. With some pushing and shoving, he moved to the front of the crowd.

'I int staying 'ere,' he shouted. 'Let me through and I will be off to get one o' they boats.'

Feldor looked at him calmly and shook his head. 'No.'

'What? You said as ow' we could choose to leave. I knew you was lyin'. You can't keep me yere,' blustered the astonished innkeeper.

'Actually, yer will find that we can.' Feldor spoke calmly, ignoring the other's anger. 'We will keep you 'ere a'cuz you are one o' they's who fed information to the mages that led to some of our people either disappearin' or dyin' in terrible ways. Those of ya who we know to have c'llaberated with the Shining One's mages, will be given no option but to stay an' fight.'

Jeg gave a roar and ran forward, expecting to crush the much smaller man, but the puck wasn't there. The Triksy gave a great leap to the side, causing the human to miss him completely. Then, spinning around on one leg, Feldor kicked out sharply with the other, catching the innkeeper a solid blow between his legs. Dropping to his knees, Jeg began vomiting up his food and his ale, clutching at himself as he did so. Feldor stood back and waited. Eventually, Jeg stood up, still clutching his stomach, and shook his head.

'No more,' he choked out, moving forward to shake Feldor's hand. Before he touched skin, he gave a shout and tried to club the puck with a clenched fist as big as Feldor's head. Again, the puck moved with incredible speed, manoeuvring around the huge body and elbowing the human in the kidneys. There followed the worst ten minutes of the innkeeper's life as every move he made was countered and he took heavy blows that much belied the size of his opponent. Finally, bloody and beaten, he collapsed on the floor, unconscious.

'We know 'oo've 'elped the buggers an' 'oo 'asn't. The rest of yer make up yer minds quick wut exit yer want, or we'll be takin' the choice away from yer.' Feldor wasn't even out of breath and spoke as calmly as before. There was a lot of shoving and pushing as various people began lining up to leave.

Half an hour later, those that had chosen to leave without a beating – and who hadn't been involved with the subjugation of the magikers – were lined up and ready to march to the harbour. The rest were standing to one side, shouting curses or crying, depending upon their nature, while their magikal guards looked on.

As time had gone on, more of the islanders had arrived, including a dozen or so of the Guardians. This caused some of the loudest complainants to quieten down a lot. Feldor checked the magikers who were there, choosing people with strong abilities, to march with him to where the mages were staying. After a quick consultation, he took half of the cat-faced Guardians with him, knowing just how helpful their magik would be against the power of the mages.

A group of fae had been keeping a watch on the mansion with its connected tower that the mages called home. A big stone wall with a row of sharply pointed railings that were cemented into the top of it, made the finished size of it almost the height of the fifteen foot Guardians, surrounded most of the property. Large iron gates blocked anyone from entering, different colours shooting up the metalwork letting the islanders know that the gates were spelled against intrusion.

With a nod from Feldor, Felse flew up and cupped his hands around his mouth. Taking a deep breath, he blew on them. His magik turned the breeze from his mouth into a clarion call of trumpets. Still hovering, he called out to the men inside.

'All those within sound of my voice, take note! We give challenge to the mages who have tried, with deceitful actions, to enslave all the magikers in this land to the belief of the Shining One. Come out now, with no trickery, and we will let you leave alive. If you try anything underhanded, we will respond with all you deserve.'

There was a short silence, then a few windows opened on every floor, including at the top of the tower. Someone called out, his voice magikally projected, but it wasn't as melodious as the puck's.

'You are Abominations!' he said, imperiously. 'We, the mages of the Shining One, are the true owners of this land. Leave now, and we will let you live.'

The magikers began laughing loudly. Not only at the presumption of the mage calling out, but at the thought that trained magik would be able to defeat that of the natural world. The mage obviously didn't like hearing the sneers and catcalls that followed the laughter and, with a snarl, he threw a metal object out of his high window.

He didn't have a chance to even gulp when the item reversed its passage towards Felse and flew back whence it came. A split second later and the room and the mage had both disappeared in a pungent puff of smoke. The large explosion removed one of the gates completely, while the other sagged sadly from one hinge. Felse gave a polite little cough behind a closed fist.

'As I said, we will let you leave, if you go quickly. The rest of you? Well, you can join your friend.' With that, he flew down and stood next to his father, who grinned at him.

'Nice speech, son.'

'Learnt from the best, Da,' Felse laughed.

The group, made up of at least one of every type of magiker in the land, stood waiting patiently. Eventually, the front door opened and a small woman, casting many a fearful glance behind her and waving a white bedsheet on a pole, crept towards where the magikers stood.

'Do we trust her, Da?' asked Felse.

'Nope,' was the laconic answer.

A Guardian placed her huge hand on Feldor's shoulder so that she could speak directly into his mind.

*Why does she carry bed sheet? *

'I think she is trying to give the impression that she is here under sufferance and that she is a victim in all this, being forced forward by their magik.'

Are they so stupid that they do not realise that we can smell her magik stink from here?

'Not so much stupid as arrogant, my friend. Dun ferget, accordin'
to they, we are the stupid ones.'

Hmmm.

The magikers watched in silence. Afterwards, Feldor had to admit
it had been a good enough plan apart from a few issues. Magikers
came in all shapes, sizes and genders. Being female did not mean
that they were less than their brethren, therefore, the magikal
community never underestimated anyone because of gender. Not
to mention the magikal scent, along with that of deceit, was
particularly strong, meaning that, for all her scared attitude, this
woman had plenty of power. Felse and the Guardian, took
immediate action the second they saw the woman begin to act.

The female mage stepped forward, with many a spurious glance
behind her at where a small group of robed figures watched quietly
from the huge windows. As she stepped within throwing distance,
she seemed to be muttering something under her breath. Then,
from one breath to the next, she threw a ball of black energy
straight at Feldor with a scream of effort.

'Da!' yelled Felse as he pushed his father out of the way of the
spinning globe of magik. Even as he knocked his father to the
ground, he felt the bite of magik hit him. As soon as it did, he
began feeling nauseous, as energy began sucking out of his body.
Another body, heavier than Felse thought possible, landed on him
and then frantically rolled off his father. He heard a groan then he
heard no more.

Feldor stood up and gave a scream of rage, sending all of his
energy and power into his voice. Windows in the mansion
exploded, showering everyone inside in shards of glass. Three of
the ten mages collapsed, two dying instantly, because of flying
glass. The female had been torn apart by the magik in his voice,
leaving bloody gobbets of flesh in all directions. As he finished,
Feldor collapsed to the floor, struggling to breath.

Air sprites begged their Elemental cousins and the three magikers
were lifted on cushions of air and flown off at maximum speed
towards the Stone Circle. Even as they disappeared into the

distance, the rest of the magikers swarmed through the gates and over the walls. Soon, each mage was surrounded and knocked unconscious by sheer numbers. Their own crafty attempt to knock out their opponents had actually led to their own undoing as the effort of combining the Black Mýste with the spell used had been tremendously taxing. This made their capture easy to achieve. Two mages died in the capture, one by their own hand and one because a Guardian miscalculated their strength and hit too hard. Soon though, all were tied up in ropes that nullified magic, leaving the human mages completely helpless. The magikers then dragged their prisoners to the inn.

CHAPTER TWENTY SIX

Dani had just finished binding up a wound on a child when she felt the coming of the three travelling on air cushions. After patting the small grindylow's butt, she looked up to the sky. The young grindylow skipped off, no worse for wear as his injury had been caused when he played with a group of children, so the damage was minor, although it had momentarily been very painful.

As soon as the cushions of air landed, Dani ran over to see what had happened, her warning shout stopped anyone touching the wrinkled beings laid out for all to see. Without conscious thought, Dani waved her hands as she called for beds, bedding and help getting the three men onto them. She demanded lots of food and drink to keep her going and a tent to surround them and the need to be left alone.

Her focus was so strong that she didn't realise that her waving hands and focused intention had lifted up one of the smaller tents and it flew over and settled down around the distracted woman. When others checked later they found that guy ropes and pegs were set firmly despite nothing seen doing anything. Trays of food and drink made their way over to the tent, as did bandages, hot water, poultices and anything else that might be needed.

Then, as she had requested, everyone stepped away, letting Dani begin her work.

The beds were set in a triangle, with Dani sitting on a chair in the open centre. She started with the Guardian and focused hard, holding his hand and sending black lightning flickering into his body. A few moments later, she released her hold on the Guardian and reached for Felse. Shortly afterwards she released Felse and reached for Feldor. The three men showed signs of being drained by the Mýste, pale and drawn, with sunken cheeks and very little body fat left on them, but Feldor was by far the worst as he had had to wait the longest for Dani's touch.

The Healer moved from one to the other, spending a few moments with them before moving on to the next. Once she completed a circle, she pulled food and drink over to fill up her flagging energy reserves. Then she began all over again. Time went on and the ones outside the tent saw flashes of the black lightning interspersed with balls of blue/white energy bouncing around the tent, both escaping every so often to fly around the camp and sinking into the worst of the injured.

It was many hours later that the flashing lights died down to a much milder flicker before they eventually stopped. Wary, no-one entered the tent for a while, waiting for some sign that it was safe to do so. With a rustle, the tent sides were rolled up by invisible hands and all could see what was inside.

The three men, still very thin but with healthy flushes on the Triksies and with groomed fur on the Guardian, slept comfortably in a deep sleep. Dani had managed to crawl over to a fourth bed and now lay, half on and half off, unconscious from her exertions. Those who ventured closer were horrified to see how skinny she had become from using her ability. Even having eaten all the food didn't seem to have helped.

The crowd worked together and made sure that there was a watch kept on the four inside the tent at all times. Once this was organised, more of the helpers went around the arena, checking out the other patients. The relief and joy of finding some folk originally expected to die, who were now sitting up and asking for food, had laughter, relief and joy rolling out from all directions.

By the evening meal, most of the patients were well enough to watch the other fighting group walking back from the inn. There were many cuts, bumps, bruises and broken limbs but all wore bright grins and there was much joking and laughing among them. The laughter died down when they saw the open sided tent with the four patients, sleeping so heavily inside. Although this subdued the atmosphere a little, it didn't stop the celebration.

For the next few days, while Dani continued to sleep, but the three others began showing strong signs of recovery, the magikers and humans of the land began sorting out a council for the place they all loved, containing one of each species. When it was finished it was found to be too unwieldy, so votes were given to the masses and, very quickly, the council was whittled down to the species that actually wanted to be involved in the planning of laws, and those that were content enough to be called upon when needed for a specific job. There was also a truth-seeker among the hybrids who offered her services when and if she was asked. Lastly, the pledge was given that any hint of corruption would be treated severely. This was given using a blood oath: no-one there would go against it.

There was another vote held, wanting to know who the titular head of the council would be. With no great surprise to anyone, Feldor was voted in by a strong majority, despite his complaints.

'Aah, stop yer complanin',' laughed Felse, enjoying the joke immensely. 'At least this way you won't be sending others round the pole with your inteferin'.'

'I niver interfere.' His father said, indignantly. Then he, too, began to laugh. Felse looked at him suspiciously which made Feldor laugh even harder before he was able to splutter out an explanation. 'Don't you get it, lad? If I am working hard for the council, you are going to have to work harder for the clan.'

The look of utter disgust on his son's face set the older man off again, his laughter ringing from the trees. It was at this point that Dani called out for something to eat and they all rushed about getting her fed that the subject was shelved for now.

It took more than a week before Dani was able to get up and about. Even then, she tired very easily, and her appetite wasn't as healthy as it had been previously. Those people that could go back to their homes, did so. There were work groups sent to the houses the Shiners had used, where many magikal items were confiscated by the Guardians. Other crews then cleaned up the properties. Poisonous herbs were found planted in many of the Shiner gardens, so they were uprooted, and the soil cleansed and turned over before being left fallow until next planting.

Everything was bustle as the island cleaned up after the Shiners, houses were repaired, a new innkeeper found and a different set of gnomes at the portal. Slowly things began to improve…

Even though Feldor expected it, he was still stunned when Dani appeared before him one morning, less than two weeks after the short but specific battle. Feldor turned his mouth down before heaving a sigh after hearing what she had to say.

'Aah, lass, we'll miss you,' he murmured into her hair as he hugged her. Struggling to hold back years, he pulled back. 'I owe you my life, girl, but more importantly,I owe yer, Felse's. If ever I can do anything, let me know.'

'Keep on doing what you have begun here,' Dani said, smiling. 'And don't let anyone know I am going.'

Why not?' the puck asked, confused,

'If you do, they will want to give me a great send-off but, to be honest, I am really not up to that. The Zylphas and I would just like to go as soon as we can, without a fuss.'

'Tell me which way ye're headed, I might be able to help.'

Closing her eyes, Dani spun slowly in a circle, her senses working. Then she stopped and held her hand out. She opened her eyes and looked to where her finger pointed.

Feldor nodded in satisfaction. 'Right. Well, next island ain't very big an' it's fairly deserted of magikers. If you are travelling in a straightish line though, there's a Shiner place over in that direction. Take a left and over there is Belcroft, also known as Dragon's Isle. Much bigger than this place, with lots of smaller islands over the far side that they farm, mostly. It is a mixed FreeLander place, with humans and magiker together. Island's leader is a bloke called Geraint, he's a wolf shifter. Nice guy, married with two grown sons. Tyler is the Harbourtown sheriff and Jake is with Search and Rescue.'

There was much said here that Dani didn't understand but she decided against clarification. Time was moving on swiftly and, having given her word not to leave without the Zylphas, she still had to find them and hope they were able to pack their carry sacks without being noticed. She gave Feldor another hug and a few personal messages to other friends before she slipped out. When she shut the door behind her, she felt a nudge against her side.

'Whisper?' A low purr answered her, so she sank her hand into invisible fur and followed where it led.

She saw that they were heading for a small hut, set away from the other dwellings. When she arrived and went indoors, she had a surprise waiting. Both Zylphas were already there, smiling their strange, triangular smiles. Also there was the old woman who had called herself Nelly. With a joyful cry, Dani hugged the old woman and then the two insectoids.

'Now my lovely,' the Goddess smiled. 'I know you want to slip away so I will make sure that you will be hidden from sight until you leave this land. Feldor was right, my dear, you are heading for Dragon Island, I have given Whisper the way to get there. That is where you will come to rest, at last.' With a beaming grin, she gave the Healer a loving smile and another hug, not seeming to see the flash of sadness that flickered over Dani's face. Turning, she gave the Zylphas both a hug too before stepping back and waving her hands while muttering a few words.

To Dani, it felt as if a cool shower of water had poured over her from head to toe. It wasn't unpleasant though. Immediately it seemed as if the world was a teeny bit less bright and slightly muffled. With a smiling nod, the Goddess disappeared, leaving the others feeling a little bemused.

Shaking her head in befuddlement, Dani grinned up at the two males by her side, and the huge kat sat in front of her.

'Alright, my lovelies,' she said. 'Let's go.'

Moving stealthily, despite knowing they couldn't be seen by anyone, the four of them moved through the town, carefully avoiding anyone else. Once they reached the edge of it, they were able to pick up the pace a little, which they did with alacrity.

By the time evening fell, they were less than ten miles from the portal, so they chose to settle down for the evening by the side of a swift flowing stream. Pob set out his cooking implements as well as items of food, while Bertal and Dani hunted around for firwood. A filling meal of duck, roasted over the flames, along with some round tubers cooked in the embers, followed by a creamy pudding of grain and fruits and they were all stuffed full.

Leaving Whisper munching on its own duck, Dani washed the used plates and things before returning to camp. She lay down in her sleep sack, her mind busily working. Pob was getting visibly younger. Not yet at the danger mark but Dani knew that she must find a way to send them both back home very soon. While her mind was worrying about the problem, she fell asleep, without realising that the Zylphas were watching her carefully.

'You know she will try and get rid of us,' said Bertal. 'We can't let that happen.'

'Stop worrying, boy,' Pob replied. 'We will wait and see what happens . No use borrowing trouble.'

With that, both males exchanged glances of understanding with Whisper, then they lay down in their own bedding.

Meanwhile, Feldor had had a very trying day. Felse had run in, just a few moments after Dani had left, crying out that the girl was missing.

Trying to explain that Dani had left voluntarily had caused confusion, much cross-talking and mix-ups . When Feldor finally managed to get his son to understand that Dani had gone, Felse gave him a dark look of betrayal before storming from the office.

It soon became clear that the hurt boy had not kept Dani's leaving a secret. A few moments later a knock on the door had a group of brownies coming to find out the truth, before complaining that he had been a little underhanded in the way he had kept her going a secret. Before they had finished, two hybrids and a group of Fly-By-Nights had come in, to add their comments in the rapidly dwindling space.

Feldor managed to get rid of the group at last, locking the door behind their departure before the next lot could enter. He wrote out a formal declaration regarding the Healer's departure and had it magically appear in many of the businesses plus the inn and certain homes. Within five minutes everyone knew what had happened and the head Triksy had disappeared until, he hoped, the furore had died down.

CHAPTER TWENTY SEVEN

Arriving at the portal, Dani was pleased to see that it was in a much better state than the first one had been. She didn't know that there had been a spot check a few days before, which had polished up the few areas that had begun to slip.

When they tried to pay for their passage, it was very firmly turned down. It hadn't been because of Whisper this time, it was simply a way for the people of the land to show their appreciation of Dani's actions as well as the Zylphas participation in getting rid of the Shining One followers.

This portal was on top of a platform. Going up five steps, the group found that it was plenty broad enough for them all to stay in a group. One of the gnomes started the magik and waved as they all disappeared from the view of the others.

Stepping off of the portal's landing platform, Dani was again pleased by the smartness of the uniforms, area and changing hut. They didn't linger over-long at the station, all of them eager in their own ways for the journey's end.

Walking down the pathway, it soon became more overgrown and less easily seen. Trusting that the shadow kat knew where it was going, the Zylphas and Dani kept up a decent, though not over-rushed, pace.

Soon, instead of any road or track, they were moving over fields. There were a lot of waterways, meaning some retracing of steps to find easier ways across some of the broader channels. In the distance, animals with short legs, fat bodies and long necks moved across the landscape. Nearer at hand, they heard the buzzing of insects and the *"plop"* of something dropping into the water.

Seeing the very occasional ruin as well as a bridge or two, showed that there had been natives that lived here long ago. Who these had been, none of them knew as, apart from the structures, no other evidence was easily available.

The further inland they moved, the boggier some of the places became. Taking an unwary step, Bertal found himself waist deep in a foul smelling pool. Thrashing about, trying to get out, he managed to swallow large amounts of foul tasting water. Frustratingly, instead of helping him, his companions were too busy laughing at his predicament. When he finally managed to get out of the filthy hole, his curses were a wonder to hear as was his vomiting.

They moved along, Dani and Pob trying to stay firmly upwind of the noxious smelling Bertal. The next incident was when Whisper decided to explore a nest of eggs, which it had found, a day or so later. As it patted at one experimentally, a large reptile with huge jaws came running speedily up on squat legs. The kat gave a yowl and ran away, even as the others climbed trees. Once all were safe and the toothy reptile had lost interest, they all laughed uproariously, clinging to their branches and ignoring the kat's glares at them over its injured pride.

They continued on, still giggling occasionally. Dani was still trying to think of a way to send the Zylphas away so wasn't paying that much attention. So when she put her foot down and it landed in space, she wasn't quick enough to grab hold of anything to stop her flying down the steep slope that had stayed hidden from her sight. Yelling in pain and terror, she found herself going flying for a split second before she landed with a sudden bump before sliding down further. This continued until she reached the bottom and rolled for a few yards until hitting a grass tussock and stopping, winded.

Pob, Bertal and Whisper followed her down, but at a much safer pace, swallowing their laughter until they found out how she fared. Once they reached the ground and saw that she was unhurt apart from some bruises, they couldn't hold it in any longer. The laughter became worse when Dani found that she had literally lost the seat of her pants. Indeed, Pob laughed so much, he got hiccoughs.

They were nearing the other side of the island now. Dani was puzzled about what would happen when they reached the shore as she had been told that there was no portal or ferry service. Deciding to wait, they stepped out from the trees and walked over a stretch of smooth white sand.

Busy looking at a pod of merpeople playing in the deep blue water a short distance away, Pob didn't watch where he put his feet. Suddenly he gave a yell and the others turned to see him disappearing down into a hole.

Rushing over to check him out, they knew he was doing alright with the amount of swearing that floated up to them. While discussing ropes and other ways to get him up, the kat gave a sigh, shook its big head and disappeared. When he reappeared it was with Pob clinging to its back and spitting out sand.

Brushing the Zylpha free of the tiny insects, sand and bits of foliage took their full attention so they all jumped, including the kat, when a very polite cough sounded from behind them.

'I am sorry to interrupt,' a smooth, masculine voice said. 'Is there anything we can do to help?'

Turning, they saw a tall man. He looked a little strange, but handsome enough, Dani supposed. His hair resembled seaweed and his eyes…suddenly she gave a delighted shout of recognition.

'You are a Water Elemental! You look like my friend, Zutana.'

The male stared for a few seconds before grinning, showing off dagger-like teeth.

'And you are the Healer we have been told to watch for,' he said, in delight. Turning, he gave a fluting whistle and the pod of Water Elementals that had been playing in the distance suddenly began swimming quickly inland.

A full evening of shared stories, information and explanations followed. The Mers provided a large fish which Pob promptly gutted and cut up into steaks. After offering to cook some for the pod, which raised some confused looks and polite rebuttals, he cooked enough for the four of them. Once finished, Dani took a deep breath and turned to Pob.

'You have been wonderful, and without your help, I wouldn't have managed to get this far. But it is time for you to go home now.' The two Zylphas stared at her, not saying a word.

With a sigh, Dani continued to them both. 'Pob, you only have a short time left of your life. In my eyes you now look like a ten year old child. Bertal, you too are growing older. If you wait, you may not be able to get Pob home. My destination is literally just over the water. With the help of the Mers, if they don't mind, I will be able to get there in the next few days. Then, I will settle down to die. So you see, you coming any further is a waste of your precious time.'

The Zylphas thought about it for a few minutes, then Pob spoke to the Mer that had first approached them.

'Will you get her there, over to the Dragon's Isle?'

'Of course,' the Mer replied, easily. 'She is a Friend to all of us, so we will help in whatever way she needs us to. There is a small sailboat, kept safely in a cave, just a little way up the coastline, that we can tow with her resting in it. She will need food and water for four days of travel over the water and then, once she arrives there safely, we will return the boat.'

There was silence for a few minutes, and then Pob gave a slow nod.

'So, Danielle Wintersborn, our journey together will end in the morning. Let us spend the evening celebrating.'

And so they did. Songs of home were sung, the Merpeople sang their own haunting tunes and stories were told by Dani and the two Zylphas. Gradually, as the night darkened and the stars glittered, the Mers slipped back into the water, one by one.

Pob and Bertal laid out their sleep sacks, smiling over to where Dani had already fallen asleep.

'Think she *will* die?'

'Dunno,' replied Pob. 'I reckon that, no matter what she thinks, her magik and the gods ain't done with her yet though.'

With those words of wisdom, the two Zylphas settled down to
sleep, already missing the Healer's company.

Charlie followed Dani's trail slowly. With all that he had heard
from Nobby and Gilly Flower, along with the doubts he already
carried about Willoughby, he needed some thinking time. Gilly
Flower had managed to remove a charm spell, one that would have
him fulfilling Willoughby's instructions despite any doubts. Now
the doubts were even stronger.

No Guild connected Hunter could decide to end a search without
good reason and the Master of the Guild would definitely not
accept Charlie's bad feeling as good enough. There was also the
fact that Nobby had held back some major information regarding
Charlie's quarry to take into consideration too. That wily wood
gnome knew something about the servant girl he wasn't saying.
Charlie wanted all the possible information before making a
definite judgement.

All in all, Charlie would take a much slower pace and unravel each
clue and sniff out every answer. There were never any time limits
on a search as no search was predictable. So, chewing his lip,
Charlie accepted the fact he might lose his back pay, and his
payment from Willoughby. He also knew that if he was able to
find any evidence of Willoughby lying or holding back on vital
information, he might end up with a bigger bonus, thanks to the
Guild. Whatever happened, it was time to stroll and not run.

Hitching up his knapsack and beginning to whistle, Charlie moved
onwards, looking forward to meeting this girl and seeing what was
so special about her.

End of Book Two of the Chronicles of Yerat

www.ingramcontent.com/pod-product-compliance
Lightning Source LLC
Chambersburg PA
CBHW0615342107 26
48287CB00006B/1948